His face was shadowed by a large Stetson...

And Dana's daughter, Krystal, was right beside him. A mix of feelings flooded through her, and she grabbed Krystal, pulled her into the safety of her arms. Words and sounds, all meaningless, burbled from her throat as she clutched the child against her.

Krystal cried out in protest. "Mommy, you're squishing me."

Dana loosened her hold and pushed Krystal behind her, thinking only to keep the child from returning to the man's clutches. "What are you doing with my child?" she demanded, now for the first time getting a look at his face. His handsome face.

Nico stared at the woman before him. He could see how close to hysterical she was, how concerned she was for her child. Surely she needed him. And he was grateful...for Dana Harper looked like every man's fantasy....

ABOUT THE AUTHOR

For Molly Rice there was never any doubt that she'd become a writer. At the age of four she began a lifelong obsession with notebooks and pencils, which only recently transformed itself into an obsession with computers. Somewhere in between, she discovered the excitement of the public library, and the rest, as they say, is history. Molly has set this book in her home state of Minnesota, where she lives, in St. Paul, with her husband.

Books by Molly Rice

HARLEQUIN INTRIGUE
315—SILENT MASQUERADE
348—UNFORGETTABLE

HARLEQUIN SUPERROMANCE
440—WHERE THE RIVER RUNS
490—CHANCE ENCOUNTER

Krystal's Bodyguard
Molly Rice

Harlequin Books

TORONTO • NEW YORK • LONDON
AMSTERDAM • PARIS • SYDNEY • HAMBURG
STOCKHOLM • ATHENS • TOKYO • MILAN
MADRID • WARSAW • BUDAPEST • AUCKLAND

This book is dedicated to "my boys" from the Jesuit Novitiate of St. Paul: Gerard Engen, SJ; Jeffrey Essmann, SJ; Daniel Hendrickson, SJ; Mark Kramer, SJ; Patrick Medinger, SJ; Erik Oland, SJ; Michael Rosinski, SJ; Mark Ryan, SJ.

The 2nd-year novices: Darcy Blahut, Deron Lawrence, Rob Bufton, Ian Gibbons, Christopher Collins and John Sullivan. The 1st years: Steven Rodenborn, Stephen Winters, Phillip Cooke, Timothy Manah and Michael Swan.

To the staff who have helped me all along the way: Fr. Pat McCorkell, Fr. Mike Harter, Fr. Jean Paul, Br. John Masterson and Kathryn Anderson.

And especially to Margaret Rawlings, the best friend and partner I've ever worked with—someone who knows how to feed the spirit as well as the body and who has always been there for me.

And finally to Michael McManus, still one of "my boys," and always in my heart.

ISBN 0-373-22432-X

KRYSTAL'S BODYGUARD

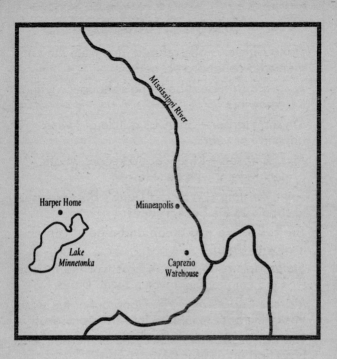

CAST OF CHARACTERS

Dana Harper—She refused help from the only man who could protect her.

Nico Scalia—He'd be Dana's shadow...without her knowing.

Krystal Harper—She was a little girl wise beyond her years.

Mrs. Johnson—Kindly housekeeper who'd protect Krystal with her life.

John Yearling—Why did Dana's boss want her to fade into the background?

Joe Lake—He was a cop and a good friend in love with Dana.

Stella Martinson—Nico's boss worried that he was too emotionally involved with Dana.

Marcus Caprezio—With Dana out of the way, this crime boss would be free from prosecution.

The Carter Brothers—Accused of murder, these boys had no use for Dana Harper.

Charlie Donegan—This white-collar criminal wasn't happy with Dana on his back.

Chapter One

Nico Scalia took the stairs two at a time, anxious to clear up the paperwork on his last case, ready to be free for his next assignment.

The reception area was like a hospital ward with its circle of glass-walled offices surrounding it. Mindy Jacobson, the receptionist/secretary, sat in the middle, monitoring the needs of the staff as well as the flow of clients.

Nico waved at Mindy as he moved around the circle toward his own little cubicle.

"Nico, hey, wait, there's someone here to see you."

"Not now, Min, I'm pumped, gotta get those reports done while the mood is on me." He kept going.

The phone rang before his Stetson hit the hat rack and his bottom the seat of his swivel chair.

"Nico, she's been waiting an hour to see you, says she wants to hire you, won't tell me what it's about and Stell's not in."

She? A woman?

He hadn't noticed anyone sitting in the guest chairs in the reception area. He peered through the glass. His gaze traveled over three empty chairs and then widened at the fourth. It was a woman all right. Or would be in about ten more years. The kid's feet didn't even touch the floor.

"Yeah, right. Very funny, Min," he said into the phone, "tell Stell I said, 'good one.'"

He hung up and withdrew the file from his right-hand lower drawer. As he lifted his head his eyes met the piercing blue gaze of the kid. She didn't seem to be moving. So the joke wasn't over yet. Okay, he could play it out along with the best of them. He punched Intercom. "No calls, Nurse," he cracked, "I'm incommunicado for the next hour."

"What about the kid, Nico?" Min whined.

"She'll have to wait," Nico said, refusing to be drawn into the practical joke.

He swiveled around and hit the Enter key on his computer. The screen lit up with page one of the file on his last case. He prepared to enter the notes from his file folder, his focus totally directed at the work in front of him.

Ten minutes passed, then fifteen. He slumped back in his chair in disgust. He couldn't pull it together. At the rate he was going, the report would be thirty pages long and such a mishmash that even he wouldn't recognize the case he'd completed. Either that or it would be so brief he'd leave out half the vital details. He searched his desk drawer for the pack of cigarettes he knew he'd shoved in there. His hand met cellophane and closed around an empty pack. Damn. When had he smoked the last one? Probably the last time he'd tried to write one of these reports.

It was great when he got teamed with someone on a case so he could con the partner—or partners—into filing the report. Or at least do a share of it.

He tapped a pencil against his cheek and without being too obvious about it, scanned the reception area. The kid was still there. Someone was taking the prank to the limit.

He returned his attention to his work. Ten minutes later he gave up.

He picked up the phone, set it down, glanced down at the papers in front of him, adjusted his seat in the swivel chair, picked up the phone again and fought for control over his nerves. Though he had avoided contact with the blue eyes staring at him through the glass wall of his office, he had not been able to avoid their impact as they followed his every move.

He punched Intercom and then Mute.

"All right, Mindy," he said when the secretary picked up, "joke's over. Give the kid the dollar you promised her and let's get back to work."

"I swear, Nico, she's the real article. Been here all afternoon, won't see anyone but you. Honest."

He blew out a sigh of exasperation and darted a quick glance at the kid. What was she, about seven? Eight, tops. He had nieces that age. What the hell was a little girl doing here all alone without a parent? It dawned on him then.

"Okay, Min, so your baby-sitter didn't show up and you had to bring the kid to work with you. We understand. Now do you mind if I get some work done here?"

The phone rang the minute he set it down. "No calls, Mindy," he said sternly.

"That is not my Tiffany, Nico," Mindy said, sounding almost as exasperated as he. "Says her name is Krystal Harper and says she isn't leaving until she has her appointment with you."

"Appointment?" He took a breath, lowered his voice. "You made an appointment with a kid for me?" Two agents passed his office and glanced from the little girl to Nico, their expressions curious. They didn't have *the look*. If they were in on it, they should have *the look*.

They didn't, and he knew from poker games with them that neither one could pull it off straight-faced.

He looked at the kid again and back at his computer. The cursor hadn't moved two inches down in almost an hour. It blinked maddeningly, taunting his frustration.

He slumped back in his chair, letting out a sigh of submission. "Send her in, Mindy, but I'm warning you, if you ever pull something like this again, you're fired."

"You can't fire me, Nico, you didn't hire me," Mindy said calmly, getting the last word as always.

Krystal Harper walked sedately into Nico Scalia's office.

She used the armrests on the chair to boost herself up and back, her pink-sneakered feet barely clearing the edge of the seat.

Nico cleared his throat and sat back, propping one leg on the edge of his own chair's armrest. He steepled his fingers and gave the little girl a forbidding look.

"This is a business, kid," he said, "and I'm a busy man. What's on your mind?"

"I saw you on TV," the child said. Her smile revealed a gap where two teeth were missing, which explained the slight sibilance in her speech. "They said you cracked a case the police couldn't solve."

Nico nodded, not bothering to hide behind false modesty with a child. In his best Humphrey Bogart imitation he twisted his mouth and said, "So? You got a murder you want solved? Somebody killed your dolly?"

The kid giggled. The sound loosened something in his chest. Why play high-and-mighty with a little girl? She was a kid; he knew about kids, liked them a lot in normal circumstances.

He lowered his leg and leaned forward, his elbows on the desk. "Why would a little kid like you need a private investigator?" he asked, gentling his voice.

Krystal sobered. "I need you to be a bodyguard for my mother."

"Your mother? Why do you think your mother needs a bodyguard?" He was intrigued despite himself. He had a lot of nieces and nephews and couldn't visualize any of them coming up with this kind of agenda.

The little girl's eyes widened earnestly. Nico thought he'd never seen quite that shade of blue eyes before.

Krystal scooted forward on the chair and placed her arms on the edge of Nico's desk. "My mom is getting scary letters and phone calls and even though she works with the police a lot, she doesn't tell them about it and she acts nervous and scared all the time."

"Your mom's a cop?"

Krystal shook her head. "My mom is a prosecuting attorney in the adult criminal division of the Hennepin County Attorney's Office." She said it with well-rehearsed ease, her face and voice glowing with pride.

Nico thought about her mother. Lady lawyer. Not Nico's favorite kind of animal. Most of them were barracudas. Seemed like almost the minute they passed the bar they crossed some invisible line and became as masculine as it was possible to become without a sex change. And the ones from County were the worst.

"So, listen, Kiddo," he said, "if what you say is true, why doesn't your mom get help from the cops—why come to me? I don't come cheap and your ma can get all the help she wants for free."

Krystal shook her head again and a look of impatience twisted her mouth, squinted her eyes.

"She doesn't admit she's getting threatened, and she would never tell the people she works with, anyway."

"Why not?"

"There are only two other women besides my mom in her division."

Nico was surprised. The Hennepin County Attorney's office was huge and in this day and age he'd expect the ratio of genders to be narrower than that. Still, he didn't see what that had to do with anything. He said so.

Krystal was completely off the chair now, leaning on the desk, one finger toying with the variety of pens and pencils in the leather cup, her head cocked to the side. She straightened and glared at Nico for his ignorance.

"They said on the news that you were really smart," she said with a sigh. Nico had the impression she was disappointed in him. He felt the way he did when, as a kid, he'd let his mother down.

Mustering bravado, he shrugged and gave her his helpless look. He knew he was prolonging the interview but if even half of what the kid was telling him was true, he was intrigued. Thursday, he had no date tonight, he could stay late to finish his report.

"Women in the workplace have to work harder, show more grit, go the extra mile, keep their emotions under wraps. It's a man's world out there and women have to make themselves fit in."

Nico felt his jaw slacken and then quickly snapped it shut as he headed off an urge to laugh. The kid sounded like she was making a speech at a professional women's group and he realized she was probably parroting her mother's gospel, verbatim.

He envisioned the mother as one of those man bashers, a libber who wore flannel suits with ties, sensible shoes, and had a haircut that would have passed muster in a Marine boot camp.

He looked at the feminine little girl before him and mentally shook his head. A shame. This pretty little thing would probably grow up emulating her mother and trade in that soft lovely promise for the butch exterior she believed would move her ahead in the world. Exactly why he avoided most career women.

"Listen, Ms....Harper is it?"

Krystal nodded. "Krystal Harper. My mom's name is Dana Harper."

Of course, he should have made the connection; Harper's name had been popping up in the news a lot lately, meaning she was on her way up, maybe being groomed for the top job if John Yearling had his eye on a senatorship.

It didn't change anything though, this was not the kind of work he preferred and this interview had no validity since the prospective client was a minor.

"Ah-ha, Krystal." He wanted to let her down lightly.

"Well, the fact is, Krystal, we don't really do much bodyguard work in this agency except on a limited basis. We're mostly investigative and I couldn't investigate..." He stopped, a new thought popping up. "Say, how do you know your mom's getting threatening letters and calls, did she tell you?"

The little girl's cheeks flushed. "I...I saw one of the letters myself. And you can tell when she gets a bad phone call 'cause she looks real scared for a minute and then when she sees me watching, she straightens her face and pretends nothing's wrong." Krystal nodded. "But I know."

"Yeah," he said softly, "I see. But like I said, I can't really help you. For one thing, it's against the law for me to work for you because you have to be twenty-one to hire a private investigator."

He didn't know if twenty-one was the actual age. It ought to be, but the fact was he had no idea at what age a person reached majority. Maybe it was eighteen. In any case, he was just scrabbling around for a way to let her down easy.

What he didn't expect was tears.

Her eyes pooled up with them, making the blue color even shinier, dampening and darkening the lashes. And then a single tear escaped and he followed its course down her pink cheek with awe. It was the biggest tear he'd ever seen and the sight of if twisted his gut and choked off his breathing.

"Aw, kid...Krystal...please, don't, hey, come on, no, don't..." He gasped and shook his head as more tears slid from her lowered lids.

Alarmed, Nico got up, went around the desk and patted the girl's shoulder. "Okay!" he growled. "Listen, stop crying and I'll make you a deal."

She lifted her eyes to his and swiped at her cheeks with her one free hand. When she sniffed he pushed a box of tissues toward her.

"You...you'll h-help me?" she hiccuped.

"What I'll do is, I'll take you home and I'll talk to your mom. It's up to her if she wants to hire me," he said, strengthening his voice with a warning note.

Krystal nodded. "Okay," she said, wadding the tissue against her eyes. "If you talk to her I'm sure she'll be glad to have someone like you to protect her."

Nico shook his head. He wasn't so sure. Krystal's mother didn't sound like the kind of woman who'd ever admit needing a man. He wasn't looking forward to the confrontation. The trouble was, he also couldn't deal with the little girl's tears. He took her hand resolutely and leaned forward to grab her backpack. "C'mon, let's go get this over with."

"Gone? What do you mean, she's gone? Gone where?"

Dana Harper grasped the edge of the counter with the first dizzying flash of fear.

"Mrs. Johnson, please. Where did she go?"

The older woman slumped down on a kitchen chair and shook her head, her gray eyes dulled by distress. "She said she was going down the street to the Halyards's house to play with Kim. She said she'd be home before you. When I saw it was after five, I called over to the Halyards's to remind Krystal that you'd be home any minute and that dinner would be ready at six on the dot because I have bridge club tonight, you remember, and..."

"Yes, yes, Mrs. J., I remember," Dana interrupted, "but what about Krystal?"

"She wasn't there."

"You mean she'd left already? Then she should be here any—"

"No." The woman twisted her hands in her apron and her gray hair threatened to come loose from its topknot as Mrs. Johnson shook her head. Her words came out in a choked whisper.

"Mrs. Halyard said she hadn't been there."

"Then...where..."

"I don't know. I was just about to call some of her other friends when you walked in."

"Oh, my God!" Dana rushed for the phone, her hand shaking as she lifted the receiver from the hook. "I'll start calling, you go across the street and see if she's at the Barnes's."

She'd just hung up after getting a negative response from Terri Montford's father and was about to dial the Smalley's number when the doorbell chimed. She dropped the phone, leaving it to dangle from its cord, and rushed through the house to open the front door, her heart racing faster than her legs.

The man's face was shadowed by a large Stetson, his height looming, cutting off her view beyond the front entrance. He filled her vision so that it took her a moment to realize that there was a child beside him and that the child was her own Krystal.

A mix of feelings flooded through her. Relief, fear, rage. Hysteria. She grabbed Krystal's arm and pulled her forward, thinking only of getting her child away from the strange man, back into the safety of her arms. Words and sounds, all meaningless, burbled from her throat as she clutched Krystal against her.

She finally managed to squeak out a rational sentence. "Krystal, run and call 9-1-1, quick!" But she clung to the girl, her arms frozen around her.

Krystal cried out in protest. "Mommy, you're squishing me, I can't breathe!"

Dana loosened her hold and pushed Krystal behind her, thinking only to keep the girl from returning to the man's clutches.

"Mommy, mommy," Krystal cried, yanking on Dana's shirt. "Please, Mommy."

Dana turned toward the child as the man took a step forward. Fright clogged Dana's throat and she halted, uncertain which way to move. The man stopped and seemed to be waiting for her to make some kind of gesture.

"What are you doing with my child?" she demanded of the man and, without taking a breath, spun around and shouted, "Why did you lie to Mrs. Johnson?" at Krystal.

Nico stared at the woman before him, his brain barely believing what his eyes were registering, his ears closed to her cries of outrage. This was no asexual career fanatic, no male wannabe; this was living cheesecake, every man's fantasy. A wealth of wheat colored hair fell in a ponytail from the top of her head swinging with her every movement. She was wearing shorts that showed off the longest, shapeliest legs he'd ever seen, legs that ended seductively in bare feet, and a T-shirt that clung to a full bosom without the confinement of a bra.

Sanity threatened. *Oh, Scalia, you male chauvinist pig!* he jeered mentally. But it was hard to react any other way with such a vision before him in the flesh. Dana Harper was the kind of woman who brought out the worst in a man.

He forgot why he was here, what he was about, momentarily forgot his own name.

"Mommy, that's Mr. Scalia, the man from TV..." Krystal protested, still pulling on Dana's shirt to get her attention.

Dana turned back, squinting in appraisal of Nico. "Take your hat off," she ordered. He did so, looking properly sheepish, and she recognized the man who'd been featured on the news just a few nights ago. Krystal and she played a game where they watched the news and Krystal had to determine how many stories were good news and how many bad. Dana helped her analyze which was which. The story featuring Scalia ended in a draw; the bad news was that a man had been conning elderly people out of their money, the good news was that Scalia had found the evidence to get him arrested.

That didn't explain what he was doing here, and with Krystal.

"What are you doing with my daughter?"

"I brought her home. She came to my office wanting to hire a private bodyguard." His eyes were still appraising her as he spoke and Dana fleetingly wished she hadn't changed out of her work clothes when she got home. At the same time she registered what he had just said.

She looked down at her daughter. "Krystal, what is this all about?"

Krystal was about to answer when Mrs. Johnson called out as she came toward the front of the house. "She wasn't over there, Dana, and..." Words trailed away and she cried out with relief when she saw Krystal. She began to shoot rapid-fire questions but now Dana interrupted her.

"I'll tell you all about it as soon as I get some answers, Mrs. J. Meanwhile, will you make us some coffee and bring a juice for Krystal, as well, please?"

The older woman cast a curious glance at Nico Scalia but nodded her head and left for the kitchen.

"We might as well get comfortable," Dana said, opening the French doors off the large foyer with one hand while the other still firmly clasped her daughter's.

Nico followed a couple of feet behind, his eyes reluctantly leaving their study of the Harper woman's backside to take in the environment in which she lived. The doors opened onto a living room larger than average that owed its first impression to a magnificent view of Lake Minnetonka through multiple windows on the south wall. On the east and west walls of the room were glass-paned doors that opened into matching screened porches.

The neighborhood alone, not to mention the size of the house from the outside, had told Nico that this was a costly piece of real estate. Now, for the first time, he thought about Mr. Harper, wondered what he did for a living that provided the kind of money required to live in such a house. One thing he was sure of, Dana Harper didn't earn this working for the county attorney's office.

He sank into one of the easy chairs across from the couch where Dana sat, the little girl beside her under the protection of her mother's arm, and placed his Stetson on his knee.

"I think we can get this cleared up in a hurry, Ms. Harper," Nico began, getting right to the point. "It seems your little girl thinks you're being harassed through the mail and by phone calls. She thought I could help."

Dana's reaction was immediate, her expressions making rapid changes across her face until she settled for surprise. She turned to her daughter. "How did you know..."

The little girl blushed. "I saw one of the letters, Mommy. I wasn't snooping, honestly! It was that day you told me I could get a pencil from your desk and I saw this piece of paper sticking out of your bottom drawer. I just pulled on it and it came out and I read it." The child sat back. "I'm sorry, Mommy."

Dana nodded, feeling more sad than anything that her eight-year-old should have had to suffer the worry engendered by the obscene threats. But now she had to deal with the unwanted presence of this professional snoop and do so without having the whole thing become a public circus. His appearance on TV told her that he was a publicity seeker and would probably sell their story to the highest bidder. She couldn't have that, too much was at stake.

She turned back to face Nico Scalia and took a moment to study him while she formed the right words in her mind. It was easy to see why Krystal would believe him capable of protecting a woman at risk; he was tall and well-built, with dark hair, and eyes that gave him a threatening presence. A black mustache offset the sensuality of his mouth, the white gleam of his teeth. Easy to see, too, why he might be the darling of the press. A reminder that she had to get rid of him.

"I'm sorry you were dragged into this, unnecessarily, Mr. Scalia," she said, clearing her throat and making her voice firm while keeping it pleasant, "but I assure you I'm in no danger and have no need of a private investigator or a bodyguard." She smiled down at Krystal and left a remnant of it on her lips as she looked across at Scalia. "I'll be glad to pay for your time up until now, however, and maybe a little something extra to forget this whole foolish incident. If you'll just wait while I get my checkbook.'' She started to rise.

Nico leaped to his feet, his ears ringing with anger. "I'm not in the business of blackmail, Ms. Harper!'' he practically growled through clenched teeth, bunching his hat in an angry fist. "And I don't appreciate being patronized like some sleazy private eye in a B movie. Ours is a reputable firm of investigators which, I might add, has provided agents to work with many of your colleagues in the legal profession.''

Dana stared, openmouthed, at the bristling detective. His eyes were glinting dangerously and his considerable size and stance were plainly threatening. If she were in the market for a bodyguard, she could do worse. It occurred to her that he was a very attractive man and that this was the first time she'd really enjoyed looking at a man since Zack's death. If they had met socially, she might actually have been inclined to flirt a little. Of course the Stetson would have to go, and she'd like to see him in something other than denim jeans and jacket and those silly cowboy boots.

But then his next words echoed in her mind, distracting her from the critique of his physical attributes and haberdashery.

"If you were paying more attention to your job as a mother, your kid wouldn't have ended up in my office, all alone, looking for help. You may not need a bodyguard but I'd say you certainly do need someone to look after Krystal and...''

Dana's outrage would have burst forth in a volley of verbal shots if the sound of actual gunfire hadn't just at that moment rung out from the direction of the kitchen.

They almost knocked each other over as both adults and the little girl reacted to the sound, rushing in the direction of the gunshots.

Mrs. Johnson lay on the floor, blood forming a circle beneath her right shoulder, one leg pointing, like an arrow, toward the heap of glass shards from the broken window next to the back door.

"Krystal, dial 9-1-1," Dana shouted for the second time that evening as she knelt beside her fallen housekeeper and Nico Scalia ran out the back door, attempting to spot the shooter.

Chapter Two

The flashing lights of police cars eerily lit up the night, strobing reflections off the trees that rimmed the east side of the property. Dana watched the affect from a window, her mind almost numb with fatigue and guilt. Her boss, John Yearling, had been talking to the detectives and now he joined her at the window just as Joe Lake came up on her other side and put an arm around her shoulders. "You okay, Dana?" Lake asked softly.

As if she was the one who'd been hurt. She shook her head. "I'm not the one who got shot, Joe. I just want to get to the hospital to make sure Mrs. Johnson is all right." She turned to her boss, looking for support.

Yearling nodded. "I think they're about through here, Dana. Listen, don't come into the office in the morning, you're going to have plenty to take care of around here."

"I'll take you up on that, John, but don't hesitate to call me if something comes up that can't wait."

He was about to turn away when Dana stopped him. "Do you think this was Caprezio's doing, John?"

The county attorney shrugged and shook his head. "I can't call it, Dana, it's too iffy. For one thing, I don't see Caprezio's people screwing up like this. If they had a hit on you, you'd have been the one who went down and you wouldn't have got back up.'' His face was grim though his eyes were compassionate.

This was the moment to tell him about the threats, but when she opened her mouth, she couldn't let the words come out. She said instead, ''I guess that makes it unlikely we'll find a suspect.''

John's day had been as long as hers. She recognized the signs of exhaustion in the shadowed eyes, trembling hands. ''We'll put interviewers out in the street, maybe we'll come up with backdoor answers.''

On her other side, Joe nodded and squeezed Dana's shoulder. ''This could very well have been almost anyone you've ever prosecuted, Dana.''

Dana shivered. ''You're right. Which makes me feel even more responsible for Mrs. J. I'll feel a lot better after I see for myself that she's going to be okay.''

''I'll drive you over, Dana,'' Joe offered. Dana was about to refuse and then realized she wasn't in any condition to drive into town. ''Thanks, Joe. I'll just be a minute changing my clothes.''

She was about to start up the stairs when she realized that with Mrs. J. out of commission, she had no one to stay with Krystal. Could she take her along to the hospital? A glance at her watch told her it was nearing midnight.

Krystal had fallen asleep, still sniffling, in Dana's arms at around eight and Joe Lake had carried her up and put her to bed. The comings and goings of the crime scene crew hadn't wakened her and Dana hesitated to do so now. She glanced over her shoulder and saw the private detective, Nick Scalia, talking to one of the cops. He looked up and their eyes met. As if reading her mind, he strolled to the bottom of the stairs and looked up at her.

''Something I can do, Mrs. Harper?''

''As a matter of fact there is, Mr. Scalia,'' she said,

turning toward him. "I need to get to the hospital but Krystal's sleeping. I don't want to wake her and I wondered if…" Her words trailed away as it dawned on her that she was asking the man to baby-sit. She started over. "Look, I'm really sorry you got hung up in all this. I tried to explain you were an innocent bystander but the police don't leave anything to chance and you were on the premises, an eyewitness, more or less."

He smiled and shrugged off her concern. "You're not satisfied with the telephone reports from the hospital, I take it."

She tried to return his smile, found her lips stiff and unyielding. "Yes…that is, I was going to see for myself and that's why I…"

The idea didn't seem to bother him. "Sure. You go ahead. I'll stay."

She was about to suggest some kind of remuneration and then recalled his earlier reaction when she'd offered him money for what had only been a kindness on his part.

"Thanks. I'll make it quick as I can." She turned and hurried up to her bedroom.

It was while she was slipping into gray corduroy slacks and a soft, white sweater that the big picture finally opened in her mind. If Krystal had been in the kitchen, she could have been the one wounded…or worse! For the first time Dana saw that she hadn't really given proper credence to the threats. They seemed to be directed solely at her, and she'd felt up to the task of protecting herself, but this incident tonight proved that they could mean danger for anyone in her life.

According to the doctor, during their last conversation by phone, Mrs. J. was going to be hospitalized for only a few days and able to return to work in a few weeks.

But after tonight would the housekeeper ever feel quite safe being here alone with only Krystal?

She pushed her feet into loafers and snatched a gray jacket off its hanger in the closet. Maybe Krystal had been right on the money. Maybe they did need a bodyguard. She left the bedroom with a clear image of Nico Scalia in her mind. A large man who obviously took very good care of his body, he was both lean and muscular. And something about the set of his jaw, the glint in his brown eyes, told her that he could be dangerous if crossed. The kind of man who could easily protect one little girl and one elderly woman.

Scalia was waiting at the bottom of the stairs. "Take your time, Ms. Harper, the night's already gone for me, I can stay as long as it takes." His smile was reassuring.

Dana stopped on the last step so that her face was almost level with his. At this proximity she could smell his aftershave, the clean soapy smell of his skin that even five hours of havoc hadn't obliterated. She gave him an even look. "How about indefinitely, Mr. Scalia?"

"Whatever it ta... Oh, I see, you're kidding, right?" He chuckled.

"No, actually I'm not. I'd like to hire you, Mr. Scalia. As a bodyguard," she said in a near whisper, conscious of Joe Lake and the other detectives milling around nearby.

Nico let out a low whistle. "I wondered if you were going to see that this goes beyond mere threats. But I figured you'd ask your own people for help."

"You misunderstand me, Mr. Scalia, I'm not hiring you to protect me. I want you to act as bodyguard for Krystal and, of course, Mrs. Johnson when she's here."

"I told you before, I don't usually hire on as a body-guard," Nico said.

She made a pointed survey of his wide shoulders, his

long, strong-looking legs; the total picture of masculine power. "Are you licensed to carry a gun?" she asked.

"Yes, of course."

"Well, then, you're certainly equipped—in every way—so I guess it's just that you consider the work beneath you. It certainly won't put you in the limelight, get your face plastered all over by the media."

Nico bit back a vulgar retort and shoved his fists into his pockets. This dame could certainly use a bodyguard if her tongue was always this sharp and unrestrained. But he hadn't missed the obvious study she'd made of his person and he couldn't keep his mind from doing its own quick study of what it would be like to spend some time getting to know her, testing the depth of her reserve.

Still, this wasn't the kind of job he liked to take on.

"I agree, Krystal should have someone looking after her until they can find out who the shooter was, but as I said, I'm not really a bodyguard."

Joe Lake came up just as Nico made his statement. He pushed his arms into a football letter jacket and nodded at Nico. "I wouldn't say that, Scalia. You have the qualifications. The cops can't spare 'round-the-clock protection and we don't know this freak won't try again. Why don't you give it a try? Maybe for forty-eight hours. We should have a line on the guy by then."

Nico grunted. "Yeah, right. Like you guys have such a great record for crime solving."

Dana stepped between the two men who had faced off as if to start throwing punches. "That's not fair, Scalia. I'm trying three criminal cases presently, thanks to the work of the Minneapolis police, and I'm only one of thirty-nine prosecutors who's up to the armpits in criminal suits."

"I guess this wise guy thinks because he solved one case, he's some kind of hero," Joe Lake said over her shoulder. "Maybe you better look elsewhere for security."

"No way," Nico snapped. "I'd love to see you put your money where your mouth is, Lake. I'll take it on for forty-eight and let's see you guys hold up your end." He directed his gaze to Dana. "That is, I'll do it on two conditions."

Dana breathed a sigh of relief. "And they are?"

Nico started to tell her, glanced past her at Lake, and said instead, "We can discuss it when you get back."

THEY WEREN'T even out of the drive before Joe Lake put his hand on Dana's knee and resumed an old conversation.

"You know, Dana, if you'd have accepted my proposal you'd have a man around the house all the time, and you wouldn't need to hire a bodyguard."

She laughed lightly while removing Joe's hand. "I don't need a man to protect me, Joe, and if I did, I wouldn't consider that a justification for marriage."

Joe's profile reflected his chagrin, his mouth tightening to a thin line, his jawbone jerking as he ground his teeth. His voice was a little desperate as he responded, "You know I love you, Dana, I've told you often enough."

She tried not to let sympathy color her tone. "I know, Joe, and I wish I could say I returned the feeling, but I think of you as a kind of brother, Zack's and my best friend. Honestly, I don't know what I would have done without you after Zack was killed, but I can't marry you just to repay your kindness." She put her hand over his and squeezed gently. "I love you enough to feel you deserve better than that, Joe."

He laughed suddenly, the air in the car turning decidedly lighter. "I had to try. Didn't want to blow my record."

Dana breathed easier. "Yeah," she said fondly, "you were never one to let an opportunity pass you by." She thought about that, about how Joe had always had a reputation for being a womanizer. Zack and the other cops had groused about Joe's ease with the ladies, often with a tinge of envy coloring their remarks. Personally Dana had often wondered why Joe had never married, given his obvious pleasure in the company of women. Despite being a bachelor for forty years, he was the one who always remembered the little things women liked. He was great with all the other cops' kids and Zack had admitted that it was Joe who reminded him of their anniversary date and birthdays.

Her thoughts were distracted when she spotted a KXLI remote van parked in front of the Super America store and recalled the circus that could have gone down at her house tonight.

"Thanks for keeping the press at bay, Joe. I know that took some juggling."

Joe shook his head. "Not all that hard. The stations know if they want access to crime news, they have to cooperate when we tell them to hold off on a story." He gave her a quick glance, and one of those grins that turned most women around. "Not to mention that I called in a few markers."

They laughed about that, each recalling Joe's special propensity for anchorwomen. He'd been seeing Cilly Baker from Channel Four when Zack died and since then he'd dated at least two other TV personalities from the other stations. Until he'd suddenly surprised her with a marriage proposal and as far as she knew, hadn't been dating anyone since, despite the fact that she'd turned him down. Numerous times.

Joe turned the car left onto Highway 394, headed toward the city. When they'd joined the light, late-night line of traffic he said, "You asked Yearling about Caprezio. Any particular reason you zeroed in on him?"

The car's heater had kicked in and Dana unzipped her jacket and settled back. "I don't know, I suppose it's like free association. I think 'Caprezio—murder,' 'murder—Caprezio.' Sort of like 'hand—glove.'"

"So you think it has nothing to do with the fact that you're prosecuting Marcus Caprezio?"

Dana shrugged, glancing over at her friend. "Nothing—or everything." She was tempted to tell him about the notes but once again felt something holding her back. Was it her innate obstinacy? Zack had always accused her of that, said she got her back up the minute she thought she might sound needy. It had been the real crux of their marital difficulty. Unfortunately she'd only recognized that after her husband was gone.

"Well, I'm inclined to agree with Yearling. If it had been Caprezio, the hit would most likely have met its target."

"Meaning me?"

"Yeah, who else? Unless Mrs. J. is enhancing her cookies with hard stuff and stepping on some drug lord's toes."

They both laughed at the absurdity. And were instantly reminded of the solemnity of the situation.

"I just hope Mrs. J. can find it in her heart to forgive me," Dana said, sighing.

"Why? Did you shoot her?" Joe turned to glance at her, a wry smile on his lips.

"You know what I mean. If I was the target, and she got in the way, well, it wouldn't have happened if she didn't work for me, after all."

They were a block from the hospital and Joe's response was swallowed up by the noise of an ambulance that had just pulled out of the garage on their right.

They spent only a few minutes at Mrs. Johnson's bed-side. The elderly woman looked grayer, more pale against the white linens, her eyes dim when she opened them briefly.

"She won't come out of the anesthetic for quite a while, but she's stable and the bullet came out clean," the doctor said, gesturing for them to join him out in the hall.

"The bullet?" Dana asked, automatically thinking like the prosecuting attorney she was.

"Detective Haroldson took it as soon as we got it out," the doctor said, wearily running a hand over his round face. His hands were long and capable-looking and didn't match his pudgy face at all. She gave a brief prayer of thanks that he was competent and had given her house-keeper his best. She thanked him and reminded him to call her if there was any change.

On their way out, they stopped at admitting where Dana signed papers identifying her as the person respon-sible for any costs not covered by Mrs. J.'s medical aid.

Back in Joe's car, she fell asleep almost as soon as she snapped her seat belt on and leaned her head against the window. She slept all the way and when they pulled into her drive and she awakened, she thanked him blearily and staggered into the house thinking of nothing but bed.

It wasn't until she saw Nico sprawled on the couch in the living room that she became completely alert. He jumped up as she came down the three steps into the room.

"You look beat," he said.

"I am. Did Krystal wake up?"

"Yeah. I got her a drink of water and talked to her for a minute and she went right back to sleep." He leaned a hip against the wing of one of the chairs flanking the fireplace and folded his arms across his chest. "I think we should get something straight right up front," he said.

Dana sighed and slumped down into the nearest easy chair. It took her a moment to sort her thoughts, to recall where she and Scalia had left off.

"You said your decision to take the job was based on a couple of conditions, Mr. Scalia?"

"Yeah, and the first one is that we skip the formalities and use first names. Frankly, I'm not used to this 'Mister Scalia' routine."

Dana wearily gestured acquiescence. "And?"

"Our living in the same house is going to crowd you a little, even given the size of this place, but in order for me to do my j—"

Dana's gasped, "Living together?" surprised Nico midword.

"Well, yeah, of course. How else would I watch out for the kid if I wasn't with her 'round-the-clock?"

Dana blew a sigh of dismay. This was all getting so complicated, so messy. She shook her head. "I don't know," she said irritably. "I guess I thought you'd come over before I had to leave for work and leave when I got home in the evening."

She didn't have the market on irritability. His expression matched her own. "In other words, you thought you'd hire me to take Mrs. Johnson's place in her absence. Maybe throw in a little light housework while I was at it?"

"No, not at all. Of course not!" Dana shook her head vehemently, her voice rising to cover something that felt like guilt...or shame. "You don't have to twist everything I say," she snapped, turning away from his accusatory glare.

"I think I do," he said as he moved to make sure she

couldn't avoid his eyes. "It seems like the only way to wring the truth out of your meaning."

"Okay. So I misunderstood the term 'bodyguard,' so sue me," she said, jumping to her feet. "You do whatever you have to do. You'll find an extra set of keys in the drawer of the table in the foyer and there's a guest room at the top of the stairs on the right." She brushed past him and made for those stairs. "I assume you'll want to go to your own home to pack some things. As for me, I'm going to bed."

She left the room without a backward glance, uneasily aware that it only "seemed" like she'd had the last word.

It wasn't until she'd reached the top of the stairs that she heard him go up to the foyer. Had he stood there the whole time, debating about taking the job, after all? A frisson of fear cooled her skin. She had to curb her unruly tongue. She couldn't leave Krystal to just anyone's care, not now when the threats had escalated to action.

She stopped on her way to her own room to check on Krystal. Even in sleep the little girl held her favorite stuffed animal to her chest, as if protecting it from nighttime terrors. The panda had been a gift from her daddy.

Krystal had tried to relinquish it at one point, insisting she was too old for stuffed animals, but when the box was packed to go to Goodwill, Krystal had changed her mind.

Dana smiled at the pair and pulled the blanket up over her child's shoulders. She placed a kiss on Krystal's cheek and was rewarded with a frown and a snuffle. She tiptoed out of the room, leaving the door ajar so she'd hear if Krystal awoke and needed her during the night.

Or what was left of it, Dana thought, dragging herself down the hall to the master bedroom.

She almost fell into bed, so tired she was sure she

wouldn't hear Scalia even if his return were heralded by a marching band.

But she was wrong. After half an hour of tossing and pillow plumping, she turned on her lamp and attempted to read herself to sleep.

Her thoughts persisted even against the lure of Mary Higgins Clark's latest mystery. Her own mystery was far more compelling.

She froze midthought when she heard sounds from below and then realized it was Nico reentering the house. She lay back against the pillows and breathed a deep sigh of relief. She would never have admitted it aloud, but it felt good to have someone to share the fear with; someone, and yes, a man, to make her home feel more secure.

She thought she could hear him moving around in the guest room though it was located at the other end of the hall. She could visualize him preparing for bed, doing the things men did, like emptying his pockets onto the dresser, hanging his pants over a chair back, going into the hall bathroom to shower.

She imagined him standing under the spray, his body glistening wetly, his dark hair slicked back off his forehead. Abruptly it occurred to her that it was as if she were spying on him, if only in her imagination.

"Losin' it, Harper," she muttered, snapping off the lamp, turning her face into her pillow, willing her mind to relinquish such tantalizing thoughts.

Maybe it was time to consider dating again, as her friends constantly urged her. She was certainly ready if this was her reaction to the first man who came along, and a man she barely knew, at that.

She turned over, tucking her hands under her cheek, staring at the tree outside her window, its branches eerily etched in shadow and moonlight.

Granted, Nico Scalia left nothing to be desired in a

woman's fantasy; tall, dark, handsome, he moved with the grace of an athlete and the self-assurance of a movie star. And it had been impossible to overlook his competent ease with Krystal during the trauma of the evening. She wasn't sure she'd have been able to calm her daughter down as dispassionately and tenderly as Nico had. Her own nerves had been so frayed, only her resolution to remain professional in front of her colleagues and calm in front of her child had kept her from going to pieces.

But this was no time to be thinking about the man-woman thing. Aside from the very real danger to herself and Krystal, there was the continuing pressure from her job and the three cases she would be prosecuting over the next few months.

A soft knock at her door startled her. She gasped and then called out, "Who is it?"

The knob turned and the detective's figure loomed in the doorway.

"This room is off limits, Scalia," she snapped, disgusted by her momentary fear.

He lounged against the door frame, an arrogant smile creasing his cheeks, exposing large, even teeth. He'd taken off the denim jacket and the white T-shirt he'd worn beneath it clung to his broad-shouldered upper body, molded to each and every muscle.

"Are you suggesting my being in your room is too much temptation for you, Ms. Harper?"

A warm feeling moved through Dana's stomach and flushed her cheeks.

She pulled the sheet up under her chin. "Of all the nerve," she said, her voice sounding weak even to her own ears. "I see your ego is equal to your boot size."

"Yeah, women really seem to go for the boots," he said, deliberately choosing the wrong interpretation of her insult.

"It so happens that I find boots, outside of a mucky barnyard, appallingly tacky."

His voice was low, smoky, threatening. "Then I'll be sure to take my boots off before we get cozy," he said.

Dana blew a raspberry at him. Nothing seemed to stop this guy's stampeding ego. "What do you want, Scalia? I'm tired, I'd like to get to sleep."

Nico decided to forego the word games that came to mind. He'd probably gone too far as it was. Something about her made him want to strip away all of her cover, to needle her into exposing the woman beneath the facade. But she wasn't playing tonight.

"You didn't give me the alarm code, and I noticed a camera on the wall over the front door, where do you activate that?"

"The code is one-zero-seven and the alarm beam is activated by the wall switch at the top of the stairs, next to the window, behind the drape."

"Got it. Thanks."

And with that he was gone, the door closing firmly behind him.

Dana let out a whoosh of air and shook her head, her blond, layered hair swishing around her chin at the front, the back brushing well below the shoulders of her pajama top. "What a jerk!" she muttered aloud.

She punched her pillow a couple of times and tested it for comfort. She'd wasted far too much time dancing a verbal two-step with the detective, she wasn't going to give him another moment's thought.

She turned off the lamp and wiggled down under the covers.

Think about work, she told herself in her sternest inner voice.

She directed her focus toward her work and pictured,

within her mind, the file of notes on the three cases that predominated her workload.

Her mind's eye had scanned only the first page of notes before she fell asleep.

Chapter Three

She awakened to bright sunlight, its heat tickling her face. It took a moment to recall the events of the previous night and then she jumped out of bed, alarmed at the lateness of the hour, concerned about Krystal.

She found her child ensconced at the kitchen table, eating an orange and watching Nico fit a piece of glass into the opening of the side-yard door into the kitchen.

"Then why did the guy shoot at our house?"

Dana stopped in the doorway, unnoticed. Obviously they were in the middle of a discussion. She stepped back, out of sight, and waited, along with Krystal, for his answer.

Nico spoke around the glazing point he held between his teeth. "Could be the guy made a mistake, thought this was someone else's house."

"Ha!" Krystal's retort was far more sophisticated than Dana would have expected. "So you expect me to believe Mommy was getting those notes and phone calls but that had nothing to do with Mrs. J. getting shot? I don't *think* so," she drawled sarcastically.

Dana held back a snicker of amusement at her daughter's stance. Nico Scalia had his hands full if he thought Krystal was a typical eight-year-old.

Nico spun around and glared at Krystal. "Sarcasm is not an attitude one likes to hear from little children."

"I'm not a little child," Krystal protested. "And you're just trying not to answer my question."

Dana heard Nico's short, derisive chuckle. "No, you're probably a midget, thirty years old with a college degree."

Krystal giggled. "No, I'm not. But I know grown-ups make up stuff when they don't want us kids to know something."

"Listen, kid, you know everything I know. The rest is just guessing." His sincerity rang with respect for the little girl. He wasn't talking down to her. It warmed Dana to hear that in his tone. He sure had a better attitude with underage females than he did with grown women.

"Okay, then tell me what you're going to do to get the guy and make sure he doesn't hurt my mom," Krystal ordered.

Nico's sigh quivered across the room, heartfelt and deep. Dana heard him pull out a chair as he settled across from Krystal.

"The thing is, Krys, your mom doesn't want my help. She wants to handle things herself and I can't make her accept my help if she doesn't want it. But I'll promise you one thing, the cops are working on it right now and if the shooting last night had anything to do with those threats against your mom, they'll find out about it and they'll do something about it. Meanwhile, you really don't have to worry, you know, because I'm here and you're safe. Right?"

Krystal thought about it. "Yes, Nico." She was silent for a moment and then she started to laugh.

"What?" Nico asked.

"Well, if you're here, Mommy's safe, too, isn't she?

I mean, nobody's going to come and hurt her if they know you're here, even if she did only hire you for me.''

Nico's laughter joined the child's. ''Hey, that's right, kid. But just between the two of us, I haven't forgotten you're the one who really hired me, so in a way, you're my boss.''

They were so busy congratulating each other, they didn't hear her step into the room.·

''This sounds suspiciously like a conspiracy,'' Dana said, making her voice as firm as possible.

The two of them jumped guiltily, midlaughter. Nico leaped to his feet and nearly stumbled over his chair. ''G'morning,'' he said, fumbling as he righted the chair.

The sight of her in morning dishevelment took his breath away. This had to be the test of true feminine beauty, he thought, a woman who could look this good only minutes after awakening, without benefit of makeup, in a plain cotton robe, her hair a mass of loose, uncombed curls that caught the sunlight and danced and shimmered around her face. She was a far cry from his original picture of her in basic business attire, despite the rigid expression of disapproval on her face.

''Sorry, Mommy,'' Krystal said, looking shamefaced.

Dana's smile broke across her face unexpectedly and she let loose the laughter she'd been holding back. ''Okay, I'll forgive you in exchange for a cup of coffee,'' she said, settling in a chair, her hands folded expectantly on the table in front of her.

They almost fell over each other, rushing to serve her the coffee, and she laughed again as she put her feet up on the chair Nico had vacated and put her hands behind her head.

''Ah-hh,'' she sighed, ''my very own servants. I love it.''

Krystal giggled as she set the cream pitcher in front of

Dana but Nico gave her a baleful look along with the mug of coffee he plunked on the table. She grinned and began spooning sugar.

"Been to the hardware store?" she asked, looking up at him. He was something wonderful in the morning, dressed in jeans and a T-shirt, revealing all the musculature of a very fit male. His hair was still damp from a recent shower and she could faintly detect the combination of soap and aftershave on his skin.

"Yeah, we figured we'd let you sleep in and have the work done before you got up."

Dana looked over her shoulder at the door. "Looks like it's almost finished." She sipped coffee. "Where did you learn to repair broken windows?"

Nico grinned and went back to the door. Over his shoulder he said, "We were always breaking 'em when we were kids so my dad insisted we learn how to fix 'em."

"Smart Dad," Dana said. She turned to her daughter and pulled her against her side in a one-armed hug. "Now let's see, how can we teach this little gremlin to repair broken dishes."

"I only broke two," Krystal declared.

"Yeah, but you're only eight, think how many you'll have broken by the time you're ten."

Krystal saw it was a good time to change the subject. "Mommy, Diane's mom said I could come for a play date tomorrow if it's all right with you and Mrs. J. already told her I could so…"

Tomorrow was Saturday. Not usually a workday for Dana because she tried to spend her weekends with her daughter. But if Krystal was going to be playing with Diane, Dana could get in some badly needed extra work time.

Dana turned to Nico, her eyes begging the question.

"Long-time friends?" he asked.

Dana nodded. Her eyes signaled approval based on his agreement. He shrugged. "You remember the rules we went over this morning, right, Krys?"

Krystal nodded eagerly. She ticked them off on her fingers. "No leaving a place without you or Mom picking me up, even if you're late and not even if it's right in the neighborhood. No time, nowhere, no joke," she added firmly.

Nico laughed. "Those last are her words, not mine," he said, shaking his head. "She's quite a little clown."

"Must get it from her father," Dana said, grinning. She tousled Krystal's hair. "Okay, you can call Diane and make the arrangements, but no begging to stay the night. I want you with me at night. Got it?"

"Yeah, yeah, yeah." Krystal started to run for the phone but Dana pulled her back. "I mean it, Krystal, no overnights for now."

"Promise." Krystal held up two fingers. Dana let her go.

Nico had been applying putty to the edges of the pane. He finished the job, wiped the putty knife clean with a rag and came to join Dana at the table.

He turned the chair backward and straddled it, resting his arms across the top. It was a posture common to men, but for some reason it struck Dana as far more suggestive with a man of Nico's build. She averted her gaze, pretending to find something of interest at the bottom of her cup.

"Are you planning to be home all day?" Nico asked.

"I think I'll go into the office for a few hours," she said when she could no longer avoid looking at him. "Despite Yearling's generosity, I can't afford to lose a whole day right now. My caseload is bulging at the seams. I have two important appointments this afternoon that I really don't want to put off, and I need to stop by the hospital and see Mrs. J. first.''

Nico nodded. "Well, I'm sure Krystal and I can keep busy for a few hours. For one thing, I have to run over to my own office, see my boss and pick up a contract for you to sign. Krystal will get a kick out of returning there as a bona fide client. You don't have to worry about her.''

Dana felt sure of it. Krystal was still on the phone babbling happily with her friend. She tousled the child's hair as she passed her on the way up to shower and dress for the office, humming to herself.

When she returned to the kitchen, she found that Nico had cleaned up the remains of breakfast, put away the tools he'd used to fix the window, and left a note assuring her that he and Krystal would be home before her.

STELLA MARTINSON looked over the contract, hesitating before adding her signature to it. She peered at Nico over the half glasses perched on her nose. "You're sure you want to do this, Nico? We have plenty of other people who prefer security work.''

Nico avoided his boss's eyes. "And your point is?''

Stella put down the pen without using it. "My point is, it doesn't have to be you.''

"The kid is already used to me," Nico said. He found a bit of lint on the tweed sport coat he'd put on before coming into the office and brushed it off.

"Nico?''

He couldn't avoid eye contact any longer. He raised his eyes and grinned sheepishly at Stella.

"Okay, so I'm intrigued. This could turn out to be good for me and the agency." He heard the defensive tone in his voice and his grin faded.

"You're not going to get personally involved, are you? Remember the last time you—"

"No," Nico interrupted. "This is altogether different. In the first place, Ms. Harper is no simple, helpless bimbo, and secondly, she doesn't even want my help."

"I don't understand."

"She wants me strictly for the kid—and for the house-keeper when she's there, I guess."

"How does she exclude herself?" Now Stella was intrigued. "And for what reason?"

Nico shrugged. "She's been getting threats. Won't turn them over to the cops. Won't show 'em to me. Won't consider hiring us to guard her, and says it's all because she's perfectly capable of taking care of herself."

"Oh, that was evident when somebody shot her house-keeper," Stella scoffed, her green eyes glinting.

"Yeah, well. So now she's hired us to make sure the old lady and the kid are safe. The premise is, the cops are going to find the shooter and put an end to the danger."

"In our lifetime?"

They both laughed. "In forty-eight hours, or so," Nico said, grinning.

"So much for small talk," Stella said wryly. She picked up the pen and signed it with her usual flourish. "See what you can do about changing the lady's mind, Nico. Sounds like she's shutting out the reality that she's being targeted. Truth is, I don't like the idea of her traveling all over the city without cover." She picked up the phone to signal their interview was over. She had just dialed the number and Nico was at the door when she put her hand over the mouthpiece and called out, "But don't—" she darted a warning glare at him "—don't change it by using your manly charm. One of these days you're going to charm yourself right into more trouble than either of us can get you out of."

Nico left the office with the contract in his briefcase, whistling under his breath, Krystal happily holding his hand.

JOHN YEARLING ANSWERED the intercom and learned Dana had just come in.

"I thought I gave you the day off," he said when she was seated across from him.

"Thanks. Half a day was more than I needed," she said. "Anyway, I had two appointments that seemed too important to put off."

"Pertaining to the Caprezio case?"

"Yes, as a matter of fact."

"That's what I wanted to see you about." He cleared his throat and gave Dana a piercing look. "I'm wondering if it wouldn't be better for you to turn that case over. You've got quite a full load as it is, and what if I'm wrong about Caprezio's involvement in the shooting? I don't like to think that an assignment I've given you has put you and your daughter in danger. Wouldn't it be safer to replace you as prosecutor?"

Dana stared at him, aghast. "No way!"

"Come on, Dana, this isn't any kind of reflection on your work or your ability. In fact, I would have expected you to see this as a favor. After all, it gives you more time to prepare for your other cases and a little more personal time. I know you've been putting in an awful lot of overtime that you could have been spending with Krystal."

"Kystal understands that there are times my work has to come first."

"But why should it, if I can ease things up for you?"

"What is this really about, John? You don't usually do these kinds of 'favors' for any of your people."

"My people don't usually get shot at, especially the women on my team!"

"Ah, so that's it." Dana sat back in her chair, her elbows on the armrests, her fingers steepled together under her chin.

"Point." She leveled a steady look at her boss. "If the person behind the shooting was after me because of one of my cases, they'll go after anyone who is prosecuting. I'm as capable as anyone on your staff of protecting myself. I've been through the academy's self-defense courses. I have high scores in target practice, and I'm licensed to carry a gun."

Before John could respond to that, she leaned forward and said, "And a more pertinent point? Your removing me from the Caprezio case might be construed as gender discrimination. How would that go down with your constituents? Last I heard, more than half of them were women."

She could see, by the way her boss's face paled and then flushed, that she'd struck a nerve.

"Damnit, Dana, I was only looking out for your best interest."

"Well don't!" She leaped to her feet and leaned on the edge of Yearling's desk. "Don't coddle me, don't try to protect me, and most of all, don't underestimate me. I haven't asked for any preferential treatment and I don't want it. What I want is to do my job. The job that includes cases that might even present danger."

Yearling shook his head and slumped back with a heavy sigh. "You're a hard case, Harper."

"Yeah, well ask yourself this, Yearling. Would you be making this offer to any of the men on the staff?"

John waved a dismissive hand at her, refusing to get

into a self-defense position with her, especially since her points, including this last, were well taken. "Go. Slay dragons, win indictments, make headlines. I've got work to do."

Dana wondered how he'd react if she did a little jig in front of his desk. Discretion being the better part of employment, she walked sedately from the room, keeping her back rigid, her head high.

In the outer office she saw that Carol Adams, John's secretary, was waiting with an expectant look on her face. The woman never missed a thing that went on in the department. Dana gave her a thumbs-up and a big grin.

"One more for our side," Carol said, returning the smile and a victory sign.

"Once more into the breach," Dana said, turning in the direction of her own office.

But once back at her desk, she sobered, turning in her swivel chair, facing the view of downtown Minneapolis from her window. But her eyes were looking inward, seeing once again the details of her husband's murder.

Zack and Joe had been on a week-long stakeout of a warehouse owned by Caprezio that had been fingered as a depot for the storage and sale of illegal weapons. Zack had gone out for coffee and upon his return had been shot in the back out on the street in front of the old abandoned building the cops had been using for surveillance. On the street, in plain view of anyone walking, or driving by, visible to anyone looking out of a window facing the street. Yet no witness had been found and though the cops had worked the case harder than any they'd ever had, they'd come up empty and had to move on to new business that was fast piling up.

Dana had made a helluva scene when she'd learned that the task force was shutting down on her husband's murder. Lieutenant King, in charge of the task force, had tried to explain that the case wasn't really closed but that with no evidence, they couldn't justify spending the money and the manpower to keep chasing their own tails. At the time Dana had been positive that the Caprezios were responsible for the hit.

She closed her eyes and rubbed them. Was she viewing the prosecution of Marcus Caprezio as payback? And if so, would she push harder than normal, maybe even invite retaliation from the first family of crime in Minnesota? She shuddered and opened her eyes.

They hadn't been able to convict in the past, but she had no doubt whatsoever that Caprezio Sr. wasn't above murder when it came to protecting his organization. And now his only son was on trial for murder. How far would Alphonze Caprezio go to stop the wheels of justice from putting Marcus away for life?

Dana took a deep breath and placed her hands on her desk. She had to let go of those suspicions from the past if she was going to do an honest and competent job of prosecuting Marcus for this current indictment. With renewed determination, she powered up her computer and pulled up his file.

IT WAS ALMOST SEVEN when Dana arrived home to find the scene in the kitchen very much the way she'd left it that morning. Only instead of doing repair work, Nico was at the stove, whipping up something with a heavenly fragrance. And Krystal, a lazy child by nature, was busily setting the table as she chatted with Nico, her voice and movements very upbeat.

"Did I miss something in your job description?" Dana asked, peering over Nico's shoulder at the pan that contained the source of that wonderful smell.

He edged her away and scolded, "No lid lifting, please. It slows down the cooking."

"Well, ex-cuu-use, me!" With a sniff of feigned hurt, Dana went to the sink to wash her hands. She suppressed a giggle. Slows down the cooking, indeed. Big deal. It wasn't as if he was creating some exotic gourmet dish like veal piccata, for heaven's sake. More likely a Hamburger Helper-type thing. She turned to Krystal as she dried her hands.

"Isn't that the good china, Krys?"

"Uh-huh."

"Well, we usually save that for special occasions, don't we?"

The little girl frowned at her, putting her hands on her hips. "Mommy, family is more important than outsiders. Why would you want to put your best foot forward for strangers and give only your second best to your own family?"

Mouth agape, Dana turned from the child to the man. "You're teaching philosophy to eight-year-olds now, Scalia?"

Nico shrugged. "Works for me." He cast a fond grin at Krystal. "And she's a good student."

"Humph." Dana sat down in her accustomed place at the table, wincing at the sight of the damask napkins she kept carefully wrapped in plastic to keep from yellowing.

She might have felt less grumpy if Nico's point hadn't been well taken. After all, who was more important than one's own family? What she didn't need was for Krystal to learn it from someone else, particularly the handsome, devil-may-care type dishing up...*veal piccata?*

"Ohhh," she sighed, "I might have known." The sigh became a moan at the first taste of perfection.

Nico accepted the implied compliment with a nod and a grin. "The kid said it was your favorite dish."

He was complacently forking a side of spaghetti al pesto onto Dana's plate as Krystal said, "I'm not a kid."

Then Dana said, "Don't call her 'the kid.'" He looked from one to the other and they all laughed.

For a moment Dana had a sense of déjà vu, her mind glimpsing past memories of a man, woman, and child laughing over a meal at this very table. The spasm of memory turned to pain as she observed the bright look on her daughter's face. It wasn't that Dana was male dependent. Not at all. Nor even that she was still grieving over Zack. But she knew Krystal missed having a dad, having a sense of a complete, normal family life.

As if reading her thoughts, Nico said, "This could become a nice habit."

Dana shuddered and put down her fork. "For your information, Mr. Scalia, we weren't eating bologna sandwiches and frozen dinners before tonight, and let's not forget this is a temporary situation." She turned and gave Krystal a warning look that deterred anything the little girl might have been about to say.

To herself Krystal secretly agreed with Nico. This was nice. The whole day with him had been special and she'd had a sense, all through it, that she'd been right in picking him for the job. She'd noticed right away how, together, Mommy and Nico looked like one of the couples in those swanky car ads in the magazines. She could just picture them all dressed up in fancy clothes stepping into a long black limousine, sipping champagne, dancing around a huge sparkling ballroom. She sighed aloud and poked desultorily at her dinner.

"Something the matter, Krys?" Nico asked.

"Maybe you'd prefer a peanut butter sandwich, hon," Dana said. "I know veal isn't one of your favorites."

Hurriedly Krystal picked up her fork and put on her best smile. "Oh, no, Mommy, this is great, I love Nico's cooking. I didn't used to like veal, but Nico's is better than the stuff I had before, honest."

Dana gave the child a dubious look, but Krystal was already busy eating again with apparent relish.

"This is really excellent," Dana said, lifting her eyes to Nico's face across the table. "Thank you."

"You're welcome," he said, returning his attention to his own plate.

He ate with gusto. Dana couldn't help noticing that he also ate Continental style, keeping his knife and fork in his hands without ever setting them down. When he reached for his wineglass, he transferred his fork to the same hand that held the knife, never setting it across his plate as she did. Intrigued, she continued to observe him through her lowered lashes. The British, she knew, ate like that, and she'd always considered it a trifle tasteless, but Nico made it look elegant.

It disturbed her, though, to see Krystal attempting to mimic Nico's movements. Funny, she'd never thought Krystal was father obsessive. She'd certainly never been so enamored of her uncles, Zack's brothers, nor of Joe Lake, who was her honorary uncle and godfather. Of course Zack's two brothers lived on the west coast and Krystal had only seen them about twice in her life. And Joe was her godfather, more part of the background of the child's life.

With Nico it seemed almost like hero worship, the way Krystal blatantly looked up to him. But then Dana realized that was appropriate since Krystal had first seen Nico on TV, being lauded by a newswoman who gushed over his ability to solve a crime that had eluded the local police and the FBI. Children did view anyone they saw on TV as larger than life.

Satisfied that she had the answer, and that in time Nico's appeal would dim with proximity, Dana finished her meal with warranted pleasure.

Both Krystal and Dana refused dessert, Dana wanting

nothing to detract from the pleasure of the entrée and Krystal itching to get to the family room to watch a favorite TV show before bedtime.

Dana excused Krystal and scraped the last of the sauce from her plate with regret.

"That was the best piccata I've ever had," she reiterated as she got up and began clearing the dishes. "Thank you again." At the sink she turned on the taps and began rinsing the tableware. Over her shoulder she asked, "Where did you learn to cook like that?"

Nico came up behind her and reached around her for the sponge.

"At my mother's knee," he said, his words carried on his warm breath, caressing her hair, the back of her neck.

Her own knees seemed to weaken and a plate slipped from her fingers. Nico's reflexes were better than hers; he caught the plate before it could break against the porcelain sink.

Dana froze, waiting for him to step back, to free her from the accidental prison his arms made around her.

Instead he leaned in closer, inhaled deeply and breathily said into her hair, "You smell like wild clover. Does your fragrance come from a bottle?"

Her head cleared. She ducked and slipped out from under his arms, moving briskly and purposefully toward the table. "I don't know what you're talking about, Scalia. I wash my hair like any other woman, use soap, dab on a little cologne. No biggy." But her hands trembled slightly and she made fists and took a deep steadying breath before relaxing her hands and reaching for a cup and saucer.

Nico chuckled. "The lady doesn't take compliments well."

"The lady doesn't fall for every loose line that comes down the pike. And you might remember that you're here in a professional capacity, not as a houseguest or a live-in Lothario.''

His laughter deepened. Her irritation grew. Didn't anything penetrate the man's thick ego? She plunked the cup and saucer back on the table, heedless of their monetary value, and spun around. ''Listen, since you've obviously nothing else to do, why don't you finish up in here and I'll go to my study and get to work.''

''Hey,'' she heard him gripe as she left the room. ''Not fair. I did the cooking.'' This time she was the one to laugh and she kept going, ignoring his plea that he'd behave. She didn't trust his promise any more than she trusted his line.

Chapter Four

Dana detoured to the family room to check on Krystal.

"Twenty minutes to countdown, sweetie," she said, tousling her daughter's curls. Krystal nodded, her eyes glued to the screen.

Dana sighed with exaggerated exasperation. "If you can hear me, Krystal, I'm going to my study to work. When your show is over, please turn off the TV, get in your jammies, brush your teeth and then call me on the intercom and I'll come up and tuck you in."

Again Krystal nodded and this time she murmured, "Yes, Mommy."

Knowing that "Family Matters" on television held more interest for an eight-year-old than family matters in real life, Dana settled for that and went down to her study.

Her first step was to line up the files in the order she'd go through them. That done, she activated her computer. She dialed a number on the phone attached to her modem and entered the password that would link her with the computer in her office at city hall and set to work.

She bent to her work with purpose. Only today she'd had a meeting with a federal forensic accountant who had assured her that if she could justify a warrant to break open Caprezio's books, he could find that single thread, normally invisible to the average person's eye, that would lead to a hidden and more accurate picture of the don's business and ultimately to proof of *enterprise corruption*.

Two birds with one stone, Dana thought with anticipatory satisfaction. Marcus in the state penitentiary for murder, his father in a federal prison, his Mafia-like empire destroyed. A coup for the FBI who had been trying to nail Caprezio for years, but most especially for the county attorney's office and Dana's career.

She was poring through notes and researching the computer files that defined the murder investigation when Krystal's voice came over the intercom.

"Mommy, I'm ready."

"Right up, sweetie," Dana said, almost reluctant to leave her work now that it had taken on its own rhythm.

But Krystal was her first priority. She hurried up to the child's room.

"Nico's nice, isn't he, Mommy?" Krystal said, coming out of the bathroom with a shining face and dressed in pajamas and robe.

Dana tucked in one side of the bedding and pulled the other side up loosely, so Krystal could get easily into bed. She sat down on the edge of the bed and caressed her child's soft, smooth cheek as Krystal came to stand in front of her, bending to rest her elbows on her mother's knees.

"Hmm? Oh, yes, of course. Nico's nice. And you—" she tickled Krystal under the chin "—you're nice too."

Krystal giggled and then grew serious. "Nico says he can help you, Mommy."

Dana was picking up the library books lying beside the bed, stacking them neatly on the nightstand. "Help me with what, dear?" she asked as she looked at the title of the book in her hand. Nancy Drew. Gosh, was Krystal old enough for Nancy Drew already?

"You know, help you find out about those notes and stuff."

Dana looked up, startled. Krystal's blue eyes nailed her, rousing feelings of regret and even a little guilt. It was bad enough her father had died, how would she have taken it if they were to have divorced? Looking back, she recalled the thought had crossed her mind frequently in that last year of Zack's life. It got the grieving all mixed up with guilt and remorse.

"Honey, I told you…"

"I know. But Mommy, how can it hurt your career if Nico helps? He's a private investigator so he has to keep your business private and nobody will find out."

Dana laughed and hugged Krystal. "You're so logical, my love, and so grown up for your age." She changed the subject. "Nancy Drew books were my favorite, too."

"Way back when you were my age?"

"Yeah, way back then," Dana wryly mimicked. "Only I guess I was more like ten when I started reading them."

"That's because children are more mature today than when you were little, Mommy," Krystal pedantically quoted some grown-up source.

"Too true," Dana said sadly. Fleetingly she thought about the cases of child crimes that were discussed with ever-increasing and frightening frequency at work. The thought reinforced her priority for assuring that Krystal learn family values at home.

"Prayer time, sweetie," she said.

Krystal got down on her knees, put her elbows on the bed, put her palms together and tucked them under her chin.

The prayer was pure Krystal.

"And God bless Mommy and Grandma and Grandpa Taylor even if Grandma Taylor is too bossy sometimes and acts silly for a grown-up, and all my friends. And, God, please make Mrs. Johnson get well fast and don't let that bad man come back again. Thank You, God. Amen.''

Dana smiled and bent to kiss Krystal good-night. ''That was lovely, dear, but I don't think you should tattle on Grandma Taylor.'' They both giggled. And Dana added as a last and sober note, ''And, honey, I don't want you going to sleep worrying about anything. Nobody is going to come back here now that the police have increased their patrols in the neighborhood, and don't forget we have Nico here, as well.''

Krystal hadn't forgotten.

As soon as her mother had left the room, she scooted out of bed, fell to her knees, reclasped her hands and said in a near whisper, ''God, I forgot something. No, I didn't forget exactly,'' she corrected, fearing God would detect a lie. ''But I didn't want to upset Mommy. Please, God, help Nico find the bad guys and bless him, too. And, God...'' She lowered her voice to a whisper. ''Make Mommy like him. Ame—'' She stopped and then added firmly, ''A lot! Amen.''

NICO CAME to the door of Dana's study and cleared his throat.

''Yes?'' She didn't look up.

''Will it disturb you if I turn on the TV in the living room?''

''Hmm? No, go ahead.'' Her fingers flew over the keyboard.

She was hardly aware that Nico had been at the door, barely registered the sound of the television voices through the open door. It might be like looking for a needle in a haystack, but she was determined to find that elusive clue.

She didn't know what drew her attention from her work. Perhaps it was movement she caught peripherally as Nico got up to lower the volume, got up again to change the channel, and once more to readjust the volume.

What was the matter with him? Why wasn't he using the remote like most men? He bent forward to fiddle with a dial and her eyes registered his tight butt, long, muscled legs, broad shoulders. He stood erect and gazed at the set a moment before deciding he was comfortable with the picture. A low chuckle confirmed that he was content with the program.

Finally he settled in the easy chair across from the TV set, his profile illuminated by the table lamp at his side.

She noticed that he was wearing chinos now, rather than jeans, and a neatly laundered, short-sleeved polo shirt. Best of all, he'd exchanged the boots for loafers. With socks! She mentally applauded that. She'd always thought there was something so affectatious about the fad that had men wearing leather shoes over bare feet. She realized she was allowing her thoughts to be distracted by Krystal's bodyguard and scolded herself for using such cheap methods to avoid working.

With a sigh, Dana returned her attention to her computer.

After a few minutes she realized that she'd been staring at the screen but seeing nothing. She looked up and saw that Nico was sprawled in the easy chair, his attention focused on the TV screen, his long legs stretched out before him. She noticed the way his dark hair curled around his ear, almost touching the collar of his polo shirt. Did he need a haircut or was that his preferred length and style?

She shook the thought away, disgusted that she'd al-

lowed herself to be so frivolously distracted. Again! She
swiveled her chair away from the sight of the man.

The screen saver pattern had filled the monitor screen,
a precaution for keeping the wrong eyes from reading the
screen if the user left her work for more than a few
minutes. She hadn't realized she'd been distracted for
that long. Feeling foolish, she pushed Enter and restored
the screen.

When she discovered that she still couldn't concentrate, she got up to close the door between the study and
the living room.

Nico looked up as she stood at the door, her hand on
the knob.

His breath caught in his throat. The sight of her suddenly appearing there had an unsettling affect on him.

Their eyes met. There was a kind of pleading in her
soft blue eyes, something desperate that he hadn't seen
before.

Hot. The word came to him from the terminology of
the street; it fit her perfectly. She was hot!

Bellisima. The word came to him from his father's
language, his eyes seeing her as his father would, all soft
curves, the golden halo of her hair, her poise, her innate
elegance. His father would consider her a goddess. He
thought about her feistiness and realized it was an attri-
bute that made her more approachable, less goddess and
more woman.

"Am I disturbing you?" he asked.

*Yes, that's the word exactly. You disturb me, and I
don't know why.* Dana shook her head. "No, I...yes, the
television..."

"Sorry. I'll go into the family room."

"No, that's okay. I'll just shut the door." She did that,
abruptly cutting off any further protestations from him.

Feeling shaky, and bemused by that reaction, she returned to her work, determined to make herself concentrate. It took a few minutes but she finally found her focus and settled in.

Sometime later a knock at the door penetrated her consciousness.

"I'm going to make some fresh coffee, would you like a cup?" Nico asked, popping his head around the door after she'd called out, "Come in."

She glanced at her watch, surprised to discover she'd been working over two hours. "Yes." She stretched and then self-consciously crossed her arms over her chest when she saw that his gaze had followed the sensuous movement. "I could use a break," she said, avoiding his ardent expression. "I'll be along in a minute."

Coffee was already brewing when she entered the kitchen. Once again she sat at the table and observed the easy way he moved around her kitchen. As if he'd been living in the house for months instead of barely twenty-four hours. He was obviously a man who could make himself at home anywhere. She found that thought disturbing and then rationalized that as a private investigator, he might often be called upon to settle in unexpected places for long periods of time, especially if he did a lot of surveillance work. A niggling thought that he might have made his way through a long line of other women's kitchens was quickly scotched and considered unduly cynical and none of her business anyway.

Nico carried two cups of steaming coffee to the table and went to the refrigerator for the cream she used. He didn't know why it gave him such a kick to wait on her. Was it a power ploy, a kind of control? He decided that wasn't it. More likely a matter of conditioning.

He'd been raised by a doting, nurturing mother, but his father had tempered that by insisting on independence for all of his children. Not a typical Italian male, old dad, though he treated his wife—and for that matter, all women—with Old World charm and gallantry.

He remembered his father insisting Mama teach the kids to use the laundry machines, the stove, the iron, while he gave lessons on the proper use of the gas-fueled lawn mower and lined them all up to show them how to change a tire, check and replenish car fluids, and restart the old furnace in the basement.

The four boys were not exempt from Mama's lessons, the girls included in Dad's. As papa had pointed out many times, with pride, "Anything happens to me and Mama, my kids could run this house by themselves. They'll never need help from outside to take care of them."

"Want some dessert now?" he asked as he joined Dana at the table.

She shook her head. "This is fine," she said, stirring her coffee. "I don't want anything to override the memory of that wonderful dinner," she said, shyly smiling.

They sipped in companionable silence for a few moments and then Nico spoke.

"Do you mind answering a question?"

"Shoot." Her hair swayed across her cheeks as she lifted her head and turned to look at him.

He watched her pull it back, hold it there with two hands for a moment and then let it spring back. An automatic, unconscious habit he'd seen her exhibit frequently in the short time he'd been there. He knew she'd get up at any time, seek out a rubber band and impatiently pull the whole shimmering mass into a ponytail. Half an hour later she'd discard the band and let it all swing free again.

Nico drew his gaze from her hair. "Why haven't you turned those notes over to the police? That would be the first thing the average citizen would think to do."

Dana hesitated, debating how much to confess to this man, a veritable stranger. But then she recalled the conversation he'd had with Krystal that morning, and his attitude toward the police department's efficiency in crime solving.

Some instinct made her trust him. "The legal and the court systems here in Minneapolis are very patriarchal and...almost chauvinistic. A menacing combination for a woman trying to keep a foothold against the built-in odds. If they find out I'm being threatened, they will become so protective, it will hinder my freedom to do my job. That's the first thing." She waited a beat and then added, "The other thing is that I don't entirely trust the police department."

Nico had his cup to his lips but set it down without drinking.

"What? But why? Your husband—"

"I know, I know." Dana waved a hand dismissively. "But maybe that's why. I've never been completely satisfied with the way his murder investigation was handled."

"And that's because..."

"Because I think they gave up too soon, and maybe the reason they did was because they didn't want to be discovered with egg on their faces so they decided the sooner the case was quietly pushed to the back of the closet, the quicker the public would forget that they hadn't been able to solve it." She wet her dry mouth with another swallow of coffee. "And maybe someone was paid to distort the facts and contaminate the evidence."

"You're talking about your husband's fellow officers." Was that tone, that look on his face, meant to chastise her?

Dana's chin jutted defiantly. "So that means one of

them couldn't have been on the take?'' She laughed bitterly. ''When did you become so biased in their favor? What are you, an ex-cop?''

''Yeah,'' Nico said quietly. ''But you're wrong about me being biased. I was only playing devil's advocate.''

But Dana was still digesting his admission.

''You were? When?''

''When I reminded you that whoever covered the ev—''

Dana's fist hit the table. ''I meant, when were you a cop?'' she asked through clenched teeth.

''A long time ago. Another time, another place.''

Dana's gaze was searching. ''I confided in you,'' she noted pointedly.

His look matched hers and held for a long, drawn out span. Then he said, ''Five years ago. St. Paul P.D. Detectives. Vice.''

''Why did you leave?''

Nico got up and refilled their cups before answering. When he sat back down, he saw that she'd unearthed a rubber band and pulled her hair into a ponytail. He smiled inwardly and then sobered as he considered his answer to her question.

''I didn't like the way the department overlooked certain infractions.''

''So you were a by-the-book cop. That doesn't surprise me.''

''Not that, so much as that I couldn't stomach the inequities.''

''Such as?'' She had her elbow on the table, chin on her hand, enrapt by his revelations.

Nico smoothed his mustache and then slumped back in his chair, arms crossed over his chest. ''It didn't make sense to me that the same cops who arrested the hookers were also accepting their favors. It made even less sense that we'd bust dealers and then some cops would pocket the goods for their own private use. It seems to me if prostitution and drugs are vices, and illegal, they're off limits for cops, too." He shook his head. "Especially for cops."

"Makes sense to me," Dana agreed. "So why didn't you just report them to Internal Affairs?"

His laugh was a short bark and his look disdained her naiveté. "It was hard enough on my parents, having a son on the force, without putting myself at deliberate risk." He stood up, shoved his hands into the back pockets of his jeans and wandered over to the outside door, peering through the window into the night.

With his back to her, Dana had to strain to hear him.

"There isn't a criminal out there more dangerous than a rogue cop. We're trained, armed, put out in the streets to mix it up with the thugs. If one of us goes bad, we have the resources of both the force and the streets to do our dirty work. And it isn't just on the streets that a guy's partner will back him up, most likely that same partner will cover for him if he's caught with his hand in the cookie jar. So then it isn't just one bad cop you've got to deal with, but two." He turned to face her, leaning back against the door.

"I'd rather go up against your average Mafia lord any day than a cop gone sour."

Dana could feel her heart pounding in her chest. It wasn't just the terrible things Nico was saying, it was the utter despair in his voice when he said them, and the look of pure desolation in his eyes.

She had the urge to go to him, to comfort him with a hug, as she would Krystal. She reminded herself they were newly met and that she had no idea how he would respond to such a liberty. He might mistake it for an invitation, or he could have one of those male egos that rejected anything that might be construed as pity. She balled her hands into fists and kept them in her lap as she remained in her seat.

She offered him trust instead.

"Would you like to look at those notes, Nico?"

He looked puzzled and then wary. "Not unless you're willing to take us on board."

"What do you mean?"

He joined her at the table, pulling the chair out to turn it around so he could sit on it backward, his arms folded across the top of the chair back.

"The way our agency works is that you don't hire a single private eye when you contract with us. You probably caught that clause when you looked over the contract I had you sign.

"It's actually the agency in its entirety that you contract with, and as many investigators as deemed necessary are assigned to a single case. In other words, when you hire me, you have access to the whole company. We have a good forensics department and do quite a bit of our own lab work. In fact, the lab also does work for other organizations. My boss's way of bringing in more revenue so the lab doesn't have a lot of down time.

"The best thing is, we can guarantee absolute privacy while an investigation is under way. We're not beholden to the public in any way so we don't have to answer to the press."

He put his hand out on the table.

"I think you should hire the agency to help you uncover the truth, find out who's making the threats, and more important, find out if the person sending them is the same person who shot at the house last night."

Dana sat forward. "You think the threats and the shooting could be coming from two different sources?" The air went out of her lungs in a painful whoosh. She shook her head, loosening wisps of hair from the pony-tail. She tried to tuck them back in but found the effort wasn't worth it.

Nico tried not to let the sight of her casual attire deter him from straight thinking. She looked better in jeans than any woman over the age of twenty that he'd ever seen. The soft, faded denim clung to her lower body as if tailored to show the sleek lines of her legs, the enticing curve of her derriere. God, she was one sexy woman and if circumstances were different…

"The shooting smacks of spontaneity, not the work of someone who'd harass you with notes and phone calls. A person like that is more of a long-range thinker, using the threats to scare you into a deal."

"That was more or less what Yearling and Joe said," Dana admitted. A glimmer of an idea formed. "Maybe the shooting was only meant to be a threat," she suggested. "Maybe the shot went wrong and met a target quite by accident."

Nico felt his admiration for her go up another notch. She wasn't letting the personal trauma keep her from thinking like the fine lawyer she was. He nodded. "That's possible, too. We need to be open to all the angles. So. Do we have a deal, Dana?"

"You understand that your first priority is still to keep Krystal safe?"

He nodded assent. "I can do both and there are people in the agency who can be called on to fill in as needed." He hesitated a moment and then added, "It's not going to be cheap so if—"

"I can afford it." She leveled a firm look at him.

Nico cleared his throat and lowered his eyes. "I guess that leads to my next question, Dana. I know what an assistant D.A. makes, and Zachary Harper was a cop…"

Dana's quiet laugh brought his eyes upward to her

face. "You want to know how I can afford this house, to live this well." It suddenly dawned on her what he was really asking was if Zack had been on the take. The unasked question would normally have raised her hackles, but after what he'd told her, she understood where he was coming from.

She met his dark brown gaze with her own blue-eyed honesty.

"My father is Daniel Taylor," she said simply, and waited for recognition to sink in.

It took less than a minute. "Of Taylor Industries?"

"Yes. I have a considerable trust fund that came to me from Dad's father when Dad took over the family business." She didn't know why she was being so revealing with him; he was practically a stranger and she knew many men would respond with avarice to her admission of wealth.

But Nico Scalia didn't react at all. It answered what he had asked and he seemed to have no further interest in the subject.

He nodded and said, "We've done some work for T.I. Not me, personally, but the agency, I mean."

She smiled. "I know. The time that T.I. hired your company it was at Zack's suggestion. Evidently the private sector has better technology and technicians for uncovering espionage, and breach of security, than the police do."

"So?"

"So what?"

"So are you going to take us on and let me work more directly with you?"

"The notes are in my study," she said, standing to lead the way.

Chapter Five

"As you can see, they're fairly straightforward," Dana said, looking over Nico's shoulder. He sat at her desk studying the notes laid out in the order she'd received them.

They seemed identical. "'C. Gets Off Or You Go Down.'"

Nico looked up at her. "'C.' for Caprezio?"

Dana shrugged. "It's not that easy. As it happens, 'C' is the first initial of either the first or last name of each of my three major cases."

"Hmm. Funny the sender doesn't realize that."

Dana felt the first ray of hope since she'd begun receiving the notes. Maybe it was better to have someone to share this with, input from another mind. She went around the desk and sat on the edge of the front of it. "You're right. The sender either doesn't follow the news, or has such a big ego he thinks of himself as the one and only 'C.'"

"You know the defendants pretty well by now, which of the three fits that picture?"

Dana thought about her three cases. "Well, first of all, it's four defendants, not three. In the Carter case, I'm prosecuting two brothers, accused together of rape and murder. But it isn't only the brothers we're dealing with, the entire Carter family has been very public about their hatred of the police and the legal system in general, loudly proclaiming that the two boys were framed, offering up such an assortment of phony alibis that we almost got buried by the sheer numbers.'' She laughed without mirth. ''We had to check out the alibis of the alibi providers on that one.''

''And Marcus Caprezio? What's his story?''

Dana plucked a pencil from an intricately carved teak cup and twirled it between her fingers as she ran the case down for him.

''That one should be open and shut. Marcus got into a fight, in a bar, with one Anthony 'Squirrel' Nunzio. Plenty of witnesses. Marcus stormed out after the bartender intervened. An hour later Nunzio comes out and a car rolls up, the driver leans out and shoots him, and the car drives off. Again, plenty of witnesses. Nobody got the license plate number, unfortunately, but the description of the car makes it Marcus's bright red Porsche. Only three of those in the twin cities. One owned by a rock musician who was on tour in Europe on the date, his car in storage. The second owned by a Porsche dealer. Airtight alibi. He had driven to a dealer's seminar in Chicago. Any number of people could account for his presence there.''

''The third, of course, is Caprezio's.''

''Anyway, it was enough for us to bring him in. And lo and behold little Marcus Caprezio hadn't covered his butt. He has no alibi for the time slot.''

Nico frowned. ''Weird. If he did finger the guy, why wouldn't he have covered himself with an alibi? Any of the people in the Organization would have put up for him.''

Dana's eyes turned steely as she talked about it. ''Right. Unless Marcus's rage was such that he just lost it and didn't regain it in time to set up an alibi. Or, and I like this one better, he's so damned cocksure that he figured he was above the law and never even thought he'd be arrested and need an alibi.''

Nico wasn't comfortable with that, but let it slide for now.

"The third?"

"Surely you've heard of 'Prince Charlie,' the darling of the media? He's been seen on TV more often than Charlie the Tuna."

Dana tossed the pencil back in the cup in a gesture of disgust. "Charles Donegan is either the most stupid white-collar criminal I've ever run across or he's brazen as hell. It appears that he's spent most of the stolen funds on his wardrobe. He's always impeccably, and expensively, custom-tailored—to the nth degree.

"He preens like a peacock for the news cameras and since he's been out on bail, delights in giving press-conference-type interviews that sneer at me in particular and the court system in general."

She sighed, stood and stretched. "So much for finding a clue in the message of the notes."

Nico followed her movements. Her sensuality shook him. "Don't do that," he said abruptly, his voice harsh.

"I beg your pard..." Dana's words tapered off as she realized what had just occurred. A mischievous grin lit up her face.

"Maybe this job is too much for you to handle, Scalia. Maybe you better have your agency put someone else on it."

Nico was on his feet and around the desk so quickly that Dana was caught off guard. His arm around her was steel, his hand at the back of her head firm. He pulled her face close to his and his hand rippled fingers from her brow to the corner of her lips, gentle as the soughing of a spring breeze. His mouth was inches from hers, breath warm and sweet, the danger of his warning more formidable by the contrast.

"I can handle anything you dish out, Ms. Harper, and then you better be prepared to play the game to its conclusion."

She was mesmerized by his eyes, chocolate brown turned almost midnight black and by the husky threat in his voice. Her knees weakened while her heartbeat strengthened. Was he going to kiss her? And if he did, was she going to allow it? Without making a conscious decision, her lips parted, her head tilted ever so slightly, her eyelids drifted down.

He let go of her abruptly and she fell back against the desk, catching her hip on the edge.

"Very funny, Scalia," she snapped, rubbing at her leg. Was it relief, embarrassment, or disappointment that raged through her? She snatched up the notes and shoved them into a drawer, avoiding his eyes as he moved back to the chair behind the desk.

"You know, this seems like a pretty heavy caseload," Nico said, acting as if the moment had never happened.

"We're all overloaded in the county attorney's office. Or are you just suggesting my load is heavy for a woman?"

Nico laughed. "Women are still touchy on the subject, eh?"

Dana's color heightened. "We wouldn't need to be if men didn't still act like they were doing us a favor letting us move beyond the reception area."

Nico wasn't going to touch that. His own boss was a woman and he admired her to the max, but he knew there were still plenty of men out there who hadn't moved from the caves out into the light of the late twentieth century.

"Actually, I was wondering if it was possible that

someone figured if you were bogged down with work, you wouldn't be able to do justice to any one case."

"You mean…but that would imply that John… No way! I'd swear on my life that Yearling is clean."

Nico shrugged. "You'd know best. It's my job to be suspicious of anyone and everyone. You say he's clean, he's clean. If you don't mind, I'd like to go through your files, familiarize myself with the cases."

"Of course."

He shuffled through the folders, arranging them so that he would have room on the desk to jot down notes under each as he went through them.

But Dana was still seething and unwilling to look openly at the source of her frustration. She focused instead on what she'd interpreted as Nico's chauvinism. "You wouldn't be questioning the weight of my load if I were a man, though, would you?"

He gave her a level look. "Yeah," he said calmly. "I would."

It popped the balloon of anger and left her nothing to cling to as she tried to avoid facing her still-simmering desire.

"It's late. I'm going to bed."

"Good idea," Nico said.

She was almost at the door when he stopped her with a question.

"The cops haven't seen the notes at all?"

"No. I had them checked out on my own with the lab people. There are no clues as to the identity of the author." She hesitated, her hand on the knob. "You know, those kinds of threats aren't so unusual in felony cases. Most of the time they're just blowing hot air, hoping to scare us off."

"You haven't even shown them to Joe Lake?"

She turned back. "No, not even Joe."

"But you're pretty good friends, right?"

"He was Zack's partner, his best friend. He's my friend, too."

"Nothing more?"

Was the question professional or personal? Dana shrugged, either way the answer was the same. "Nothing more," she said. She didn't add that that was due to her feelings and not Joe's.

She peered across the room at the handsome detective. Was he sniffing out the territory, checking to see if any other takers were stalking her? He appeared to be already involved in the work. Apparently his interest in her was minimal and his questions had been strictly professional.

"It's all there, in those folders," Dana said, waving in the general direction of her desk. "You shouldn't need me for anything else."

But he was engrossed in what he was reading. He barely mumbled a "Good night." It took all of her control not to slam the door as she left the room.

ALONE, Nico let got of the deep, shaky sigh he'd held back. This was walking the edge, he knew, the very thing Stella had warned against. He knew better, had been burned before. So why was he courting disaster now?

Because of a woman who had masses of wheat-colored hair, eyes the color of bluebells, and a mouth that begged to be kissed, which only added to her allure. *And doubled the danger.*

He sighed again and forced his attention to the files in front of him. He was here to do a job; if he did it well, he'd be out of here in a couple of days. Everybody could go back to their normal lives, Stella would be happy with the completion of another job, and he'd be assigned to a nice, impersonal, slightly boring, tax evasion case.

He opened the first of the files. He'd been reading only

a couple of minutes when he was distracted by a sound at the door. Simultaneously his head swung up and his hand went to his underarm holster.

"Nico, I had a bad dream and Mommy's in the shower and I didn't want to be alone and..."

Krystal's voice trailed off on a hiccup, punctuated by a dry sob.

Instinctively he opened his arms and the little girl bounded across the room and catapulted herself onto his lap to snuggle against him. He stroked her hair and crooned promises of safety until she'd quieted and then he softly asked her to tell him about the dream.

"It was so scary," she said, the two s-words made sibilant by her two missing front teeth. Nico smiled above her head and tightened his embrace.

"First it was just a party, and that wasn't very scary, but then I noticed it was all Daddy's friends from the police and Mrs. J. was going around with a tray, giving everyone drinks and then I went to her to get a drink, too, but instead of drinks, there were a lot of guns on the tray."

Krystal began to cry then, weeping rather than sobbing, more out of sadness than fear, Nico thought. He pulled a tissue from the box on the desktop and dabbed at her tear-streaked face but didn't try to stop the crying. Instead he gently rocked her in his arms, waiting until she'd cried herself out, every so often dabbing with the tissue. When she seemed to be recovering, he handed her a fresh tissue and she noisily blew her nose.

"It's no wonder you had a dream like that, Krys, I'd be more surprised if you didn't. But there's some good stuff in the dream, you know."

"Like what?" Eyes the color of bluebells gazed up at him beseechingly. He felt a strange clutching in his chest. A definite aching, but not painful so much as yearning.

Her small body was warm and damp against his and her sleep-tousled, silky hair tickled his chin. The smell of soap and little-girl sweetness filled his nose.

"Like the fact that all your dad's buddies from the force were there and you know they'll always look out for you, right?"

Krystal nodded, gave another small hiccup. "What else?"

"Well, let's see. If Mrs. J. was handing out guns, then the dream was telling you that she was back in control, no longer a victim. It probably means she'll be up and well and back here to take care of you very soon. The doctor said she wasn't badly hurt at all."

"You talked to the doctor?"

"No," he shook his head. "But your mom did, and she said Mrs. J. is already on the mend."

Krystal sniffed and nodded. "Uncle Joe told me that, too."

Uncle Joe? Krystal called Joe Lake "uncle"? Did that mean what it usually meant? Was there something going on between Dana and Lake after all? Despite her firm denial?

His thoughts were interrupted by the sound of shouts from the hall. Dana burst into the room, her eyes wide with fear.

"Nico! Krystal's not in her bed... Oh." She came to an abrupt halt as she spied Krystal safely tucked up on Nico's lap. Damp wads of tissue on the desk told their own story.

"Bad dream, honey?" she asked as she approached the pair, her arms held out.

Nico transferred the child to her mother. "She's fine now."

Dana rocked from side to side, clutching Krystal to

her, her heart still racing from her recent fright at finding her child's bed empty.

"I'm okay now, Mommy," Krystal said, straining against her mother's embrace. "Nico took care of me."

She slid to her feet as Dana's arms loosened their hold.

Dana looked over at Nico. "She was sleeping peacefully when I looked in before I went to shower," she explained defensively.

Nico nodded. "Probably the sound of running water penetrated her sleep and triggered the dream."

He knew something about the slight paranoia of single moms. His sister, Kenna, was trying to raise three kids without a husband to help and she often read criticism where none was intended. It didn't help that Gary was always after her to take him back, showering her with gifts and attention he'd neglected to give her before the divorce. She fluctuated between being Gary's girlfriend and the mother of his children.

Dana had far more reason to be paranoid. He smiled at her and said, "I did what anyone would do."

"Thanks. I'm glad you were here for her."

Nico shrugged and glanced meaningfully at the paper-strewn desktop.

Dana got the message and took Krystal's hand. "Come on, hon, we'll go back to bed and let Nico get on with his work."

In the silence that filled the room when they'd gone, it took a few minutes for him to draw his attention away from the image of Dana in a nightshirt, her long bare legs exposed to the thighs, her breasts thrusting against the soft knit. The back view as they'd left the room had been equally as enticing. Unbidden, the thought of Joe Lake encroached. *Uncle Joe.* Lake and Dana Harper. Now there was an image he had to squelch if he was ever going to get back to work. It took some doing, but he finally immersed himself in the information in front of him.

DANA LAY AWAKE for a long time, her ears straining to catch any further sounds from Krystal's room while trying to detect sounds from the first floor. She knew Nico would be hours at the desk, the files were sizable.

Her mind drifted to the picture of the man holding the little girl on his lap, the trusting look on her daughter's face, the easy comradery that had sprung up almost instantly between Krystal and Nico Scalia.

She tucked her hands behind her head and gazed up at the ceiling. The posture brought her breasts upright, reminding her of the incident down in her study. She lowered her arms and crossed them over her breasts, aware of the tingling the memory incited. He'd meant to kiss her. She couldn't be wrong about that. Something had changed his mind. Someone, perhaps. Did he have a special woman in his life? Why not? He was drop-dead gorgeous and highly visible, thanks to the press. There were probably plenty of groupies out there just waiting for one of his dark-eyed glances, the sight of him brushing his mustache with his fingers as he assessed a situation.

She growled, a low sound of disgust deep in her throat, refuting the imp's judgment, and rolled to her side. This was a business relationship and she was professional enough to keep it that way.

She squeezed her eyes shut, damning herself for thinking about this, damning her body for remembering the moment and wanting more. She'd been contentedly celibate for three years. Why did her body have to begin making demands now?

"Krystal," she muttered aloud, pushing her face into her pillow, "what have you gotten me into?"

THE MAN HUNG BACK in the shadows of the shallow woods across the street from the Harper house. From where he stood he could see the cop car parked in front and the glow of the cop's cigarette in the dark.

All of the houses on this street were backed by Lake Minnetonka, its waters lapping at the edge of backyard lawns and docks. It wasn't likely that they had a cop sitting in a boat watching the back of the property.

The cop car was facing the other direction and the cop didn't seem to be doing anything but making himself visible, perhaps his assignment only to scare off anyone who meant to approach the Harper residence with nefarious intentions.

Keeping his stride slow but even, he walked with purpose toward his target. If the cop looked into his rearview mirror at that moment, he'd surely spot him, even in the dark.

He kept going, silently planning an explanation should the cop suddenly get out of his car to question his presence on the street.

Scarcely breathing, he reached the house of the neighbor without incident. With careful stealth he made his way along the side of the house to the back, along the back, crossing a section of lawn, a patio, another section of lawn and then stepped onto the Harper's property.

Done! Easy as pie. So much for police surveillance; the Harper house was about as well protected as Yankee Stadium.

There was a gazebo in the middle of the backyard and he crept toward it, eased the screen door open and slipped inside. He sat for a while, surveying the house, feeling the satisfaction of trespassing without being caught. It was the sort of one-upmanship he most enjoyed, even though no one was around to appreciate his derring-do.

He sat like that for half an hour and then got up to

leave. He had no note with him, had only intended to stake out the place. But as he was about to make his way back the way he'd come, he had an urge to leave some proof of his prowess, something to let the Harper broad know he'd been there, that she was vulnerable, despite the cops, and that he was invincible. He searched his pockets, found a matchbook from the Hilton Hotel and wedged it between the frame and the screen door of the gazebo.

Chapter Six

Dana crossed the parking lot, clutching files, books, and shoulder bag to her chest as she fumbled for her keys. The lot was still quite full for a late Saturday afternoon, but she spotted her blue Lexus, four cars down, just as her fingers located the keys. She breathed a sigh of relief, grateful she wasn't going to have to set everything down to search the depths of her purse.

She didn't notice the man creeping along the next aisle of cars.

She was only a few feet from the Lexus when the man jumped out from behind a car, shouting obscenities, causing her to throw up her arms in fright, a scream caught on the edge of her suddenly dry throat. Books, papers, keys went flying. The man gripped her arm and shoved her back against the car.

She recognized Henry Carter, his grizzled face permanently etched with rage and frustration, his voice graveled by nicotine, whiskey and menace.

"What are you doing here, Mr. Carter? What do you want?"

She was aware of activity nearby, people passing in and out of the parking lot in cars, in and out of the government building on foot. She had only to scream to alert others to her whereabouts, to the danger this man posed.

"I wanna know why my boys is in the slammer while others far worse goes free."

"I'm not going to talk to you until you let go of my arm," Dana said, clenching her teeth. "I could have you arrested for this, you know."

Her bravado didn't faze the old man, although he let go of her arm, but kept her pinned to the car by planting his body directly in front of her. His fetid breath was almost more painful than his hold had been.

"Yeah, I know how you cops operate," he growled. "Them that has money greases the palm and walks out and them that don't pisses in the wind. My boys are rotting in jail for something they was framed for. My boys wouldn't never do nothin' like them things you say they done. My boys was framed by dirty cops!"

Dana used his absorption in his own litany to ease away from Carter, far enough to take a deep, cleansing breath of air polluted by nothing more nauseating than car exhaust.

"We have enough evidence to prove the boys did it, Mr. Carter," she said calmly, risking a moment to glance around for her keys. They lay on the ground only inches from her right foot.

"Planted by dirty cops!"

She shook her head, calling on all her patience. She'd been through this with Carter Sr. before. "No, Mr. Carter, evidence taken from the victim and the crime scene, evidence that could not possibly have been planted."

There was spittle on the old man's chin and the zealous glint of purpose in his eyes. "You got ways. I watch TV. I know you got ways and them ways is what got my boys framed."

He pounded his fist on the top of the Lexus to emphasize his outrage and Dana flinched and then used the moment to bend and swiftly grab her keys. Without the element of surprise on his side, Henry Carter was just a frail old man, poor personal hygiene his strongest weapon. She didn't like the idea, but if she had to, she could shove him out of her way, even knock him down, and take off.

She'd give it one more shot of reason.

"Mr. Carter, I shouldn't even be discussing this case with you, but since you're so obviously misinformed, let me assure you that we wouldn't be taking this case to trial without absolute proof that your sons did, indeed, commit the crimes of which they are accused."

His voice turned oily, his smile crafty. "You mean like you got proof on that Caprezio fellow?"

"I'm not at liberty to discuss..."

"Yeah," he shouted, thrusting his face toward her, "you can't discuss that everyone knows them Caprezios is Mafia and they can walk away free but poor boys like mine who ain't got no connections got to rot in jail for somethin' they didn't even do."

"Caprezio didn't walk away free, Mr. Carter. He met the bail and will have to report for his trial. Your sons had the same opportunity to meet bail."

"No thanks to you," Carter jeered. "I heard you tell that judge not to give my boys no bail. And then even when he did he made it so's there wasn't no way we could pay it."

"I'm sorry. That's how the system works."

She really wasn't sorry. If she'd had her way, there'd be no such thing as bail for any of the criminals who stood accused. But the legal system's policy of "innocent until proven guilty" gave everyone the opportunity to spend as little time in jail as possible until a verdict was reached in a court of law.

"Yeah, I can see how sorry you are, lady, but I'll tell you this, you're going to get a lot sorrier."

"You're angry with the wrong person. I'm just doing my job. The system—"

"The system stinks and so do you!"

Dana had had it. There was no getting through to this man who refused to accept that his sons were capable of committing the crimes of which they were accused. Either that, or he just didn't accept that they should have to pay for their crimes. The fact that they had rap sheets longer than the length of this parking lot did little to dissuade him from his convictions.

"Get out of my way, Mr. Carter, I have an appointment and you've already made me late." She gathered her papers and thrust her key into the lock, holding herself tensed and ready to fight back should the man touch her again.

He leaned forward and his breath dampened her hair as he said into her ear, "You ain't heard the last, Miss High and Mighty, my boys get sent up and you're goin' to pay."

Dana spun around, rage boiling up in her chest. "Sending threatening notes through the mail is a federal offense, Mr. Car—"

But the man had disappeared as quickly as he'd come, leaving her shaking with anger, fear and frustration.

She got into her car, willing her pulse to slow, her breathing to return to normal, before she attempted to navigate the early evening rush-hour traffic. But when she tried to insert her keys into the ignition, she found her hands shaking too badly to make them function. She dropped the keys twice and then sat back, clenching her hands in her lap.

Responding to frustration, she'd warned Carter about the notes, but did she actually believe he'd sent them, even given his verbal threats?

Actually, the language of the notes didn't match Carter's northwoods style, the penmanship too neat and precise. And what about the phone threats; the voice on the phone seemed somehow altered, as if someone were speaking down a long pipe and reading from a script. Obviously the use of voice disguise, but could Carter alter his voice to that degree and where would he learn about such devices?

Her hands covered her eyes as she rubbed her forehead, almost willing myriad questions out of her mind.

"Hey, Dana, you okay?"

Her head jerked around at the unexpected voice outside her window and she gasped aloud.

It was Joe Lake, his face peering in, a frown creasing his forehead.

"Dana?"

She rolled down the window. "Lord, Joe, you scared me."

"Are you okay?" he repeated.

"Fine. What are you doing here?"

He gestured toward the next row of cars. "On my way to my car, spotted you sitting here. I thought for a minute..."

"What?"

He shook his head. "Nothing." He studied her face. "You look tired."

"I am. It's been a long day and just minutes ago I had a run-in with Henry Carter."

Lake put his hands on the door frame and leaned forward. "What kind of run-in?" he demanded.

Dana put her hand on one of his and shook her head. "His usual mindless rhetoric against the law, Joe, nothing I couldn't handle."

"You're sure? You know, I could probably find an excuse to throw him into the cage right along with his scumbag kids."

Dana's laugh was short, tinged with irony. "Right. And wouldn't the press love that? The council is still breathing down our necks after all the adverse publicity from the Harbinger trial."

"That was bullshit," Lake said, pushing away from the car door and spitting over his shoulder. "Harbinger was guilty as sin! You know it and I know it and so did the jury."

"Yeah, well, the press chose to believe Harbinger's protests and you know they'd just love to catch us in the act of planting evidence or concealing facts that might exonerate one of our defendants."

Lake changed the subject abruptly. "Why don't you follow me out to Berrigan's? I'll buy you a drink to wash the taste of politics—and old man, Carter—out of your mouth."

"That sounds like a plan," Dana said, grinning, "but Mrs. J. isn't back yet so I have to get right home to Krystal. At those prices, I can't afford to use Scalia as a baby-sitter."

Lake looked surprised. "He's still there?"

"Sure. A couple of days, remember? Your idea, if memory serves."

"Yeah." Joe frowned. "Wish I could say we've got the thing wrapped up and you can let him go."

"Nothing yet, huh?" Dana let a little of the fear she was feeling into her voice. "You think it was one of my cases, Joe?"

Joe shook his head and gave a gusty sigh of frustration. "Not a clue, but we're not ruling anything or anyone out, Dana. Ballistics reports aren't back yet, we're hoping there's at least a fingerprint on that bullet we dug out of the cabinet."

She turned the key in the ignition. "Keep on keeping

on, Joe, I'm counting on you guys to lift the veil. And now I'd better get home to my daughter."

He nodded and stepped back from the car. "Say hi to the kid for me."

"You got it." She smiled and put the shift in gear. Joe stood and watched as she backed out of the space. She stopped the car just before turning and called out of the window, "As soon as this is all over, the drink's on me, Joe."

He grinned, nodded, waved.

Dana pointed the car toward home.

ONCE AGAIN, Nico had the kitchen awash with delicious aromas and Krystal setting the table and happily chattering about starting school again in two weeks.

"I could get used to this," Dana said, grinning, as she headed for the stairway off the kitchen.

"It's going to cost you," Nico said, his voice rife with innuendo.

Dana, one foot on the stair tread, stopped and looked over her shoulder. Was that sexual innuendo? Did he mean...

He laughed at the expression on her face and shrugged his shoulders, his hands held out, palms up.

"My bill," he said, looking innocent. "I was referring to my bill."

Dana glared and continued up to her bedroom. His bill. Yeah, right.

She found herself humming in the shower, an edge of excitement fluttering in her stomach. She turned off the faucets and looked down at herself, water sleeking her skin. What was going on here? Her nipples were pebbled and she reached for a towel to cover herself though no eyes but her own were exposed to her shameless reaction to...

To what? To a man in the house? To a *particular* man in the house? To Nico Scalia? She slumped against the wall and put her face into the towel.

How many men could appear even more masculine while cooking? And what kind of mind did she have that had registered—in just the few seconds it had taken to pass through the kitchen, say hello, and head for the stairs—the way his muscles rippled in his arm as he stirred something on the stove, that his Dockers clung enticingly to a very sexy butt as he bent to check something in the oven, that squinting against the steam from something in a pot made his jawline even stronger than usual.

"Okay, so he's gorgeous," she muttered aloud, tossing the damp towel aside and reaching for another. She worked in a world populated with men, most of them attractive to some degree or other, so why now, with this man, was she having all the responses of a teenager involved in her first flirtation?

She toweled her body and as she applied lotion, she thought about Krystal. She, too, was reacting in an obvious way to Nico Scalia. Truly, she had never seen the child happier. And once again she worried about the effect on Krystal when it was time for Nico to leave. It wasn't as if Krys didn't have plenty of male attention in her life. All of the detectives who'd worked with Zack were more than willing to include Krystal in any of their family gatherings. And Joe Lake was always willing to stand in as a surrogate dad. Krystal was a favorite with all the guys, but it was clear that it was Scalia who was a favorite with her.

Dana moved into the dressing room that separated bathroom from bedroom and began to dress in the culottes and T-shirt she'd laid out. Her first instinct had been for a flowered, spaghetti-strapped sundress in honor of Nico's culinary skills and the formality of Krystal's table setting, but caution, or self-consciousness, prevailed and she decided to play it casual.

Despite her earlier musings, Dana was surprised when, after dinner, Krystal offered to clear the table and then announced that she was going to take her bath and then get into her pajamas.

"Then I'll be ready for bed when my programs are over," the little girl announced.

Dana held the coffee cup to her lips, not drinking, just staring over the top at the stairs up which Krystal had just disappeared.

"Maybe she's coming down with something," she murmured, stunned.

"She has a crush on me," Nico said, chuckling.

"Oh?" She turned to stare at the man. Something in his blithe tone of voice needled, rousing her maternal instincts. "How do you know that?"

Nico shrugged. "I come from a big family. I pretty much understand kids."

Dana relaxed, slumping back against her chair, lifting her cup back to her lips. She took a sip of the hot brew and then looked into the cup.

"Did you buy a new brand of coffee?"

"No. I just used what you had in the canister."

"Well, did you add something?"

Nico grinned. "Water."

"Very funny." She shook her head and brushed her hair back from her face. "I don't get it," she said, sighing ruefully. "My coffee doesn't taste like this."

"I've had your coffee. It's pretty good."

"Yeah, but not great."

"And mine is?"

She stared at him across the table. The sun had already begun to set and darkness was imminent. The candles

Krystal had insisted on lighting were sputtering in the slight breeze from the open window beside the table. In this half light, the shadows that crossed Nico's face made the finely etched planes harsher, stronger, dangerous.

"It's not appealing, this business of being better at everything than everyone else."

He didn't smile. "You don't know that I'm better at everything."

She forced a smile. "You're certainly better at coffee." She gestured at the remains of dinner. "Not to mention cooking."

. "And I didn't know you wanted me to be 'appealing.'"

I don't.

When she didn't respond to that, he said, "The counselor at a loss for words?"

Dana cleared her throat and tightened her resolve. "Don't go there, Scalia, I don't intend to play games with you, word games or otherwise."

"Ah, then my warning met its mark." He grinned. "Rules of living together, eh?"

"We aren't 'living together'!"

His chuckle had a mixed effect on her nerves.

She stood and began to clear the coffee things from the table. When she moved around the table, he stood, too, and they almost collided.

"Sorry," they said in unison.

In the kitchen they both reached for a pot at the same time, again apologizing, with Nico bowing to Dana's murmured, "You cooked, I'll clean up."

But he didn't leave the room. He sat on a counter and watched as she scraped leftovers into refrigerator containers, filled pots with soapy water and began stacking the dishwasher.

"Are you going to sit there and monitor me?" Dana

wondered why she sounded so rude where there was no call for rudeness, but she didn't apologize.

"I was getting my thoughts organized. Seemed like a good time to report what I'd accomplished today."

For a moment she was taken aback. How could she have overlooked so completely what the man was really here for?

She turned around, reaching for a dish towel to dry her hands. "Yes, I'd like to hear," she said, moving to the table where she could give him her full attention.

"Well, first of all, I brought the contracts back. They're on your desk and after you read them and sign them, you'll officially be represented by our agency. Meanwhile, Stella Martinson and I went over my notes and sketched out a tentative working plan. First order of business, we put in a caller identification box. If you get another of those phone threats, we'll have access to the number it came from."

"Good idea," Dana agreed. "Wonder why I didn't think of that? The phone company called and offered me the service a few months back, in one of their routine marketing calls, but I couldn't see the need, at the time, and I'd forgotten about the service."

"Well, they don't always work. The caller can request to have his or her number blocked. Or he could be making the calls from a different pay phone each time. But there's always a chance and we don't want to overlook any possibilities."

He leaned back, his head against a cupboard door, and closed his eyes. "Stella suggested backup and I'm inclined to agree."

"Backup?"

"Yeah." Nico opened one eye and looked over at her warily. "Someone to back me up with Krystal so I'm free to spend more time working directly with you."

Dana thought that over and then a light of suspicion sparked in her mind. "You mean, do guard duty on me!"

Nico pushed himself upright, giving her his full attention. "No," he said, shaking his head. "I mean work with you while letting certain people get the impression that you have someone at your back."

Nico held his breath. He was all for making sure Krystal was safe, but it wasn't the little girl who was receiving threats. Why did Dana refuse to see that she was the source of the author's malice? Some of it, he knew, was pride, some of it her unwillingness to trust the police, that much she'd admitted. But he sensed there was something more. It seemed to him that finding out what that was would be as rewarding as finding out who was threatening her.

"Strictly an illusion, right?"

"At least until and unless it should become necessary to make it more."

Dana's reluctance was a mystery to her, as well. The idea of having her every move shadowed by a bodyguard felt just as intrusive as having someone out there trying to scare her off.

She finished the thought aloud. "But I suppose if I'm going to hire you, I should go along with your game plan."

Nico nodded, trying not to let relief light up his face. "No sense spending the money otherwise."

"What next?"

Dana suddenly needed to be on her feet, putting distance between herself and the detective. She went back to the sink.

"We thought we should set up surveillance on Caprezio and Charlie Donegan, catch one of them in the act of mailing one of those notes. We talked about doing the Carters, as well, but that seemed hopeless, given that the defendants are still in jail and the Carter clan is so big and diverse, that we wouldn't know where to begin. Stella reminded me if Caprezio and Donegan came up clean, it would finger the Carters, anyway, by process of elimination.''

It reminded Dana that she hadn't told Nico about her scrape with Henry Carter. She put a bowl of leftovers in the refrigerator and turned to him.

"I should probably tell you what happened just before I came home, today." She repeated the details of the incident as nearly verbatim as she could recall.

Nico got off the counter while she was talking, moving around until he finally settled at the table. When she got to the part about Joe Lake showing up, he interrupted.

"Did Carter see Lake? Do you think that's what scared him off?"

Dana considered and shook her head. "No. Carter had his say and took off minutes before Joe came on the scene."

"And what was he doing there?"

"I don't know. He said he was on his way to his car and spotted me. I guess I assumed he had some business with someone in the government center. Or that he just happened to use the same parking lot as I. The police department's just across the street in the courthouse."

"Hmm. You don't use the ramp in the government center?"

Dana flushed and bent to rub at an imaginary spot on the sink with a rag. "I haven't felt safe in the ramps or the underground where I have an assigned space," she said in a low voice.

Nico got the impression she hated admitting that. "I think you're wise to stay as much out in the open as possible," he commented. He was about to move on to another subject when the phone rang.

They both stared at it and then Nico nodded and Dana went to answer it.

It was Shelly Kouros, one of Dana's best friends and a one-time co-worker. As was her wont, she started speaking the minute she heard Dana's voice.

"Sweetie, your new baby-sitter is gorgeous!"

"Baby-sitter?" Dana rubbed her forehead and glanced uneasily at Nico who was clearly listening to every word.

"Yes, that adorable hunk who delivered and collected Krystal today. I tried to lure him in for coffee while Krys and Diane were rounding up Krystal's stuff, but he seemed in a hurry to get away."

Substitute "coffee" for "gossip," Dana thought, turning her back to Nico. She loved Shelly, they'd been friends since before their daughters were born, working together as clerks before Shel gave up her law career to become a full-time wife and mother, but her friend loved a good gossip and anybody was grist for her mill.

"Um...yes. Well, he's just a fill-in until Mrs. J..."

"Oh, I know all about that and I was thinking maybe you'd like to come for dinner, you and Krys and of course Mr. Scalia, while Mrs. J.'s out of commission."

"Oh. Well, um, gee, that's sweet of you, Shel, but you see, actually..."

She turned around and shrugged helplessly at Nico who was frowning at her, trying to figure out what had her so rattled.

"I know you're very busy, Dana, probably tearing home to get a meal on the table after a long day, and here I am with the leisure to start dinner anytime I feel like it. You know how I love to help out when I can."

Another Shelly trait, making it sound like she'd be doing you a favor if she got her own way. She could envision dinner with the Kouroses, Shel pumping Nico through every bite he swallowed.

"I am busy, hon. I appreciate your invitation, but things are so up in the air just now that I really can't think ahead to when I'm free," she said firmly. She quickly changed the subject. "But I do appreciate your having Krystal over to visit. We'll have to have Diane here when Mrs. J. is back."

"Oh...well, of course we love having Krys. Anytime. She and Di are like sisters. Anyway, if you're sure..."

"I'm sure," Dana said. "Let's talk about it when I'm out from under, so to speak."

She got off the phone with a sigh that mingled relief and disgust.

"Mrs. Kouros," Nico said, grinning.

Dana slumped on a chair at the table, forgetting her need to keep physically distant. "Yeah. Shelly means well, but I suspect her motives when she invites the three of us to dinner."

Nico laughed. "She struck me as someone who might be writing a book," he said. "You know, all research, never mind the amenities."

Dana's laughter joined his. "That's Shel. Right to the point and right to the heart of the scuttlebutt. If there's romance afoot, she's the one to always sniff it out first."

She was sorry she said that as soon as the words were out and she saw the expression that lighted Nico's eyes.

His voice, though low, hummed with innuendo.

"You know what they say, love, 'if there's smoke, there's fire.'"

Chapter Seven

Dana stared at Nico and then shook her head. "In your dreams, buddy."

She was sure she appeared perfectly cool as she got up and returned to the sink, but she had to fight to keep from telling the man off. She had worked in a field dominated by men long enough to learn that the best way to deal with the arrogant male ego was to simply ignore it. Her ability to keep her emotions hidden from view had worked in her favor in the courtroom, as well.

Behind her she heard Nico's soft chuckle and her hands found the dishcloth and wrung it until her knuckles grew white. There was some small satisfaction in pretending the cloth was Scalia's neck.

He muttered something about adding Shelly to the suspect list, which caught her off guard.

She turned to face him, her eyes wide. "What?"

Nico shrugged, his expression even. "Just a thought, Harper. You know your friend better than I do."

"I can assure you, Shelly is the last person in the world to wish me harm. She's a bit of an airhead at times, and yeah, she loves a good gossip, but she is my friend, Scalia." Her voice underlined the word "friend."

She punched Wash on the dishwasher with more force than was necessary. "I suggest you keep your suspect list limited to my professional life. There are no skeletons in my closet, nothing in my personal life to warrant scrutiny or suspicion. No secret animosities among my friends.''

Nico's experience warned that this was not a given. Despite her protests, most people's lives overlapped. Friendships were often formed in the workplace, enemies made over back-fence slights. Still, he kept his counsel, merely nodding in agreement.

"Okay." He got up, planning to go up to the guest room to retrieve his briefcase. He stopped with one foot on the bottom step, remembering what he'd meant to ask her. He stuck his hand in his pocket, withdrew the matchbook.

"By the way, have you been out back in the last twenty-four hours?"

Dana frowned. "Out back?" She shook her head, puzzled. "No. I don't think so." She saw that he held something in the palm of his hand. "What's that?"

"Do you have a yard service?"

"Yes. What *is* that?"

He held it out and she crossed to him and took it. "It's just a matchbook. So what?"

"When does your service come?"

She had to think a minute. She stared at the matchbook cover. The Hilton. She hadn't been to any of the Hilton hotels since...

"Fridays," she murmured. "They come on Friday. Where did you get this?"

"It was stuck in the door of the gazebo. Found it when Krystal and I walked down to the dock."

"Well, so what? Probably been there...I don't know, maybe Mrs. J. found it in the grass and stuck it in the door to..."

Nico was shaking his head. "Look at it, Dana. It's in

mint condition. It hasn't been outside for more than twenty-four hours, at most.''

"Why twenty-four hours?" She turned it over and then over again. He was right, it was in good condition.

"It rained night before last for about forty minutes."

It struck her then, where he was coming from. "Someone was out in my backyard sometime yesterday."

"Most likely last night."

She looked at the matchbook and then up into his face. He looked so solemn she almost laughed. "Probably a neighbor kid. A teenager cutting through the backyards to get home before curfew. A closet smoker, hiding the matches so his folks wouldn't find them."

He nodded. "That's not a bad scenario. But, unfortunately, it won't wash."

They were silent for a minute. "If it were anyone else, why leave the matchbook?"

"To show you that they could. That you're not as safe as you think you are."

Dana eased into a chair, still clutching the matchbook in her hand, her eyes fixed on Nico's face. "I like my scenario better," she said hoarsely.

He joined her at the table. "So do I, but it doesn't fit for me," he said, his voice heavy with regret.

She put the article on the table between them. Suddenly she leaned forward, grabbing Nico's hand without thinking. "Fingerprints!"

Nico shook his head. "I already dusted it. Nothing."

She let go of his hand and slumped back, her mouth open. "You have your own fingerprint kit?"

He grinned. "I'm a detective. It's what I do, remember?"

She grinned back. "Do you have a magnifying glass and a deerstalker hat?"

He laughed. "No, but I'd know how to find them if I needed to."

They sobered.

"So that pretty much tells us this wasn't an innocent incident," Nico said. "The temperature hasn't dropped below sixty-five in the past week, there'd be no reason to wear gloves, which is obviously what this guy was doing. And by the way, Dana, I want you to start making it a practice to keep your security system activated at all times. Even when we're home."

Dana nodded. A cold chill had run up her back and settled at the base of her neck. She put her hand up and rubbed the spot but it didn't go away.

"We've had a patrol car out front for two nights, did you check to see if—"

"Nothing," Nico interrupted. "But to tell you the truth, I think the Chief put a cop out there just to scare off anyone driving by with intention to harass. I don't think one officer in a car can cover all the bases. And I think that's what our backyard caller intended to prove."

"I don't see any of the Carters hanging out at the Hilton," Dana mused, pushing the matchbook around in a circle with one finger.

"I don't think there's a clue in that," Nico said, seeing where she was trying to take this. "Matchbooks are found everywhere with no real connection to their advertising. Besides, we have three Hiltons in the Cities, even if we could prove one of our suspects had been to one of them, it wouldn't prove they'd been in your backyard."

"Suspects," Dana said. "As a matter of fact, we don't really have any suspects."

Nico nodded agreement. "That's true. We're assuming that the shooting and the threats are connected, which points to your three prosecutions, but they may be totally unrelated.''

"Still, it has Caprezio written all over it to me.''

Nico shrugged. "Yes and no.'' He stood, picking up the matchbook in the process. "Sometimes an item by itself doesn't tell us anything, but surrounded by other bits of evidence it can start to unfold a story.''

Dana remained at the table for a few minutes after Nico'd gone upstairs, pondering the thought of an intruder on her property. She'd agreed only to the minimal security setup of alarms at the front and back doors and the first-floor windows with a motion detector pointed from the front door down to the end of the long hall. Half the time she didn't even bother to activate the system.

Up till now they'd been perfectly safe.

She'd never worried about Krystal going outside alone once she was sure her little girl understood the rules pertaining to strangers. The only other rule they'd cautioned was that Krystal was never to go onto the dock or down to the water's edge unless accompanied by an adult. She had never disobeyed that edict.

Minimal as it might be, there was a cop car out front, and more important, a detective on the premises; they were as safe as they could be for tonight.

She didn't realize until she'd arrived at her study door that she'd been turning on lamps along the way, creating a trail of light behind her, as if that could scare off hobgoblins and drive-by shooters.

She stopped in the doorway of the study and gazed across the dark room to the window that overlooked the backyard. Turning on a light would make her visible to anyone standing outside. She pulled her hand from the switch and crossed the room in the dark.

At the window she peered out. A half moon illuminated the yard, bringing some things into focus, casting others in shadow. Did some of the shadows have the outline of human form? She could see the gazebo from this vantage point but could not see into its screened interior. Could someone be lurking inside, peering back at her across the shadows?

Suddenly she thought she could feel eyes staring at her. She took an involuntary step back and felt a presence behind her.

She spun around, crying out in fright. And stepped into Nico's arms.

His hand intercepted the scream that rose in her throat. "Shh, it's okay, it's me." Cautiously he removed his hand.

"Why did you sneak up on me like that?" Dana gasped, fighting to catch her breath. Her legs were weak and trembling and she was grateful for the support of his arm around her.

"I wasn't sneaking," he said. "I wanted to see what you were seeing out of the window and I didn't want to attract attention if there was actually someone out there. Did you see anyone?"

She shook her head, her hair drifting with the movement, brushing against his cheek. He could smell her shampoo, the spicy fragrance that was her signature cologne.

"Nobody."

"Something spooked you. Besides me, I mean."

She sighed and took a step back, lifting her head to look into his face. "I spooked myself, actually," she said, feeling foolish while at the same time needing the haven of his arms. "I didn't see anyone, I just let my imagination run wild for a moment."

Nico knew there was no reason to keep his arm around her any longer but looking down into her upturned face, feeling her heart beating against his chest, hearing the ragged edge to her breathing, his own pulse quickened and a faint stirring in his loins made him pull her closer.

"This isn't an easy time for you," he murmured, his lips brushing the top of her head.

Dana felt her body moving of its own accord to fit against the length of him, her hands sliding up his chest sensing the erratic rhythm of his heartbeat.

She inhaled his clean, masculine fragrance. "It's easier having someone to share it with," she whispered.

A cloud moved in the sky, giving the moon's rays a direct shot at the house, in through the window behind them, bathing them in a soft glow of illumination.

It felt like a benediction, gave Nico the courage to tilt her chin so that their eyes met. He read the vulnerability there. And more. Desire? As if testing it, he bent to press his lips to hers, half expecting her to draw back.

He didn't exert any pressure, make any demands. His lips were just a gentle caress across her own. Dana understood that he had only opened a door; he was leaving it to her to decide whether to go through. Her hands slid upward, crossing the hard expanse of chest, cupping the girth of his shoulders, moved up the strong column of his neck to settle in the crisp wealth of hair at the back of his head. Tendrils of curls snaked around her fingers and she marveled at the vibrant, lively quality of it.

He was a magnificent male specimen and her hands trembled with pleasure at the indulgence of the feel of him. Her lips parted and she sighed into his mouth as he read her invitation and deepened the kiss. His mustache tickled her top lip and then, as he increased the pressure, it added to the erotic sensations the kiss ignited.

Excitement darted through her nerve endings, pooled in her stomach, heated her skin. Nico's hands were no longer comforting but had begun a seductive exploration of her body and she leaned in to facilitate his search even as her hands continued their own survey over him.

She felt as if she'd died and gone to heaven. How could she have forgotten the pleasure to be derived from this kind of human contact?

Thoughts of the past, of Zack, contrasted with the present, reminding her of the situation that existed in the here and now and of how inappropriate this was.

Nico heard her murmur though he couldn't make out the words. He interpreted them as words of passion. Without breaking their kiss he turned in a circle so that Dana's backside rested against the desk. He was lifting her onto the edge when she cried out, pushing him away.

"No, Nico, don't, please..."

He stumbled back in surprise, caught off guard so that he nearly fell. His mouth still hummed with the feel of hers, his senses still buzzed with desire. Dazed, he could only stare at her, not comprehending the disruption.

Dana folded her arms across her breasts, her hands holding her elbows. She gazed at him, eyes heavy with pain. "I'm sorry, Nico, so sorry. I shouldn't have started this."

"You didn't start...I mean..." He faltered, shook his head.

"This is wrong," Dana said, her voice strengthening as reason slowly usurped passion.

"Wrong?" He couldn't quite focus, couldn't understand why she was talking when they could be kissing, touching. He took a step toward her, his hand outstretched. His legs felt weak and his pulse still thrummed.

Dana held her breath, frightened of him, of herself, of her own runaway passion. If he touched her again she feared she wouldn't have the power to resist. Her body felt like one huge ache, every part of her wanting him.

And looking into his face, fused with desire, she could see the reflection of her own feelings. His eyes had darkened to black and his lips were fuller than usual beneath his dark mustache. His cheekbones and jawline were more pronounced, the skin stretched taut against them. His masculine beauty seemed almost surrealistic in this small room. He belonged on the pages of a magazine or on the television screen where she'd first seen him. Fleetingly she wondered if she would have found him easier to resist if his physical charms were less compelling. She shuddered to think she might be that shallow.

She took a deep breath and moved with purpose to the light switch. "Time to put paranoia behind us," she said as the lamps came on, "and time to get busy. I had an interview with a witness today. I think my notes will interest you. Now where..."

He watched her bustle around the desk, searching for her notes, listened to the bright, breezy tone, and recognized that she was feeling some residual embarrassment.

"Are they in that folder on the right?" he asked, matching his tone to hers though he had to clear his throat before he could speak.

She understood that he was attempting to ease her feelings of awkwardness and she was grateful. What a really nice man he was, she thought, knowing that many men would have continued to push for, or refused to acknowledge her right to terminate, intimacy. And she could think of no other man who would have been as sensitive to her feelings in the aftermath.

"Yes," she said, a smile tempering her confusion, "here they are." She removed a sheaf of notes transcribed by a department stenographer.

Nico let out a ragged sigh, took the notes and then sat in the one club chair, leaving the chair behind the desk to Dana.

At the top of the page was the witness's name: George Bertram Vale, and the date: September 2, 1996. His address, Nico noted, was only a block from the warehouse owned by Caprezio, Inc., which Harper and Lake had under surveillance the night Harper got shot.

It was typical Q&A and the typist had transcribed it exactly that way into the computer.

The witness, Mr. Vale was being questioned about seeing the red Porsche and its owner, Marcus Caprezio, pull up outside the family-owned warehouse at the corner of Thirty-fourth and Lake on the night of the Nunzio murder.

He'd read halfway down the second page when he saw what she meant for him to see.

Q: Was it normal for people to use the warehouse after business hours? No, let's put that another way. Did you ever see anyone going in or out of there at irregular times?

A: Yeah. Lots of times. We called the police a couple times but nothing ever came of it.

Q: You never heard anything more, then, as to what the police found?

A: Nah. We talked it over. The neighbors, you know? It seemed like the cops were covering for whatever goes on over there because Caprezio is…well, you know what they say?

Q: Did you ever see or hear anything that would warrant that implication, Mr. Vale?

A: Well, there was that shooting two, three years ago. You know, that cop got shot?

Here, Nico stopped reading and glanced over at Dana. The witness must have been referring to the death of Dana's late husband. She was busily typing at the keyboard of her computer, unaware that he'd come to that part of the transcript. He wondered how she'd responded to mention of the shooting. It wouldn't be recorded in her notes.

He lowered his eyes to the page.

A: Some of us heard the shots. We expected the cops would question us but nobody ever came around. So then, finally, when there didn't seem to be much in the papers about it, the shooting I mean, and we heard on the news that the police didn't have no information to go on, a couple of us went over to talk to the chief. He gave us this big song and dance about being good citizens and all but the bottom line was what we had to say didn't help none. Said the case would never be officially closed, bein' a murder and all, but that the cops had to move on to things they could do something about. We felt like something was bein' pushed under the rug, you know, but like we done all we could and that's the way the ball bounces. Anyways, after that, seemed like nobody was doin' nothin' about the traffic in and out of the warehouse. Some of the folks even think it's a crack house but the cops don't show no interest.

There was more but apparently Dana had brought Mr. Vale back to the case she was prosecuting, the killing of Nunzio.

Nico put the transcript back in the folder and set it on the desk.

Dana looked up, a question in her expression.

Nico nodded. "Yeah, sounds like you're not the only one with the feeling the cops buried your husband's case. But there's no new information there, that I could see."

Dana's eyes brightened with hope. "No, but don't you think if we questioned the neighbors something more might come out that would give us some answers? Isn't it clear the police hardly investigated at all?"

Nico rubbed the back of his head. "Dana, you didn't hire me to investigate your husband's death and I'm not sure I'd let you waste the money if you tried."

She expelled a sigh of exasperation. "This isn't about money, Scalia, and you don't have to worry about how I spend mine. If you don't want to help me, fine." She turned her back on him, faced the computer. "I can do this on my own."

Alarm sent a frisson of cold up his spine. "What do you mean?"

She spun the swivel chair around, her chin pugnaciously thrust forward. "I mean that I'm going to talk to Mr. Vale again and to any of his neighbors who are willing to talk with me. I mean I'm not going to let the police go on pretending Zack's death was an accident. I mean, Mr. Scalia, I'm going to levy an investigation on my own."

Nico shook his head, admiration for her warring with fear for her safety. If Zack Harper's case had been a cover-up, bought and paid for by the Caprezios, she could be setting herself up as a target and pretty likely next time the shooter would hit his mark. What puzzled him about the thing, though, was the fact that there'd been no cover-up in the Nunzio case. He expressed his questions out loud.

"Don't you think it's funny that the same people who might bury your husband's case wouldn't cover for Marcus?"

"We have witnesses this time," Dana reminded him.

Again Nico shook his head. "Witnesses can be bought off, not to mention other ways they've been made to change their stories, or disappear altogether, for that matter.''

Dana pulled the scrunchy out of her hair, letting the abundance of gold fall to her shoulders. ''There's something I didn't tell you about...'' She hesitated and then seemed to make up her mind. ''We're cooperating with the Feds on the Caprezio case. It's all very hush-hush and I'm trusting that what I tell you won't go beyond this room.''

She barely waited for his nod of assent.

''We might normally have waited until we had more than just circumstantial evidence to take this to the Grand Jury for an indictment, but the Feds have been looking for a way in for years and they asked us to move on this with what we had. By bringing Marcus to trial, we could use any evidence we found to develop a case for *enterprise corruption* against the Caprezio empire.''

''How firm is your case for trial?'' Nico asked.

Dana picked up a pencil and drummed it on the desk. ''Not bad. This is the first time we've got one of the Caprezios into a courtroom and we're counting on their reputation to sway the jury if there's any doubts left in their mind by the meager amount of physical evidence.''

''And speaking of that, how come the defense didn't ask for a change of venue?''

''To where?'' Dana said wryly. ''There isn't a corner of the state they haven't got some kind of operation. With all the gambling opening up throughout Minnesota, we know there's mob money floating in all directions, even if it's wearing legitimate cover. Apparently their counsel recognized the futility of a plea for change.''

''All of that doesn't make this any more viable. It seems to me with all the work on your calendar, you don't really have time to spend looking for cold evidence in a three-year-old case.''

Dana's grin revealed a dimple in her right cheek and rekindled Nico's desire for her. "That's why I need you to help me, Nico," she said, her voice a seductive whisper.

"Are you stooping to feminine wiles, Ms. Harper?" But it didn't matter what she answered; he knew he was going to do anything she asked and worry about consequences later.

Chapter Eight

The unexpectedness of Nico's deep voice at her ear sent tingles of excitement through Dana and she felt herself flush as she glanced at the people seated around her desk. She tried to keep the tone of the conversation impersonal.

"I'm in conference at the moment, Mr. Scalia, can this wait?"

"Sorry. I wanted to catch you before you made other plans. Can we meet for lunch?"

"What about Krystal?" Dana asked, uncomfortably aware that the mention of her daughter's name made it clear this was a personal call.

"My mom's invited Krystal for lunch. Some of my nieces and nephews are there for the day. Krystal will fit right in."

Dana swiveled away from the group so that she had her back to them and lowered her voice. "Your mom? Really, Nico, I don't th—"

"Not to worry, Dana. She'll be perfectly safe there. My brother-in-law, Carmen, is there. He's a cop on the St. Paul P.D."

She couldn't argue with him without enlightening her colleagues and she had no desire to prolong this conversation.

"All right," she snapped. "Just tell me where and when."

"Is twelve-thirty good for you?"

"Yes," she said, glancing over her shoulder. Harve Mackey was looking at his watch and Mary Quan was gazing out of the window, looking very bored. "That's fine. Just tell me where."

"How about Pagoda?"

"Yes. Fine. 'Bye."

She slammed the phone down and turned back to the others with an apologetic frown on her face, her tone clipped and businesslike. "Where were we?"

THE PAGODA had been one of the city's more familiar landmarks until the renovations of the downtown area had required that it be torn down to make room for the Nicollet Mall and many new buildings, including the City Center which now housed the new Pagoda.

She found Nico already seated at a table overlooking the street and let him hold her chair for her before she reprimanded him for disturbing her meeting.

"How did I know?" He shrugged his shoulders. "Besides, it was important."

Dana pushed the menu aside and took a sip of water. "So what's so important? And why is my child at your mother's house? I don't even know your parents, for heaven's sake!"

Nico chuckled. "Can I get a word in here?"

Dana sat back, chin out, her right hand impatiently tapping the bowl of a spoon on the tabletop. "Go!"

"Okay. First of all, Hello, Dana. How are you? I'm so glad you could join me."

He grinned and she glared at him but kept her mouth shut.

He laughed aloud. "Okay. Moving right along. My

folks have a ton of grandkids always underfoot and I'm sure you'd find the folks' home an acceptable environment for Krys even if it isn't in Wayzata.''

"I wasn't protesting out of snobbery," Dana defended, "but first of all it seems like an intrusion on your folks, and secondly, I like to be informed—no, *asked*—before you entrust my daughter to anyone else."

"Don't worry about intruding. My mom doesn't see it that way. And there wasn't time to check with you first, I had to get over there right away."

"Over where?"

Nico pushed flatware out of his way and placed his elbows on the table so he could lean forward. He lowered his voice. "I decided to follow up on your Mr. Vale. I called him and asked if he'd be willing to get me a list of all the neighbors he knew were willing to cooperate to get the goods on the action at that corner. One of the people he named owns a pool hall on that block. It turned out the owner's an old friend of mine from school. Pool halls are great places for picking up the neighborhood gritty and I figured a reunion with my old buddy was in order. Turns out Max is going on vacation, leaving tomorrow, so I had to get over there pronto or wait a couple of weeks for him to get back."

"You talked to him?" Dana inched forward on her chair, eager to hear what Nico might have learned.

"Yeah. And I learned a lot more than I expected. First of all, it seems Marcus Caprezio, either on his own or on behalf of the Organization, has been trying to muscle his way into a piece of the action. Max has been able to keep him out but there have been numerable unexplained accidents that Max is sure were meant to be warnings. Then, it turns out, that's not the only business in the area that Caprezio has tried to strong-arm. Max is pretty sure some of the others caved in and are paying protection."

Dana's eyes were wide, her mouth slightly agape. She let out a gusty sigh. "Too bad we can't wire your friend and use this."

"Why can't we?"

Dana sat back, crossing her arms at her waist. "You know what I told you, about 'our friends' doing their own investigation?"

He knew she was referring to the Feds. "Yeah. So what?"

"So, we've been ordered to turn everything we find over to them, outside of anything directly related to the Nunzio murder." She sat forward again, reaching for her glass of water. She took a sip before adding, "For all we know, they're already onto this and haven't moved on it for reasons of their own."

"So we just let it slide?"

She shrugged. "Did you find out anything I can use?"

Nico's answer was intercepted by the appearance of the waiter at the side of their table. Nico deferred to Dana, who ordered a combination plate.

"I'll have the same," he told the waiter, and handed the man both menus.

"Go on," Dana ordered when the waiter was out of earshot.

"It seems the night your husband was shot, Marcus showed up at the pool hall about eleven o'clock. He was a little drunk and crowing about cleaning up the neighborhood, starting with 'the pigs,' to quote Max quoting M.C."

Dana gasped. "Do you mean he was admitting he'd killed Zack?"

"No." Nico shook his head. "More like someone else did but M.C. knew who it was, according to Max."

"But the Caprezios might have paid for the hit?"

"Not the impression I got from Max. He seemed to

think Marcus was merely congratulating someone else in his own way.''

Dana mulled that over.

Nico left her to her thoughts for a moment and then put his hand over hers to get her attention.

"Dana, maybe you could make some kind of deal with M.C., trade what he knows about Zack's killing for less time on the Nunzio thing."

Dana's eyes were glittering with unshed tears when she lifted them to meet Nico's. She shook her head. "No way. This may be the only chance we ever have to get a sure fix on this guy and put him away for a long haul. I'm not jeopardizing that."

Nico's chest swelled with admiration. What a woman, he thought, squeezing her hand to relay his unspoken feelings. She would never compromise integrity, no matter how much she might want something.

She smiled and blinked back the threat of tears. "There's got to be another way in, another way to find out what went down behind Zack's murder."

She pulled her hand away as the waiter approached with their plates.

They ignored the chopsticks at their place settings, both picking up forks instead. They ate in silence for a few minutes. When Nico filled her teacup, Dana put her fork down.

"Did you talk to any of the others on Vale's list?"

"No. By the time I finished with him, I had to get over here to meet you."

Dana nodded and picked up her fork, pushing sprouts aside to find a mushroom. Suddenly she looked up and grinned.

"You don't use chopsticks, either?"

He returned her grin. "I always think it looks sort of funny when I use them."

She nodded and they laughed in unison.

Dana whispered, "How about in those romance movies when they eat out of the cartons with them."

"Or when they feed each other food with 'em."

They were having a hard time containing their laughter and now people at neighboring tables were glancing over at them.

With some effort Dana sobered and resumed eating, avoiding Nico's gaze for fear she'd start to laugh again.

His sobriety was brought on by a sudden spasm of longing. There she sat, her hair in a proper up-do, wearing a decidedly tailored suit, primly matching her manner to the public atmosphere, and he wanted her so badly that he could barely swallow. Memories flooded through his mind, restoring the taste of her on his lips, the feel of her voluptuous curves beneath his hands.

She looked up and noticed that he was staring at her, not eating, not smiling. His expression was...

Her stomach lurched with excitement as their minds met and she was once again in his arms, her hands exploring, her mouth crushed to his in wild need.

"Nico...I..."

His eyes were smoky with desire. "You're the most beautiful woman I've ever known," he whispered.

Their hands crept across the table, palms meeting, fingers entwining, as they looked into each other's eyes.

"It's a good thing we're in a public place," she whispered at exactly the same moment that he murmured, "I wish we were alone."

Their nervous laughter lightened the mood. Barely.

Dana pushed her plate up from the edge of the table and rested her elbow there, her chin on one palm, the other still pressed up against his. His fingers moved seductively over hers, caressing...maddening...

"I have to get back to work," she said as she reveled

in his look of adoration. She didn't realize that her assessment of his wonderful face was reflected in her face.

"I know." Nico laid his napkin beside his plate and released her hand with obvious reluctance. He reached for the check. "Would you like me to walk you back to the government building?"

"Yes. But no, I'd really rather you talk to the other people on your list."

She didn't protest as he laid some bills on the check, and Nico appreciated that. Was that because she came from plenty of it or because it wasn't important in the scheme of things to her? In either case, he was grateful there'd been no fuss. He hated it even when a male companion argued about who should pay. For some reason that had always embarrassed him.

As they rose to leave, Dana said, "Are you sure your parents won't mind keeping Krystal a bit longer?"

"I told them I'd pick her up about four. I've plenty of time, yet," he said, glancing at his watch.

They parted out on the street, holding hands for a brief moment. Nico wanted to kiss her. As if sensing that, or perhaps wanting the kiss, as well, she looked furtively around. He laughed, chucked her under the chin and turned away.

Dana stood for a moment watching his graceful lope as Nico strode toward the end of the street to the parking lot where he'd left his car.

He'd be there when she got home from work, probably with dinner simmering on the stove. Her pulse escalated at the thought. They'd be alone tonight, after Krystal was put to bed. And then...

"And then we'll discuss his findings," she muttered, clenching her fists at her sides as she turned to head back to work.

A man passing her threw her a curious glance, but

Dana was too busy, silently praying for strength against the lure of rampant desire, to notice.

The blare of a car's horn penetrated her revery as she was about to cross the street at a red light. A warm rush of embarrassment heated her cheeks when she caught a look of admonishment from an elderly lady waiting to cross beside her. She grinned sheepishly and obediently stared up at the walk sign until it lit up. She joined the throng of late lunchers and shoppers moving up the mall.

Halfway across the street a sense of uneasiness penetrated and a chill stirred at the back of her neck. She halted midstride to look over her shoulder, almost bumping into a man carrying a baby on his shoulder, and met the eyes of the same elderly woman. The woman shook her head and made a moue of disgust, obviously labeling Dana as some kind of flake.

But the woman's implied scolding didn't deter from the sensation that she was being followed. She kept glancing behind her as her pace quickened, never seeing anyone she recognized, never losing the feeling of threat.

By the time she reached the entry to the government building she was nearly running.

"Yo, Ms. Harper, you okay?" Don Martinez, one of the security guards, stopped her in midflight across the lobby.

"What?" Dana turned to the man, but her glance strayed to the entrance where another rush of people was coming into the lobby.

She saw no one suspicious and turned back to Martinez. "Sorry, Don, what did you say?"

"You looked like someone was after you," Martinez said, chuckling at the absurdity. "You okay?"

"Sure, I'm fine, Don. Just in a hurry." She started to move toward the elevators and remembered her manners.

"Thanks for asking, Don," she called with a wave in the guard's direction.

He smiled, nodded, and gave her a thumbs-up.

He was still smiling in her direction as the elevator doors closed, shutting off Dana's view of him and the people moving in all directions behind him.

The feeling of unease seemed to fall away as the elevator car started its stomach-dropping surge upward. She slumped back against the wall and let out a sigh of relief. A secretary she recognized from the commissioner's offices smiled at her.

"One of those days, Mrs. Harper?"

Dana agreed with a weak smile. "Yeah," she said, straightening. "One of those days."

By the time she'd reached her own office she was berating herself for "losing it" and letting her imagination run wild. Not like her at all. She could envision sharing it with Shelly, her friend's eyes wide with projected excitement and fear.

But she had no intention of telling anyone. Dana struggled every day to keep her professional image intact, she wasn't now about to come across as the weak, frightened damsel in flight.

Chapter Nine

Dana had just pulled the Caprezio file, in preparation for her meeting with the arresting officers, when her door opened and Joe Lake stuck his head in.

"Hey, babe," he called out, "got a minute?"

"'Babe'?" Dana repeated wryly. "I take it this is a social call, Detective?"

Joe laughed as he entered the room, closing the door behind him. He pulled a length of silk from his pocket and waved it at Dana.

"You left your scarf in my car the other night, just found it when I had my car washed, and thought you'd want it."

It was hers. Dana recalled that she'd worn it the night Mrs. J. was shot. God, was that less than two weeks ago?

"Thanks. Want some coffee?"

She accepted the scarf and tucked it into her bag before going to the coffeepot on the file cabinet.

"Sure. Black's fine."

Joe settled himself into a chair, swiveling around to gaze out over the city as Dana filled two cups and carried them back to the desk.

Joe was dressed in a gray three-piece suit over a muted striped shirt. The ensemble was finished off with a burgundy and gray tie; a far cry from his usual street wear.

"Been to court?" Dana asked. She set a cup down in front of him and carried her cup around the desk to her own chair.

"Yeah. That Feller thing."

"Mmm." Dana tilted her head. "Johnson's case," she said, naming another prosecuting attorney. "How does it look?"

Joe nodded. "It's a shoe-in. Feller offed his old lady and we got all the evidence we need to convince a jury."

"From your lips to God's ear," Dana said. "How often have we presented a clean case and the jury's been swept away by the sleight-of-hand rhetoric of the defense?"

Joe grimaced. "I don't want to think about that. Every time that happens, half a dozen good cops threaten to leave the force."

They were silent a moment, sharing thoughts that plagued law enforcement people. Then Joe set his cup down and leaned back, one hand in his pants' pocket, the other drumming fingers on his knee.

"Dana, I really stopped by because Lieutenant King mentioned your call. It's been three years, honey, don't you think it's time to let go?"

Dana cocked an eyebrow at her late husband's ex-partner and tapped her fingers against the side of her mug. "I wasn't aware there was a statute of limitation on murder, Joe."

Lake rubbed his head in frustration. "Dana, don't you think the department would like to get the guy who offed Zack? Don't you think *I'd* like to find him?"

"Or her?"

"Huh?" Lake obviously hadn't caught the sarcasm in Dana's voice.

"Obviously since you have no clue as to the identity

of Zack's murderer, we don't know that it was a 'him' that took him out.''

The detective shot her a look of disgust. ''Yeah. You're right. We don't know. And that's the point, Dana.'' Increased frustration raised his voice an octave. He picked up his mug but didn't drink from it.

''What do you want us to do? We couldn't find anything to follow up on. No physical evidence at the crime scene, no threats made prior to the shoot, no witnesses, no—''

''Ah,'' Dana interjected, cutting him off midsentence, ''but how do you know there were no witnesses? Did you question the neighbors, do a door-to-door?''

For a moment Joe Lake looked blank, and then he leaned forward, a flush reddening his neck and face. ''That's standard procedure, Dana, of course we did,'' he said, his jaw clenched with anger.

She took her hands off the mug and sat back in her chair, her arms folded across her chest. She shook her head.

''Where were you when the investigation was going on, Joe?''

''What? I was…I was…'' His expression changed as he suddenly remembered.

Dana nodded. ''You were very shook up over your partner's death. They sent you home, had you go through debriefing with the department shrink.''

They stared at each other across the span of the desk.

''You didn't even get on the investigation until after the funeral, as I recall,'' Dana reminded.

''Yeah.'' Lake's voice was hoarse, as if his throat was clogged with remembered pain.

''So you don't really know what went down during that first, most important phase of the investigation.''

"Dana, I read the reports when I came back on the team," Lake said.

She laughed. It wasn't a pretty sound. "And we both read *The Celestine Prophecy,* and I still don't know how much was fact and how much fiction. Do you?"

"You're saying you think the investigation was dirty, that cops, Zack's co-workers and buddies, dumped the case?"

Outrage deepened his flush to mauve.

But Dana was in too far, emotionally, to back out now and she plunged on.

"Joe, Lieutenant King said the stakeout was about to be pulled, that the reports indicated a lack of criminal activity. But people I've spoken with tell me there's still suspicious movement in and out of there at all hours."

Lake appeared to mull that over, a puzzled expression replacing anger, and then said in a low voice, "Dana, are you accusing Zack of covering for the Caprezios?"

Her jaw slackened as the words echoed across the room and Dana's mind received them. Zack involved in a cover-up for Minnesota's first family of crime? Not likely. A flush warmed her face and the threat of tears burned behind her eyes and in her throat.

"Of course I know that's impossible," she said, clearing her throat and shaking her head. "Zack was one of the most honest cops I've ever met."

"Exactly." The single word spoke volumes. They had reached an impasse and as if to underline that, Lake stood and set his mug on the desk. It was still nearly full.

"Believe me, hon, if there was anything to go on, we'd have stayed on it indefinitely. But look—" he leaned forward, his palms flat on the desk "—if it'll make you feel any better, I'll pull the paper on it and see if we missed something, maybe go out on my own time and ask a few questions."

Dana stood, also, walking around the desk to give her long-time friend a hug. "Thanks, Joe," she murmured as his arms closed around her.

"I just want you to be happy, Dana, you know that, don't you?"

She nodded and stepped back to smile up at him. "I know, Joe, and I'm sorry if I seem a little strung out on this subject."

"Hey, who knows better than me what it would mean to you to put the perp away."

He drew her back and kissed her cheek and then moved his lips to her mouth.

Dana accepted the kiss in the spirit of friendship, expecting it to be only that, but Joe, ever the opportunist, deepened it, demanding more.

An image of Nico flashed across her mind. She jerked away, a feeling of guilt warring with the honest affection she felt for her old friend.

"My next appointment's due any sec," she mumbled, covering her feelings with a forced smile.

Joe looked down at her for a moment, his eyes sad.

"I wish you could feel the way I do," he said.

Dana decided it was a moment for supreme honesty. She nodded her head. "I know. You're the dearest friend anyone could ask for, and you've been the perfect godfather to Krystal and she loves you. It would have been so nice if it had worked out for us. But I don't love you that way, Joe. I'm sorry."

He shook his head and smiled. "Hey, I'm thickheaded but I'm not dense, Hon. You gotta go with your feelings." He gave a short laugh. "And speaking of going, I'm late for a meet with a snitch."

He was almost at the door when an impulse triggered by regret made her say, "Joe, come to dinner next week, Krystal's missed you."

"I'll give you a call," he said, waving a hand as he left the room.

She wondered if he would. She hated to lose the friendship but if Joe's feelings for her were as deep as he professed, maybe it was too painful for him to hang out with her, and in that case, she'd have to let him go. She'd be sorry, for Krystal's sake and her own. "But fair's fair," she said out loud, returning to her desk with a sigh.

Memories of times they'd shared, as a makeshift family, rose in her mind as she sat down. Dana, Joe and Krystal celebrating Krystal's first piano recital at Divanni's for pizza and pitchers of rootbeer; an all-day trek through the Minnesota Zoo; many trips to Valley Fair. The three of them at Mass together once. She chuckled as she recalled how Krystal had shamed Joe into accompanying them to church that Sunday. It hadn't taken more than a few minutes to see that church just wasn't his thing and that he was truly uncomfortable there.

The next time Krystal tried to harass him into joining them, Dana had intervened, telling Krystal that Joe had already made other plans. They'd met him for lunch afterward at Perkins where Krystal had given him a blow by blow of the service and Father Kevin's sermon.

She was still smiling when the policemen arrived for their appointment with her. Quickly she put on her professional face and got down to business.

From then on she was busy every moment until four o'clock when the secretary announced that Dana had a personal call on line three.

She didn't recognize the woman's voice. It was low and melodious, with a faint accent she couldn't quite place.

"This is Rose Scalia," the woman said. "Nico's mama."

Dana's heart lurched. "Is Krystal all r—"

"Fine, fine, Mrs. Harper, Krystal is fine," Mrs. Scalia quickly assured her. "I called only to give you a message from Nico."

Relief flooded through her. Her voice was breathless with it. "Yes, Mrs. Scalia," she said.

"Nico says to tell you that he's unable to get away from where he is for maybe another hour and would you mind getting Krystal for him. But, Mrs. Harper, Krystal is having such a good time with my grandchildren, I was wondering if you would come here for dinner, instead, and that way she could also stay a little longer."

"Well..." Dana was floored. The invitation was so unexpected for one thing and for another, the idea of dinner with strangers was awkward.

"We'd like it so much if you'd say yes," the older woman pleaded.

"Well, but really, we don't need to intrude on your dinner, that isn't necessary," Dana insisted.

"Not necessary, but you would honor us if you'd come. Even though we don't know each other, I feel as if we do because Krystal just fit in here so easily. We love her already."

Later, on the drive over there, Dana realized she'd accepted the invitation mostly because she was so curious about Nico's background. It had occurred to her that though sexual awareness had risen between them almost immediately, they were veritable strangers beyond the basic professional résumés.

Not quite true, she corrected as she eased her car into the traffic moving east on I94. She knew he had learned how to cook from his mother, that he respected both his parents, that he was good with kids, and that he had changed careers in the last five years with reasons that pointed up his integrity.

That he was totally masculine, vaguely mysterious, and sexy as hell were his most obvious traits, and would have been enough to intrigue most women, she realized as she took the Lexington exit and turned right off the ramp.

She found the Scalia house with ease, partly due to Mrs. Scalia's good directions and because she knew St. Paul, especially the Crocus Hill area.

The Scalias lived in a huge, Victorian frame that sprawled across a double lot on Lincoln. Dana skirted a fallen trike on the sidewalk and a pair of plastic, toddler-size roller skates on the cement walk to the porch steps and as she went up the first step the sound of children's voices came to her from around the side of the house. The shouting and laughter implied great merriment. She recognized Krystal's voice among the others, and she smiled in response.

Mr. Scalia answered the door, welcoming her with a flourish and a smile that echoed Nico's so totally that it was scary.

"Come in, come in, Mrs. Harper, please," he crooned in a voice that was also reminiscent of his son.

The interior of the house was cool and inviting. The fragrances of foods cooking immediately beset her sense of smell.

The aromas grew stronger as Mr. Scalia led her back to the kitchen where his wife wiped her hands on a towel and rushed to give Dana a hug as if they were old friends.

"It is an honor, Mrs. Harper," Nico's mother said, releasing Dana from her arms and stepping back to look her over with a beaming smile.

"I'm honored that you invited us, and please, call me Dana," she responded with sincerity. "I love your house," she added, spinning around to take in all the little inviting quirks of the kitchen.

"Forty years in one house," Mr. Scalia said from behind her, "gets a real lived-in look to it."

"Dinner smells wonderful," Dana said, her mouth watering from the fragrance of spices, and baking bread, that permeated the air.

"We eat as soon as Nico and Jonno get here," the older woman said, "but you come, sit, there's wine and some crackers to hold us."

Lily, Nico's youngest sister, and her husband, Carmen, were introduced as they came through the kitchen holding hands. They were very warm in their acknowledgment of Dana's presence but quickly left the room after they'd each retrieved a beer from the refrigerator.

"Newlyweds," Mr. Scalia proudly announced in a stage whisper as he filled a glass with dark red wine from the carafe on the table. He set the glass in front of her and passed her a basket of wafer-thin crackers.

Dana's next question was prevented by the onslaught of half a dozen children who pushed through the back door, all of them talking at once.

Without raising her voice, her expression serene, Mrs. Scalia brought the group to order and made introductions, her arms around Krystal and another little girl.

"This is Maria and this is Chianne," Mrs. Scalia said, pointing to the two girls who appeared to be close to Krystal's age.

Annette, Petey, Rosy and Joey ranged from kindergartner down to toddlers. Myranda, the little girl cuddled under Mrs. Scalia's arm, lived next door, but was apparently as welcome in the household as any of the grandchildren.

Krystal grinned at her mother from under the older woman's other arm and waggled her fingers. "I'm Krystal,'' she said when Mrs. Scalia had named the last of the children.

Everybody laughed and Mrs. Scalia gave Krystal an extra hug before letting both girls free as she headed back to the stove.

''Do they all live here?'' Dana asked.

Mr. Scalia looked surprised at the question. ''No, no.'' He shook his head. ''They live with their parents, our children. We're just lucky they live close by.''

Dana offered to help, but Rose pointed out that she had all the help she needed, gesturing at the girls who were scurrying in and out of the kitchen, carrying things to the dining room. Krystal seemed to be as much a part of the group as if she'd been there every day of her life. When she came over to ask, in a whisper, if sometime her three new friends could come to their house to play, Dana agreed without hesitation.

Krystal had just run off to tell the others when Dana looked up to see Nico standing in the doorway.

His eyes found her instantly and they stared at each other, oblivious of the roomful of people, for a very long moment.

''I like your family,'' she whispered when they were seated side by side at the dining room table, minutes after Jonno, a college student and the youngest, had completed the group.

''They like you,'' Nico said, grinning down at her as he handed her a basket of the bread she'd smelled baking when she'd entered the house.

The children were fed at the long table in the kitchen and their laughter and bubbling conversation could dimly be heard through the connecting door.

The conversational tenor was similar among the adults. They were a teasing group; the junior Scalias' favorite target, their parents. Rose and Dom Scalia took it in stride, giving as good as they got.

Dana sat back with a sigh of contentment, sipping espresso and smiling around at the others. "Do you eat like this every day?" she asked.

"Only when we eat here," Lou, Nico's oldest brother said. "At home we mostly live on TV dinners." He tousled his wife's red curls and jumped away as she elbowed him in the stomach.

"I didn't promise to love, honor, and cook," Jenny said airily. "Besides, that's how you got me to marry you, you said you'd do all the cooking."

They all laughed at that. And then, as the conversation turned to various stories of cooking disasters or triumphs, Dana whispered to Nico, "How did you make out with the interviews?"

Nico shook his head. He had an arm across the back of Dana's chair and leaned toward her to speak in her ear. "I've got plenty to tell you but let's wait till we get home."

At the end of the table Rose watched her son and his lady. This was more than a working relationship, she thought, and exchanged a contented smile with her husband who was always attuned to her thought waves.

It was time. Nico had dodged the responsibilities of a family for long enough. Time for him to settle down as the others had and make a real home for himself. And Rose Scalia felt that she couldn't have handpicked a better family for her son than Dana Harper and her adorable little Krystal. Okay, maybe it wasn't an absolute yet, but as she watched Dana laugh at something Nico said to her, and saw the way her son's eyes glowed with pleasure, she was sure it was only a matter of time.

As she bid them good-night an hour later, she whispered to Dana, "Call us Mama and Papa, it's better, more like family."

Chapter Ten

Nico carried the sleeping child up to her room and laid her on her bed. "I'm going to shower while you're doing that," he whispered as Dana bent to undress Krystal. "Meet you down in the study."

She could hear him whistling under his breath as he went down the hall to the guest room and she smiled to herself. It had been a fun evening. And so enlightening. She couldn't remember when she'd ever seen such a large family, and the way she and Krystal fit right in was nothing short of amazing. Dinner at her parents' home had always been more formal, the conversation dictated by the politics of the day but never allowed to become heated or punctuated with the kind of merriment that exemplified mealtime at the Scalias'.

For that matter, she couldn't recall ever seeing her own mother in the kitchen except to give orders to the cook. Like herself, Zack had been from a small family, both of his parents dead before Dana had married him. He and his two brothers had grown up in separate states, each farmed out to a different relative.

Dana's and Zack's efforts at making a home had always been a little self-conscious, as though they didn't quite have the hang of it.

It occurred to her that in just a few days Nico was

more at home here than Zack had ever been. She knew
now that he'd learned that ease from his family, almost
as if by osmosis.

Was that why Zack had been such a workaholic? Was
he more comfortable at the precinct or out on the streets
than here at home? The thought saddened her.

She pulled a nightgown over her daughter's head, pulling the little girl back as Krystal tried to roll to her side,
mumbling in her sleep.

It took her a few more minutes to get the covers pulled
up, Krystal's clothes retrieved from the floor and placed
in the hamper, the lamp turned off. She'd have time for
a quick shower herself, she thought as she slipped out of
the room, leaving the door slightly ajar.

She was about to turn in the direction of her own room
when Nico stepped into the hall and her breath caught in
her throat.

He was wearing only a towel around his waist, his
body damply glistening, his wet hair slicked back from
his forehead.

Dana licked her lips in an attempt to banish their sudden dryness, and her hands clutched at the wall behind
her.

"Hey," Nico called softly, not the least self-conscious
about his state of undress, "finished already?"

She nodded, unwilling to trust her voice. If she even
still had a voice. Her throat seemed filled with the beat
of her blood pounding there. She couldn't take her eyes
from him though at some level she knew she ought to be
running as fast and as far as her legs would carry her.
But her legs were barely holding her up as it was. She
leaned into the wall for support.

Nico took a few steps toward her, a frown of concern
on his face. "Dana? Are you all right?"

Muscles rippled in the arm he held out to her. His

broad chest and legs were darkly haired, his thighs well muscled, the planes of his face stronger with his hair, made darker by water, pulled straight back. She took mental inventory as if assessing him for a magazine layout and realized he'd easily qualify for centerfold of the year. And there he stood, in her hallway, in the flesh. And too much of it, she told herself.

"You're not dressed," she croaked. Inane, immature, naive.

"I forgot to take clean clothes into the bathroom with me," Nico said. His grin was apologetic. "I'll go get dressed," he said, starting to turn away.

"No!" Oh, God, where did that come from?

He turned back. "No?" A ferocious gleam brightened his eyes, a feral tilt shaped his lips.

"I mean..." *What do you mean, Harper?* a nasty voice prodded from inside her head.

He closed the distance between them, entering her personal space, cutting off the little bit of breath she was able to muster. His own breath was plentiful, pelting her face sweetly as he lowered his head and spoke in a near whisper.

"Tell me what you want, Dana."

"I want...I want..." she stammered. "I w—" His mouth closed over hers, and she forgot everything but the want. The need. Her hands came out from behind her to slide up his damp chest as his closed around her waist to pull her against the warm, solid bulk of his body.

They melted into each other, lips and tongues dueling to gain dominance, hands struggling for control, sighs and moans accompanying their exploration.

Dana was dizzy with desire as Nico pulled her blouse from her waistband and she pushed his hands away so that she could get the blouse over her head, too impatient to deal with the buttons. Nico pulled her bra down to her waist as she flung her blouse aside and stepped in to press her breasts against his masculine chest. The hair that fuzzed between his nipples enticingly teased hers into hard pebbles that made her cry out at the intensity. His arms folded around her, pulling her against the hard, throbbing evidence of his arousal as he tilted his head to deepen their kiss.

Dana was desperate to free her body from the bondage of the rest of her clothing, to bring their bodies into total naked contact without breaking the kiss.

When Nico suddenly pulled away, she rocked back on her heels, grabbing the wall to keep from falling. It was then she heard the doorbell.

Nico grabbed the towel that had slipped down. "Doorbell," he gasped.

Her eyes, bluer than he'd ever seen them, blinked and then squinted. She slipped bra straps up her arms and pulled them up over her shoulders. "Who could it be this late?" Her voice wasn't much stronger than his.

Suddenly Nico smacked his palm against his forehead. "Jeez, I forgot Heather." He turned and made a dash for his room and the nearest pair of pants he could locate.

"Who? Who's Heather?" she called after him.

"Heather Wilson, she's going to take my place with Krystal." Nico was already zipping up the fly of his blue jeans as he came running out of his room. He'd tossed on a short-sleeved shirt that he hadn't bothered to button.

A woman? Dana hadn't expected that. Though certainly it seemed logical to have Krystal's guard be a female since she was going to be spending so much time with the little girl.

But why did she have to come at such an inconvenient time? Dana thought as she buttoned her blouse and tucked it back into the waistband. "Or the best possible time," she wryly muttered under her breath. She was still shaky from their lovemaking, her breasts still sensitive, her lips still humming. How smart was that, to almost drag the man she'd hired as investigator to her bed? She put her hands to her flushed cheeks and decided it would be wise to take a moment to splash with cold water before going down to meet her new employee.

She stared at herself in the mirror over the sink as it hit her that Heather's moving in would mean Nico could move out. Her stomach lurched and a lump rose in her throat.

She could have sworn that his constant presence in her home had been more intimacy than she'd been prepared to deal with, and that his leaving would bring genuine relief. But try as she would, she could conjure nothing but good memories of the time he'd stayed there.

"Get it together, Harper," she whispered to her image. The face that stared back at her seemed cheerless, depressed. Her mind insisted on replaying images of Nico in the kitchen, happily chatting with Krystal as he whipped up his gourmet dinners. Nico sitting at her desk, going over her files, his face illuminated by the glow of the desk lamp, his dark curls springing back every time he ran a hand through his hair. Nico in the bosom of his family, beloved and respected, taking their teasing in stride with ease, dishing it out with a good dose of loving humor of his own.

She straightened the collar of her blouse. Her stomach lurched again as the image of him bending to kiss her ran through her mind, followed instantly by the vision of the two of them locked in a battle of passion as they fought to get closer to each other.

She sank to the edge of the tub, her legs turned rubbery, her hands shaking, her breathing gone shallow again. All that from just the memory.

Letting her imagination go wild, she pictured herself

offering to pay Nico to stay—as cook and housekeeper if need be. The idea caused her to catch her breath on a giggle. But at least she was breathing again.

"I'll tell him I want to hire him as my personal bodyguard," she said, grimacing as she rose to her feet.

"In a pig's eye," she told her reflection in the mirror. "I made it without him before, I can certainly do it again. And it will be fun having another woman in the house, sort of like having a roomie again."

A pounding at the door caused her to jump back.

"Dana, are you all right?"

"Just coming, Nico," she said, opening the door to prove it.

"Heather's waiting to meet you," he said, leading the way to the stairs. Over his shoulder he continued, saying, "Did I hear you talking to someone in there?"

"Yeah, right, I keep a spare friend in the linen closet in case I ever need someone to talk to."

Nico stopped short so that she bumped up against him. He turned and clasped a hand at the back of her neck.

"You're a sarcastic little wench, Ms. Harper." His lips hovered inches from hers, his breath warmed her mouth, making her melt as she recalled the taste of him.

It took real effort, but she said, "We have a guest waiting, don't we, Scalia?"

His jaw muscle worked and his eyes blazed as he considered sweeping her up into his arms and hauling her off to his bed and to hell with Heather Wilson.

Dana saw the danger in his stance and though part of her thrilled to it, sanity won out. She gave a shaky laugh, pushed away from him and ran down the stairs.

HEATHER WILSON KNEW she made a striking figure with her red hair, the requisite jade green eyes, and a healthy smattering of freckles across her nose and cheekbones.

Straight-legged jeans, high-heeled boots and a short, leather, bomber jacket emphasized her tall, lean figure. The grin she gave Dana, as she turned from the wall of family photos she was studying, was meant to put Dana at ease.

They shook hands and exchanged names as Nico appeared in the archway. "Want some coffee, Wilson?"

Heather looked from Dana Harper to Nico and back again, surprised that the offer came from her co-worker rather than the lady of the house. But Dana didn't seem to find it at all strange.

"Sure, that'd be great," Heather said, shrugging. Maybe Harper was so rattled by the threats and the shooting that she'd given over control to the investigator.

But as they seated themselves in the grouping of chairs near the fireplace, Heather couldn't help but notice that Dana's eyes were focused and made direct, easy contact. Obviously Harper was no frail female.

"So, Heather, you're going to be with us for a while. Did you bring your things or will you have to go and get them?"

"My bag's in the front hall," Heather said, gesturing in that direction. "And I'm officially on duty as of this moment. Unless..."

Dana shook her head. "No, I'm sure you're perfect for the job. Nic...uh, Mr. Scalia..." Her words trailed away as she realized there wasn't going to be any way to keep up the pretense of formality between herself and Nico, especially since Heather would be living there. Especially since Krystal already treated him like a favorite uncle.

"Nico swears you're the best in the agency, and I trust his judgment," she stated firmly.

"I'll need a room near Krystal's if that's possible, although I'd feel better if there were an extra bed in her room."

That shook Dana a little. Hiring a bodyguard for Krystal had merely been a precautionary measure, not something she'd have done if Mrs. J. were able to be with them. This suggested that Krystal was in actual danger.

"I didn't think anyone thought Krystal was under any real threat," she said.

A very professional, no-nonsense expression settled on the other woman's face. "What if the person threatening you decides that the best way to get to you is to snatch your daughter?"

"What?" Dana leaped to her feet. A chill rushed through her, freezing her blood, making her feel the cold right to the roots of her hair. She rubbed her arms and began to pace. "That scenario never crossed my mind," she admitted, clenching her jaw to keep her teeth from chattering.

Behind her, Heather said, "Ah, coffee, good. I think Ms. Harper could use a shot of brandy in hers, Nico."

Nico watched Dana's jerky movements, her hands rubbing her arms as if she were freezing, the way she was pacing, muttering under her breath. He set the tray down on the coffee table, went to Dana and halted her midpace by enfolding her in his arms. His hands and low voice soothed, and Dana took deep breaths and let herself grow quiet under his ministrations.

"What brought this on?"

Dana lifted her head and he could see the despair in her eyes. "Nico, I've got to give up my caseload, take a leave of absence, or maybe just quit my job altogether."

He led her to the couch, poured her coffee and put the cup into her hands. He knelt in front of her. "Dana, you can't mean that. Why would you even consider—"

"Nico, I can't risk Krystal just for the sake of my pride or even for my career. If these threats could expand to include her, I've got to remove myself from the arena."

He began to laugh, surprising both Dana and Heather.

Dana slammed her mug on the table and gave Nico a shove so that he fell back on his butt.

"Damn you, Scalia, what's so funny?"

But he'd already sobered. "Well," he drawled, not bothering to get up, "I guess the threats paid off. The sender got you off his case just as he intended and he didn't have to do anything but write a few notes."

"And shoot my housekeeper," Dana snapped.

Nico shook his head and got to his feet, rubbing his butt. "Not the same person," he boldly stated.

"Not the same... How do you know?"

It was Heather who answered as she filled a cup for herself. "The shooter was right-handed, the writer was left-handed." As if she hadn't noticed the undercurrents of personal drama that existed between Nico and Dana, she calmly stirred sugar into her cup and went back to her seat.

"How do you know that?" Dana turned to Heather.

"Our lab tech submitted the findings in his report. Angle of bullets, description of wound, position of idling car according to your Mrs. Johnson. And, of course, the location of the spent shell. The shooter could only have been right-handed. As for the notes, they are clearly typed by a lefty as evidenced by the greater pressure placed on the letters on the left-hand side of the keyboard."

Dana thought about that for a moment. "Well that should help narrow it down some. At least we can find out which of my suspects is left-handed."

Nico chuckled. "That was one of the things I meant to tell you about when..."

Both women stared at Nico as a blush heightened his coloring.

It took a minute for reality to dawn. Dana put her hand

over her mouth to hide a nervous grin. "Oh, right," she improvised, attempting to help him out. "When we heard the doorbell ring."

Nico shot her a look of gratitude tinged with relief.

Heather, clearly in the dark as to their meaning, but definitely spotting that some form of intrigue had passed between them, cleared her throat.

"So we're dealing with two sources of harassment," she said, returning to the initial subject.

"Unless it was a drive-by, victim chosen at random," Nico said, "and not intended for Dana at all."

"How often have you heard of drive-by shootings in Wayzata?" Dana asked.

"They can happen anywhere, none of the burbs are crime free these days."

They were all silent for a moment and then Nico said, "So what's your decision now, Dana, you still want to quit?"

"I suppose I could have Heather and Krystal move in with my parents for the duration," Dana said, her voice and expression etched in regret.

"We've already discussed that alternative in staff," Heather said, "and agreed it isn't a great idea."

"Why?"

"It's too obvious, the most likely place to start looking. We concluded it would be no safer than this house and only to be considered as a last resort. Actually, none of us think we'll reach that point."

Dana arched an eyebrow. "It sounds as if you think you're going to get a make on the guy."

"Oh, we'll make him—or them," Heather said. "You've got Nico on the case, and he's the best there is for sniffing out rats."

They're a mutual fan club, Dana thought, seeing them exchange a look of admiration. Or was it affection. For the first time it dawned on her that Heather Wilson was a damned attractive woman. Was there history between them? After all, they shared a career, had a great deal in common.

But she refused to allow herself to be ruled by jealousy. "Well, then, I guess there's no need for me to make any abrupt career changes at this time," she said. She stood.

"Heather, there's a twin bed to Krystal's in the attic. We can get it down and set it up in her room tomorrow. Meanwhile, you can use the room Nico's been occupying."

She hid a smile behind the pretense of a yawn as she saw the look of alarm on Nico's face.

"There isn't any need for you to be here 'round-the-clock now that Heather's here, is there, Nico?" Her tone dripped sugar.

It was clear that hadn't occurred to him.

"I...I guess not," he stammered. He pulled himself together, his face closed. "I'll just go up and get my things." He turned back when he reached the steps up to the foyer.

"Heather, why don't you come along. I'll show you where the linens are."

Dana sank down on the couch as the two of them went up to the second floor. She felt numb. How could she have thought she'd one-upped him, she wondered, when she was feeling so bereft at the idea of him leaving? And when Krystal awakened in the morning, and found him gone, she was going to be very upset.

She wanted to go to the stairs and call up to him, beg him to stay, offer to hire him on as her bodyguard.

She couldn't—wouldn't—go that far.

She comforted herself that it wasn't as if she'd never

see him again. He was still going to be working with her as an investigator, so they'd see each other frequently.

It was small comfort but it would have to do.

When Nico came down, his bag in one hand, his jacket in the other, she was waiting with a brave smile and a falsely cheerful note in her voice as she bid him good-night.

She expected to toss and turn, missing his presence in the house. What she didn't expect was the phone call from John Yearling.

"I'm sorry to call so late and with such bad news," he apologized, "but I just got a call from headquarters. George Vale was murdered sometime this evening."

Chapter Eleven

Dana found the newspaper unfurled on her desk as if someone had left it to catch her attention. She spotted the pertinent headline just as she was sinking onto her chair, one hand reaching for her coffee cup. Her hand hovered and then fell onto the desk, balled in a fist.

"Witness For The Prosecution Found Dead In Garage."

According to the story, Vale had been found by his wife who had been bringing him a cool drink and a snack. She found him lying on a pallet, his legs still under the car, a bullet dead center of his forehead.

At that point Dana stopped reading to ponder the information. Only one shot, a perfect target. She'd have to get the M.E.'s report to learn the distance from shooter to target, but unless the shot had been discharged from a foot away, the killer had to be a pro, and most likely, one of the Caprezio clan.

She resumed reading. The rest of the article had little more information to convey, except, as she expected, there'd been no physical evidence left at the scene and no witnesses. According to Mrs. Vale, she'd been in her kitchen, the windows open to the backyard with a full view of the back of the garage. She'd not seen anyone nor heard anything that could have been a shot.

Dana nodded. *Silencer.* Definitely a pro.

She refolded the paper carefully, her mind replaying the interview she'd had with Vale. A pleasant guy, likable. The jury would have responded to him. She regretted the thought instantly. This wasn't about a witness snatched from the prosecution's roster, this was about a fairly young man who had cared about his community, his neighbors, and been prepared to go all the way to do his civic duty. A husband and father who would be sorely grieved and whose death would leave a gaping hole in his loved ones' lives.

She certainly knew what that was like, from firsthand experience. A glimmer of insight lit her mind. Could Zack have been shot because he'd witnessed something incriminating and had to be stopped before he got back to tell his partner?

Her throat clutched up as she recognized the irony of the situation; as a witness, Vale had not had any definitive proof to support the prosecution's case. Dana had been using him only to give the jury a picture of the animosity between the good citizens of the neighborhood and the dark menace the Caprezio warehouse posed. With so little physical evidence in the Nunzio case, she had to strengthen the circumstantial evidence as much as possible. Even at that, a good defense attorney could tear her case to shreds, and Marcus Caprezio could end up walking.

Dana stood and went around her desk to pace the small bit of space in front of it. From now on she was going to have to keep a lock on who she interviewed for this case, and if, as they were all praying, an actual eyewitness came forward before trial opened, the person would have to be taken into protective custody.

She glanced up at the clock. Eleven forty. Lunchtime soon. But the thought of food caused her stomach to twist savagely. She wished she could cry, maybe that would let out some of the impotent rage, the frustration she was feeling.

God knows, Vale deserves to have a few tears shed over him, she thought.

A knock at the door stopped her midthought and Yearling came in, a grim look on his face, the newspaper rolled under his arm.

"Dana, I know how you must be feeling, but you have to get used to this sort of thing, it's part of the agenda in this business," he said, slumping into a chair.

She returned to her own seat behind the desk. "Still, I can't help but question my methods and—"

"Those kinds of thoughts are unproductive," her boss interrupted. "You need to be thinking objectively now. You can't bring Vale back, but you can damn well vindicate his death in court."

He got to his feet, wearily, Dana thought, concern for the older man obliterating her confusion and frustration.

"John, are you all right?"

He had started for the door. He looked over his shoulder and smiled sadly. "I will be when you nail that bastard in court and this case is closed for good."

It was a vote of confidence she badly needed. She smiled as the door closed behind Yearling. With renewed vigor and a burning desire to justify her boss's words, she pulled out the witness list and set to work.

She was still working when Nico knocked and entered the room.

They hadn't seen each other since he had moved out of her house and returned to his own apartment. If Dana wanted to fling herself into his arms, she hid it well by removing her glasses and rising to greet him with an impersonal smile. Fleetingly she thought of that last night when their lovemaking had been aborted by the arrival of Heather Wilson. She could see by the expression in his eyes that he was remembering, too.

There was an awkward moment of silence and then Nico's glance fell to the newspaper on Dana's desk.

He shook his head, sighed, and fell onto a chair. "I feel as if it's my fault," he said, his voice grim. "Maybe if I hadn't kept after him..."

"Why should you get all the blame?" Dana asked. "Didn't I initiate the interview with him?"

Nico looked distressed, rubbed his hand across his forehead. "He was a really nice guy, you know?"

Dana nodded. "I was just thinking that. And ironically, he was no real threat to anyone."

Nico did a double take. "What?"

"He didn't have any real evidence, wasn't an eyewitness to the shooting, didn't even have anything concrete on the action going down at the warehouse. I was using him to substantiate rumors and speculation, hoping the jury would be moved to add that to the circumstantial evidence we have."

"Do you hear yourself, Dana? You're saying the guy died for nothing!"

Fresh pain throbbed in her throat and left Dana speechless. Finally she shook her head and rasped, "That's why I feel so guilty. But I told you why we had to build a case with anything we could find. Do you think I'd have elected to take this case to trial with so little proof?" Her voice grew stronger. "Dammit, I was following orders." She pounded the desk so hard it made Nico jump.

"Take it easy, Dana, I was just caught unawares for a moment. I'm not blaming you for anything."

She gestured her apology with a wave of her hand. "Okay, so what's next?"

"I've got some leads to follow up on. I'll get back to you as soon as I have something significant to report."

The door had almost closed when it opened again and Nico stuck his head back into the room. "How's Krystal doing with Heather?"

She misses you, Dana thought. Out loud she said, "they're thick as thieves already."

Nico nodded but his face showed his disappointment. "Yeah, well, give the kid my love."

Dana put her head in her hands when she heard the gentle snick of the door closing.

What would be the point of telling him that Krystal was moping around, that it took real effort on Heather's part to get her to open up at all to Nico's replacement, that Krystal curled up in Dana's bed at night and talked nonstop about Nico and about his family.

She couldn't have told him how sad that made Dana feel, and how it reminded her of her own sense of loss. He was just a business associate now and they would continue to meet in circumstances that were purely professional.

Still she was too depressed to work. She decided to take an early lunch break and get some errands done. She jotted a short list of things she'd put off for one reason or another and noticed that she could accomplish all of them right in the area of the government building. It was a great day; moderate temperature, zero humidity. Perfect fall weather. She decided she'd walk.

Half an hour later she'd been to the post office, the bank and Dayton's department store. She checked her watch as she came out to the mall again, pleased with her efficiency. She stood for a moment, wondering if she could make it to the computer store and back within an hour. Any minute now, she'd be running out of toner for her printer at home, and surely that software she'd ordered would have come in by now.

Suddenly that sense of being watched returned. She

looked all around but saw no one she knew, no one who looked the least suspicious, no one who appeared to be paying special attention to her. She shook her head and turned in the direction of Third Avenue. The computer store was about seven blocks away, and out of the stream of pedestrian traffic that clogged the mall. She ought to be able to make it in good time.

In no time at all she was a block from the store, its neon sign in her sights just as she started across Tenth Street.

The taxi seemed to come from out of nowhere, barreling around the corner, bearing down on her at top speed.

Instinctively Dana took a step backward.

The hand at her back pushed her forward, and she fell to her knees as the taxi screeched to a halt with a squealing of brakes.

The scream stuck in Dana's throat as a hand pulled her roughly to her feet.

"Din't you see the light change, lady?" the taxi driver shouted as he climbed out of the cab. Dana flinched and started to explain.

"Think how much it costs us taxpayers when city officials don't watch where they're going," a low voice said from behind her.

She spun around at the familiar voice, shocked, but not surprised, to find Marcus Caprezio at her back.

This explained the feeling of being followed, the sensation that she was being watched every time she walked anywhere in the vicinity of her office. And then she recalled that hand at her back just as she'd fallen.

"You've been following me," she accused. "You pushed me."

"Hey, Ms. Harper, what kinda gratitude is that, I just saved your life."

The cabdriver came up beside them, nodding his head. "That's right, lady, I saw him pull you up outta the street. This guy's a hero, you owe him big-time."

Dana stared suspiciously at the driver. Were they in cahoots, was this a setup? But there was nothing she could charge the driver with. He hadn't hit her, after all, and she couldn't see trying to accuse him of anything when no one had been hurt.

"I'll keep that in mind," she said, "and I can't see any reason to detain you. Thanks."

The driver looked at Caprezio, a question on his face. "Yeah, thanks, buddy," Marcus said. He handed the man a bill. "And thanks for the backup." He turned an oily grin on Dana as he added, "I wouldn't want the lady to think I'd do her any harm. Wouldn't want her to think I'm some kind of murderer for instance."

Dana watched the driver get back in the car and drive off at a more reasonable speed before she turned back to Marcus.

"You're not fooling anyone, you know," she rasped.

"Come on, Ms. Harper, if I'd wanted to kill you, you'd be dead. We both know that." He brushed imaginary lint off his suit jacket front and gave her a menacing look from under his beetled, black eyebrows.

"But you're never going to feel safe, are you, lady lawyer?" And in a low, guttural snarl, added, "And you're never going to *be* safe, either."

Dana was struck dumb by horror as the man turned on his heels and strolled away.

For a moment she thought about reporting the incident to her boss but the more she thought about it, the more uncertain she became.

Yearling had put such trust in her capabilities. She had to maintain a sane and sober manner. She couldn't run tattling to him with every little threat, couldn't give him reason to regret leaving her on the case when just a short time ago he'd suggested turning it over to another attorney—a man, at that.

Anyway, it would be her word against Caprezio's and a case could certainly be made for the paranoia Marcus had accused her of, especially since she'd never reported the other threats to her boss. Not only that, but she had a feeling Caprezio would have no trouble locating the cabdriver who would back up his protestation of innocence. Especially if Marcus had set up the whole scenario just to create a new way of delivering his threatening messages. He would come out looking like a hero, wrongly accused, and Dana would come off ungrateful, paranoid, vengeful. The press would have a field day at her expense.

She looked around as she got her bearings and remembered she'd been on her way to the computer store. There was no point in wasting the trip now that she was only a block away. She'd be late getting back but she'd just stay a little longer at the office to complete her day's quota of paperwork. Feeling better, she straightened her shoulders and set her chin at a brave angle, her eyes focused on the neon sign at the end of the next block.

But she looked around carefully before stepping off the curb to cross the street.

IT WAS AFTER SEVEN, already growing dark, when Dana interrupted her work to check the time. She'd meant to be home before Krystal went to bed but apparently she wasn't going to make it.

Rubbing her eyes with one hand, she dialed her home number with the other.

"Heather, it's Dana," she said when the detective answered on the second ring. "It doesn't look as though

I'll make it home before Krystal's bedtime. Can you cover for me?''

"Sure thing, Dana, no problem. We're watching *Wizard of Oz* and I suspect Krys will be zonked by the time it's over."

Dana laughed. "Is she repeating every line of dialogue word for word?''

"Yeah, you'd think she wrote it.''

"She's watched it maybe a zillion times since she was two years old,'' Dana admitted, still chuckling. "Well, tell her I'm sorry about tonight but that I love her and I'll make it up tomorrow.''

"Will do. Oh, hey, I left a plate of dinner for you in the warming oven.''

The mention of food brought Dana's attention to her empty stomach. She'd missed both lunch and dinner and hadn't even thought of it until now. She thanked Heather for her thoughtfulness and hung up, anxious to be done so that she could get home to the dinner that awaited her.

It was a quarter to eight when she called it a day. The offices were dark as she made her way through the corridor toward the reception area, the only light the low-wattage wall sconce beside the elevator. Suddenly she heard the sound of movement behind her.

She spun around and peered into the shadows at the end of the hall. She couldn't see anything. She picked up her pace, nearly running through the gloomy passage. Once again she thought she heard a noise but when she stopped to listen, she heard nothing.

Still, she sensed she wasn't alone. If someone was back there, he was keeping out of sight, making sure he wasn't heard. Maybe she could get away without him knowing it. She slowed her step, took off her shoes and tried to move soundlessly to the elevator.

She was about to turn the corner at the end of the hall when she felt someone rush up behind her. She tried to spurt forward, but an arm closed around her throat, halting her movement.

She had time for only one scream before the grip tightened to a choke hold. She was sure she was going to black out any minute, positive death was only one more twist of that arm away when she heard another sound and then a voice shouting her name.

The arm fell away from her neck and she heard a grunt as the man pushed her forward and took off at a run.

She tried to focus and get to her feet. A wave of dizziness swept over her just as a strong pair of arms swept her up and a familiar and welcome voice begged to know she was all right.

"Go after him," she croaked, urgent fright outweighing the pain.

"Not till I know you're all right," he repeated.

"Fine, I'm fine. Go after him, Nico, he tried to kill me."

She could hear him opening doors, searching offices, running from one work area to the next, slamming doors shut, as she slowly limped to the water fountain that hung on the wall across from the elevator. She splashed cold water on her face and throat, using a cupped hand to hold the water. It helped ease the pain a little.

Nico ran back to her yelling, "He's gone. I'll call down to the lobby, see if the guard saw anyone running out of the building."

"You saved my life, Nico," Dana said hoarsely as he hung up the phone at the receptionist's desk, shaking his head.

"All I did was show up," he muttered, studying Dana's neck in the light from the wall sconce beside the elevator. Angry red marks were already blotching her skin.

"But your arrival scared him off," she insisted. "If you hadn't shown up just then, he'd have killed me."

She shuddered and Nico enfolded her in his arms and held her tightly until she moaned softly.

"Pain?" Nico asked.

Dana nodded. "I could use some cold compresses in strategic places," she admitted.

Nico held her face between his hands and shook his head. "Are you ready to concede now that you need a bodyguard, Dana?"

"There's nothing to show the attack was personal," she argued. "He might have attacked anyone who worked late and threatened his mission."

"Which was what?" Nico demanded.

"Burglary?" Dana said weakly.

"Of the County Attorney's offices?" Nico scoffed. "I don't think so. What would he have been after? Paper clips?"

Dana gingerly caressed her throat, the pain suddenly welling up again as if to remind her of what could have happened if Nico hadn't shown up.

"You can't ignore the facts, love," he said, his voice gentle, soothing. "It's not safe for you to be alone anymore, and certainly not here, at night."

She had to admit, to herself at least, that she was suddenly attracted to the thought of Nico covering her back.

She hadn't even told him about what had happened in the street earlier in the day.

"I don't want you to give up your investigation," she rasped.

"I can do that after I see you safely to your office every morning and then safely home at the end of the day. We both have pagers, you can always beep me if you're going to leave the office for any reason during the day.''

Dana agreed, recognizing that to refuse to accept his guardianship would, at this point, be sheer foolishness.

''I don't want anyone else to know,'' she warned, ''especially no one in the department. And,'' she added, pushing to make her tone as firm as possible under the circumstances, ''I don't ever want to hear the term 'bodyguard' used in connection with our association.''

''Done,'' he agreed, affection apparent in his chuckle. ''So unless you want to stop at the hospital to have them give you the once-over, let's go to my apartment so I can pick up my bag.''

SHE FELL IN LOVE with him as she moved around his living room while he was in the bedroom packing a bag. She clutched an ice bag, concocted from a plastic bag and a hand towel, to her throat, strolling from one area of interest to the next.

His bookcases were stuffed with the broadest array of titles she'd ever seen outside of a library. The books overflowed to other surfaces in the room and even to stacks on the floor near a leather recliner. A stereo system offered the choice of LP, cassette or CD; there were plenty of each in evidence on the shelves and here again she noticed his eclectic taste.

There were pictures of people on the walls and on the table in front of the window. From that window she had a clear view of the Mississippi River and Harriet Island on the other bank. She recognized those members of his family she had met, including his parents. In almost every picture that included Nico, he was holding or playing with a child, his expression one of simple joy.

A battered old saxophone was peeking out of a partially open case, suggesting long years of use and recent use at that. She could visualize him blowing bittersweet jazz on the horn and she opened the case all the way and caressed the dull brass of the instrument with gentle fingers.

She went to the couch and settled into a corner, looking around at the general decor of the room. Early Salvation Army, she thought, smiling, but pulled together into real hominess by Nico's personal stamp. Books, music, family photos, odd little ceramic pieces that had probably been humorous gifts from his siblings and cherished without self-consciousness, and plants everywhere, obviously well cared for.

There was no sign of the cop here, nothing that said this was strictly a man's home, no sense that there were things hidden from the casual eye that would suggest another persona lurking beneath the domestic facade. It was strictly "what you see is what you get," and she liked what she saw.

She had her head twisted at an odd angle, trying to read the title of a book on a table at the other end of the couch, when Nico reentered the room, his suitcase and a small matching travel kit in one hand, his briefcase in the other.

He dropped them and rushed to the couch. "Dana, are you okay?"

She straightened her head and grinned at him. "Why? Did you think my head had slipped off my neck?"

A sigh of relief, mingled with exasperation, whooshed out of him as Nico stamped away to retrieve his luggage.

"Dammit, Dana, I still think you should get checked out at a hospital. Ramsey is just a few blocks away."

She couldn't stop grinning. "Were you really an altar boy, Nico?"

"How did you..." He glanced over at the framed photos on the window table. "Oh, right."

Was that a look of embarrassment tinting his cheeks? Dana unfolded her legs and stood, giving him a sober, even look. "And you still attend church?"

There'd been a picture of Nico, as a grown man, with his arm around a priest's shoulder. They were standing in front of St. Luke's.

"When I can," Nico admitted, a question in his eyes.

Dana nodded. "It's not so hip these days, but I like to see men at Mass. Especially single men. It's a good example for the kids."

Nico stared at her. "You're Catholic?"

She nodded again, surprised he hadn't known that. But then, it wasn't something one wore on the outside that everyone could recognize.

"Krystal and I attend St. Pater Claver. It was Zack's church from childhood and I went with him because he preferred it to the Basilica, which is where my family worships. Then, Father Kevin was assigned there and I began going because I was so crazy about him. After Zack died, I realized that I'd come to think of it as my own church."

Nico began to laugh.

"What?"

"Mama always told me I'd meet the right woman for me in church." He sobered as he realized how much he'd just admitted.

Dana went to him, dropping the ice bag on the couch. She slipped her arms around his neck and raised her face for his kiss.

He bent his head and then hesitated, his mouth only a couple of mile-long inches from hers.

"Dana, this is really wrong," he warned. "We can't afford to let our emotions get in the way of the job we have to do."

"I'm through working for the day, Nico, and I want you to make love to me."

Chapter Twelve

Nico needed no further urging. His mouth closed over hers as if it were the only way to slake his considerable thirst. The kiss was deep and searching, leaving them both breathless and unsteady.

For a moment a red light filled Dana's mind, warning her of the danger of so much chemistry, but the green light of passion obscured all other thoughts and prevailed.

She pulled him closer, her arms tight around his shoulders, her hands caressing his neck. They resumed the kiss, their tongues dueling as if each were fighting for control over the other. Their hands bumped repeatedly as they tore at each other's clothing.

In mere seconds Nico achieved a state of full arousal and Dana was pulling him closer, urging his body to soothe the ache that pulsed at the apex of her thighs. Dana's blouse and bra came off and fell to the floor along with Nico's shirt. His tongue plunged the sweetness of her mouth over and over and his fingers moved so urgently over her breasts and then down her stomach that Dana cried aloud her runaway desire.

She pushed her hands down into his jeans, curving them around his hard buttocks to bring him closer to the ponderous ache.

Nico cried out and pulled the fly open, sliding jeans

and briefs down in one swift movement, unable to wait any longer to unite their two bodies.

Anticipating him, Dana slid skirt, slip and panties down so they fell to her knees. He tumbled her onto her back and then he was filling her completely.

She heard his frantic, whispered endearments, some of them in Italian, inhaled his personal scent, felt his hands caressing her everywhere, and her heart filled as completely as her body.

The fire of their lust increased their body heat and Nico suckled her nipples as if quenching his thirst. Dana thrashed beneath him. She could feel her desire building as his body engulfed hers, every movement pure heaven.

She'd never ever experienced such passion. She wanted to wrap herself completely around him, to swallow him up into her body, wanted to hold him inside forever, every cell in her body screaming for more.

Nico felt her urgency and his heart swelled with adoration, his blood thrumming with excitement, as he gave her all that he had within him to give.

They reached the crescendo of passion together, their bodies pressed so close that not a breath could have fit between them. When they climaxed he pulled her up so that she was sitting on his lap, her legs wrapped around his waist, her arms twined around his neck.

They collapsed on the floor, still wrapped together, still throbbing as they began the descent into real time.

"I'll never be able to move again," Dana whispered hoarsely.

Nico's voice was only slightly stronger. "You won't have to, love, as soon as I'm able, I'm going to carry you." But it was clear the speech had taken the last of his energy. They dozed until Dana became aware of the scratchiness of the carpet against her back. She nudged Nico.

"I need a ride," she whispered into his ear.

He turned his head and grinned at her. "I'm not sure I'm not all ridden out," he said.

"Not that kind of ride," Dana scoffed. "A ride into the bedroom, to a nice soft, smooth bed."

"If I can do that, I might be able to do more," he warned.

"I don't think so, sweetie, I think we've both had it."

"Oh? You think so?" He kissed her ever so softly and carried her into the bedroom.

He laid her down gently, taking a moment to stare down at the wealth of femininity spread there for his eyes only. Her eyes glowed with the knowledge of his adoration and she brazenly lowered her gaze to his arousal. He couldn't move. He stood there, mesmerized, as she slowly rose to her knees and inched over to the edge of the bed. Her eyes never left his as she reached out and carefully pulled him toward her.

He didn't move at first. He held her face in his hands and caressed her lips with his tongue. "You're mine, now, you know," he warned, lifting his head to gaze into her eyes.

"Show me," she murmured, lifting her body to accommodate him. His movement taunted her to the highest peak, threatening repeatedly to send her over the edge.

It seemed to go on forever. "Please, Nico, please," she begged. He responded with a movement that drove her upward. And then he began the slow withdrawal, making her cry out, excitement and frustration warring within her.

When he added a new twist, she writhed under him, her hands clawing at his shoulders.

Nico held himself still, watching her face. For some reason a flashback rose in his mind just then and a cold chill ran up his spine. What if something were to happen to her? What if he couldn't protect her for some reason?

He felt himself going limp. Dana responded immediately, rising up on her elbows, looking at him askance.

"Nico?"

"It's all right, love, really. I'm just tired. Fatigue is a real deterrent to lovemaking."

She looked skeptical but then her own exhaustion consumed her. She fell back on the pillow, her eyes already closing.

"Darling, are you sure you don't want me to…"

"Go to sleep, Dana, you don't have to do a thing."

Her heavy breathing told him she was already asleep. He eased away, moving onto his own pillow, his body curled on his side. He'd done the unforgivable, allowed his emotions to dominate, wiping out all the knowledge he'd gained from his last slip, leaving him, and worse, Dana, totally vulnerable.

He gritted his teeth and struck his pillow with his fist as he realized that a band of guerillas could have invaded the premises and he'd never have known it until it was too late.

He turned onto his back and stared up at the ceiling. He could never let his guard down like this again. He glanced over at Dana and his heart sank. That sassy, strong-willed little bundle of voluptuous beauty would never let anything get in the way of something she wanted.

He sighed as he rolled off the bed, knowing he wouldn't be able to sleep and, in any case, knowing it was best to get this over with as soon as possible.

DANA'S PURR of contentment awakened her from the light doze she'd slipped into. She turned to fold herself back into Nico's arms and found only cool sheets and the pillow that still held his unique and wonderful smell. She sat up and listened, heard the shower running. A gleeful, mischievous imp inside urged her out of bed and toward the bathroom.

She reached the door just as the water stopped running and she heard the shower door slide back. She looked down at her nudity and realized that what would have been a romantic surprise wasn't going to work now that Nico was out of the shower. She fled back to the bed, to the cover of the sheets.

Nico found her propped against the pillows, her shoulders and arms bare above the sheet tucked across her breasts, her face illuminated by the lingering fulfillment of their lovemaking.

He hesitated before speaking, every cell in his body responding to the sight of her beauty, a lump of guilt rising in his throat.

"It's very late, Dana, we should get back to the house before Heather starts worrying."

Dana's smile faltered at the cool tone in his voice, the grim expression on his face. And he was fully dressed, except for his socks and shoes.

"Is something wrong, Nico?"

He turned away, rummaging in a drawer for socks. "Nothing's wrong. I just think it's time to go."

Suddenly she felt embarrassed at the thought of exposing her nudity to him, of dressing in front of him. But she'd just made love to this man, how could she ask him to leave the room while she dressed?

Nico spared her the awkwardness, mumbling something about leaving his shoes in the living room. The door closed with a quiet click behind him.

Dana sat for a moment longer, her fist against her mouth, fighting back threatening tears.

Nico was acting like a man who'd done something

impulsive and now regretted that action. Was that all their loving had been to him? An impulse?

She stifled a sob and swung her legs off the bed. Okay, if that's how it was, she could live with it. She'd lived with worse and never forfeited her dignity or pride.

Hurriedly she began to dress, all the while struggling against breaking down, muttering under her breath about how she'd warned him off continuously but how he'd persisted in coming on to her, seducing her with exotic meals, confusing her with sexual innuendo, even going so far as to get her involved with his family.

"So much for love," she snarled, jerking up a thigh-high stocking with reckless disregard for its flimsiness.

The words were no sooner out than the impact hit her. Sometime during their lovemaking, he'd whispered that he loved her. She collapsed on the side of the bed, one leg clad, the other with the hose pulled up only halfway.

She was an experienced prosecutor, able to recognize the difference between sincerity and subterfuge. There had never been a time where she had felt that she had prosecuted, or been accused of prosecuting, an innocent person.

Nico had been sincere. She was sure of it. He hadn't uttered the words through a fury of passion spinning out of control. *Though there'd certainly been plenty of that,* she thought, smiling wryly.

No, he hadn't used the words as a means of using her, she decided. Something had happened, or occurred to him, to make him wary of an ongoing relationship.

She bent to ease the rest of the stocking up her leg. Okay, so now all she had to do was find out what the something was and make it go away.

When she joined Nico in the living room, she gave him an enigmatic smile. "All ready," she said in as cheerful a tone as she could muster.

Still avoiding eye contact, he turned to retrieve his luggage. "Would you get the door, please, Dana?" he asked, gesturing with his burdened hands.

She made a wide swath around him and held the door open. Over his shoulder, he told her the door would lock automatically.

They drove to Wayzata in silence, except for the hum of the wheels rolling over asphalt, and the questions tumbling over and over in Dana's head. By the time they were within a few blocks of her house, she decided they were going to have to reach an understanding, one way or another.

She cleared her throat. "Nico, it's clear you've had second thoughts and decided tonight wasn't a good idea. I have to assume that this has something to do with the fact that I'm your employer. If I'm wrong, I feel you owe it to me to tell me what's upset you."

Nico's laugh was a short bark of disbelief. "Oh, Lord, Dana, you're so off the track. I'm just not chauvinistic enough to let the fact that a woman is my employer get in the way of a personal relationship." He shook his head and lowered his window halfway before continuing.

"And," he went on, "I don't really think of you as my employer. Given my job and yours and the one we're both involved in, I consider us more partners than anything."

Dana started to speak but stopped herself when she realized he had more to say. She turned in her seat, her back to the door, her eyes riveted on his handsome profile.

He sighed. "I guess I should tell you the whole story." He turned onto her street, waved at the cop in the blue and white patrol car as they passed by, and eased up into her driveway.

He pressed the button that moved his seat back as far

as it would go and turned off the motor. Mimicking her position, he turned so that they were facing each other.

"Four years ago, not long after I'd joined the agency, I was assigned to security on an estate not too far from here. The assignment was temporary, meant to last about three weeks during which time it was my job to make sure nobody came onto the premises who could tamper with the security system, hide away on the acreage surrounding the house, or attempt to infiltrate the dwelling for purposes of leaving bombs, poisons, drugs, or anything that might result in harm to any of the occupants."

He cleared his throat, turning to take a gulp of fresh air through the open window.

When he turned back, Dana could see the steely look that brightened his eyes. Realizing she'd been holding her breath, she let it out quietly as he began to speak again.

"The purpose of all the extra security was the pending visit from the ambassador to Great Britain who was to meet—secretly—with the ambassadors of two other countries, and the U.S. secretary of state, on a matter of utmost political delicacy. They'd elected to meet in Minnesota because it was far from the gossip mill of D.C. and one of the better places to set up security surveillance.

"The people who were hosting the British ambassador, had two small children, boy and girl, three and four. They took a shine to me, following me everywhere anytime they could escape from their nanny. Trouble was, she was a lazy caretaker, and the kids could escape almost at will. At first, I tried to shoo them off, but they were so damned persistent, and so cute, I finally decided they were better off having someone look after them than left to their own reckless mischief."

Dana could feel the tension building, could see it in

the set of his jaw, the sound of his voice. She hung on
every word, barely breathing.

"I began to play with them while we strolled the
grounds doing my rounds. Tossing a ball or a Frisbee
with them, showing them how to fly their kites, playing
limited games of hide and seek. They were good kids.
When I set up distance limits for how far away they could
hide, or run ahead of me, they obeyed without question."

His eyes glinted with unshed tears and Dana could feel
her own throat filling as she sensed what came next.

"My partner, who worked the night shift so I could
get some sleep, kept warning me that I was getting too
involved with the kids. I laughed him off, told him a
couple of tots, barely out of training pants, were hardly
any threat to national security."

His voice had gained a tremor and it was evident that
he had to force himself to push on. Dana put a gentle
hand over his and was relieved when he turned so that
their palms joined and he held on in a tight clasp.

It was almost as if he clung to her for the strength to
finish. Her heart ached at the sound of despair in his
voice.

Abruptly Nico jumped to the end.

"We were playing hide-and-seek when I heard a
scream behind me and ran toward it to find that Daniel
had fallen into the pond and little Rosy was screaming
at the top of her lungs. Vaguely I was aware of a sound
of thrashing of bushes over to my left, beneath the wall
that enclosed the estate, but my first priority was getting
to Daniel before he could drown.

"Naturally, once the boy was safe, we searched every
inch of the grounds, but by then an hour had passed and
we found no sign of an intruder.

"Two days later, the ambassador arrived with his en-
tourage and a team from the Secret Service. When the

bomb went off, it killed two of the agents and my partner."

Even expecting it, Dana gasped at his final words. Nico had turned away, bending his head on the steering wheel, his hands clinging to the wheel. His shoulders were heaving with dry sobs. She put her hand on his back and when he didn't shrug her off, she moved over to hold him in her arms.

"It wasn't your fault, Nico, you did the only thing you could do by saving the little boy. Anyone would have."

His face was pained when he lifted his head. "If I hadn't got involved with the kids in the first place, Daniel wouldn't have been anywhere near the pond."

Dana shook her head and clenched her teeth. "Not so, my dear. You said the nanny was negligent of the children's whereabouts. They could have wandered down to the pool all on their own and Daniel might still have fallen in. Had that been the case, and if you hadn't been looking out for them, the boy certainly would have drowned."

Nico rubbed his eyes to alleviate some of the pain. "That's the only thought that kept me sane in the following weeks. But I learned a lesson about allowing myself to be distracted from my job." He gave another of those chuckles of derision. "Or thought I'd learned it."

"Until tonight, you mean." It all came together for Dana, relief competing with pity and a sense of helplessness. This was the reason Nico had withdrawn from her after they'd made love and there was little she could say to argue against his resolve. Still she tried.

"Nico, we have Heather solely looking out for Krystal, and our being together, in bed or out, is protection for me."

Nico shook his head. "Don't you see, if I'm emotionally involved with you, I'm not totally focused on what's going on around you, not concentrating all my thoughts on unraveling clues. Not watching your back. If anything happened to you, I don't know…'' He gasped at the onslaught of foreshadowed pain. ''Don't know what I'd do.''

Dana bit her bottom lip. There was no rebuttal. She could certainly understand his concern and if there was the least chance that he was right, she had to honor his feelings and cooperate with him.

''Come on, Scalia,'' she ordered, ''if we're going to take vows of celibacy, we're going to need all the strength a good night's rest can provide.''

She was already out of the car and on the driveway when he called out.

She turned back.

''When this is over…''

She shrugged her shoulders and waved a hand airily in his direction. ''We'll see, pal. Who knows, it may be like quitting smoking, after a few days you may be out of my system.''

She was still laughing when she entered the house, hoping against hope she could make it to the privacy of her room before the tears came.

Chapter Thirteen

They drove to work together as they'd been doing all week. Yearling had arranged for Nico to use the empty office two doors down from Dana's and it was agreed that if Nico was out of the office, Dana would stay in until he returned and could accompany her on any forays out of the department.

They were just turning onto the highway when Nico asked if something was wrong.

"Wrong? Of course not, why do you ask?" She fussed over a tiny bit of lint on the hem of her Black Watch plaid skirt, and adjusted the forest green blazer. Anything to avoid his penetrating gaze.

He laid a hand over hers and she twitched at the instant response her nerves made.

"You seem nervy, distracted, this morning. Is it your work? Not going well? You know, if there's anything I can do to…"

"Thank you, no. I don't need help and my work is going fine," Dana said, abruptly cutting him off.

Nico shrugged, returning his concentration to the traffic in front of them. Dana pretended to be absorbed by the passing scenery. They sank into silence for a few miles.

Why should my feelings be hurt? Nico asked himself.

She's just a little edgy this morning. Happens to everyone now and then. Probably didn't sleep well. *I sure know what that's like these days.*

Surreptitiously he threw her a glance, just the sight of her enough to get his pulse revved. The act of looking at her felt like forbidden fruit, making him want to risk the danger of one more look and then another and another after that. *And therein lies more temptation than I can handle,* he reminded himself.

The view from her window was one long blur to Dana as her mind fretted over her mean response to his show of concern.

That ought to put the kibosh on any romantic feelings he might have been harboring for me, she told herself. Her inner imp reminded her that that was their agreement. *So see, I'm doing him a favor, making it easier for him to keep to our agreement. And for me to keep to mine,* she added, keeping the record straight.

But she dared a glance at his profile, her stomach lurching at the sight. He was one of the most arresting men she'd ever met with his dark hair, still damp from the shower and already beginning to curl around his ears, his straight nose, nicely shaped black brows, the perfect look of those sensuous lips under his full black mustache. Just gazing at that mouth made her own lips hum with remembered pleasure.

She turned away from his face before her survey led to more tempting memories.

Nico coughed and covered his mouth with his hand.

Such nice manners, Dana thought, reminding her of his family and how well-mannered and warm and friendly they all were. She couldn't help but wonder if that was because they were used to Nico bringing women home.

She squelched that thought, adjusting her legs in front

of her, raising a hand to test the firmness of her French braid, and lowering her window a couple of inches.

The crossbreeze carried Dana's scent to his nostrils and Nico replayed their lovemaking and the way her fragrance played as much of an erotic part as the feel of her skin, her body closing around him.

He barely controlled the moan that threatened to escape and lowered his own window another couple of inches. He stuck his finger between his collar and tie to make breathing a bit easier, surprised to find it wasn't what was choking him.

They both expelled great gusts of relief when the car pulled into a parking space in the ramp and Dana almost tripped as she hurried toward the elevator.

The elevator was crowded, causing Dana and Nico to stand close, pressed together.

Nico stared down at the top of Dana's head, marveling at the wonderful blond hair that was already starting to form stray curls from the wisps that pulled out of her braid.

She stared at Nico's tie, mesmerized by the way it moved as he inhaled and exhaled. He coughed again, struggling to get his hand free to cover his mouth, the back of it brushing against Dana's cheek.

"You've caught a cold," she whispered.

Somber brown eyes exchanged glances with worried blue eyes.

Nico shook his head. "Just a frog," he whispered back, his gaze moving to her full lips.

She could feel his eyes moving across her mouth as if he were using the lightest pressure of his fingers. She swallowed with difficulty and inadvertently took a tiny step forward. The toe of her pump nudged the toe of his loafer. She could feel his sweet breath drifting over her face, could smell his aftershave, his shampoo, could even feel his heart pumping under his white shirt.

He inhaled her shampoo and felt her breasts beneath the prim white blouse brushing against his pecs. He wanted to step forward, wrap his arms around her. The thought had his body responding in the most obvious ways. He turned slightly, badly needing air.

She felt him shift and then felt something against her stomach that brought a flush to her cheeks. She wanted to move closer, to wrap arms and legs around him. She swallowed a gasp which made her choke and begin to cough.

Automatically Nico put an arm around her and patted her back. Almost oblivious to their whereabouts, to the other people in the car with them, their heads moved, mouth reaching for mouth.

The elevator doors flew open just as the car jerked to a halt and they were pushed out by the crowd behind them. Dazed, Dana looked around and saw that they were on the fourth floor.

"Wrong floor," she said. She turned to step back in the elevator and saw that it had emptied down to two people plus herself and Nico. She took advantage of the space to stand well away from him, willing her body to relax, her nerves to stop quivering.

He rested his back against the wall, and took deep gulps of the encapsulated air that seemed fresher now that there weren't so many lungs sharing it. He looked across at Dana and saw that she was earnestly attempting to pull herself together. He winked and grinned, happy to know she shared his discomfort.

She read the message in his face and felt her own lips curving upward in response.

With fewer passengers aboard, the elevator car made

a smoother stop at the next floor. The other two occupants stepped off and the doors closed.

"That was close," Nico said.

"Yeah. Close." She tucked her blouse more firmly into the waistband of her skirt and cocked an impish eyebrow at his briefcase.

His saucy chuckle told her he wasn't feeling the least self-conscious. She liked that about him. Nico fit in the world most comfortably.

When they reached her floor, she was able to face her colleagues with no personal discomfort and she introduced them to Nico with just the right tone of professionalism.

They walked down the corridor to her office. "Would you like to get out for lunch today?" Nico asked as they stopped at her door.

"Sure," Dana said, "I'm getting a little tired of staying in." She added, with a grin, "I take it this is an invitation, not a question."

He pretended to think that over. Finally he said, "I guess I can put it on my expense account."

"Don't bother," Dana retorted, "I'm not that expensive."

She went into her office and closed the door. He could hear her laughing and he had a smile on his own face as he crossed the short distance to his own door.

THREE HOURS LATER, after a productive morning of work, they were seated in the tiled patio room of Skip's, skylights allowing rays of sunshine to illuminate each table as if they were spotlighted.

"I'm going to do my own surveillance on the Lake Street warehouse," Nico said, reaching for the basket of rolls and offering her first selection.

Dana took a roll and placed it on her bread and butter plate. "Why?"

"There's been such conflicting information concerning the action there, I want to see for myself what's going down. And since Yearling has put me officially on your team, I don't feel I can do this during office hours since it really doesn't concern one of your current cases."

Dana sat back as the waiter set a plate of chicken salad in front of her and immediately sat forward again when he moved away. "You're going to do this at night?"

Nico thanked the waiter and stuck his fork into the soup plate heaped with spaghetti alfredo. "Yes," he admitted as he twirled pasta around his fork. "It will be late at night though, and you should be perfectly safe with Heather in the house."

"I know I'll be safe," Dana said, putting a forkful of salad into her mouth. She chewed, swallowed and gave him a benign smile.

"Because I'll be with you."

Nico almost choked on the mouthful of creamy pasta as he tried to swallow and speak at the same time. He took a big gulp of his iced cappuccino and wiped his eyes with the heels of his palms.

"No way," he said. "You're going to be tucked in bed, safe and sound and—"

"No," Dana cut in. "If you're going to do a stakeout, I'm going to be with you. And before you try to spoil our lunch by arguing with me, let me remind you that in this matter, you are my employee and this investigation is my personal baby."

Nico slumped back in his chair and stared at her. He could see by the jut of her chin, the set of her shoulders and spine, the defiant gleam in her eyes that she wouldn't back down.

Disgustedly he threw his napkin on the table and stood.

"Whatever you say, Boss. Now if you'll excuse me, I'm going to call the agency and arrange to pick up some special surveillance equipment."

Dana grinned and reached into her purse. "Care to use my cell phone?" she asked, holding it out to him.

"No thanks," Nico said with a petulant glare. "I prefer privacy in these matters."

Dana dug into her salad with renewed relish, still smiling as she chewed. She was thinking about things they'd need, like a thermos of coffee, a blanket in case it got cold—they couldn't risk turning the motor on for heat—and sandwiches against late-night hunger.

A shadow obstructed the ray of sunshine that fell across her right shoulder. She looked up into the smirking face of Charles Donegan.

"What an unexpected and unpleasant surprise," Dana said, grimacing at the man who seemed as much enraptured by his vision in the mirror across the room as he was by his encounter with Dana.

"Why, Mrs. Harper, I would have expected better manners from a lady of your stature."

"Let's not bother pretending we're dance partners, Charlie," Dana snapped. "What are you doing here and what do you want? I had hoped never to have to see you anywhere but in court."

He leaned down and said in a low voice, "You have more to lose than I have, Mrs. Harper."

It was the last straw. Dana banged her fist on the table and stood up to face off with the pompous, self-involved man.

"Now all three of you have been accounted for, you jerk," she growled.

Donegan took a step back and then laughed and sauntered away.

Nico came up behind her and grabbed her arm.

"What was that all about?" he demanded.

Dana plopped down on her chair, the breath exploding out of her lungs. She looked up at Nico and shook her head.

"That was Charles Donegan. He just delivered the third face-to-face threat."

Nico frowned and seated himself. "Third," he said, puzzled. "Who was the second?" She recalled that she'd never told him about being followed by Marcus Caprezio and the incident that ensued.

He jumped up again, his face mottled with rage.

"Where are you going?" Dana asked, frightened by the barely contained fury that seemed to come off of him in waves.

"First of all, I'm going after Donegan to knock some civility into him and then I'm going to find Caprezio and teach him a more in-depth lesson."

"Wait." Dana held fast to his arm. "You don't know what a can of worms you'd be opening."

She breathed easier as Nico reluctantly sank back onto his chair.

"I'm listening," he declared, his voice and eyes steely.

"The County Attorney's Office can't afford a media circus at this point, Nico. We don't want the press trying our cases on network TV and maybe even orchestrating the outcomes."

He didn't look convinced. She placed her hand on his arm, gently squeezed, and softly added, "I can't afford any bad press, either, Nico. The bottom line is that it would ultimately affect Krystal, you know."

That got him. She could see the tension of determination leak out of him. He drank deeply of his iced coffee and waved the waiter over.

"Can you give this a jolt of microwave," he asked the man, pointing to his plate, "and refill my glass, please?"

They resumed their meal in silence punctuated here and there by brief comments on the meal, the ambience of the new restaurant and the good service.

As Nico put his credit card on the check tray, he looked around the room. "A lot of lawyers here," he commented.

For the first time Dana studied their neighbors at adjoining tables, recognizing many fellow attorneys. She smiled and waved at a few who met her eye.

"Lord," she said, leaning toward Nico, "I hope they didn't notice my little scene."

"Or mine," Nico reminded. He brushed a wayward curl off her cheek and tucked it behind her ear. It was a casual, tender gesture and Dana put her hand over his and held it to her cheek a moment.

"Thanks, Nico," she whispered.

"*Nada,* love," he whispered back. Only a heightened awareness of propriety made him remove his hand and stand to imply that lunch was over.

Chapter Fourteen

The street was dark except for the streetlamp on the corner of Lake Street and the light at the back of the warehouse. So far there had been no visible activity at the building.

They had drunk most of the coffee, eaten the sandwiches, and spread the blanket across their laps as the night temperature began dropping.

Every now and then Nico opened his window a few inches to let in a little fresh air, but it was too cold to have it open for long, even with the blanket over them.

Nico found himself frequently glancing over at his stakeout partner, still bemused by what had taken place as they were leaving the house.

They'd been at the door, ready to leave when Dana had called to Nico to wait up.

She'd gone to the front hall closet and lifted a box down from the top shelf. Setting it on the console, she'd removed a police-issue service revolver.

"Hey," Nico had yelled, "what do you think you're doing with that?"

She was already loading it. "I'm loading it."

"I can see that, but why?"

She was sighting down the barrel, holding the gun with both hands, like a pro.

"For protection," Dana'd calmly retorted, shoving the revolver in her bag.

"Dana, honey, you don't need that, you'll be with me. I'll protect you."

She'd put the box back on the shelf and walked to the front door. She had started out and then halted, speaking over her shoulder.

"I know you'll protect me, Nico. This is for me to protect you."

Nico snickered now at the memory.

"What?"

"Just thinking about you and that gun," Nico said, grinning at her. "You looked like a kid planning to play cops and robbers with a cannon."

Dana gave him a disdainful look. "For your information, Scalia, I've had police training and certification, I can probably outshoot you."

"Maybe at target practice," he scoffed, "but how about in a live hostage situation or with a gun aimed at you, or for that matter, in the case of a moving target."

She kept forgetting he'd been a cop. He probably could shoot rings around her. She decided to bluff it out by just changing the subject.

"Doesn't look as though we're going to get any action tonight."

"You're right. Let's give it another half hour and if nothing goes down, we can come back another night."

He got the thermos from the backseat and held it up. "Want to share the last cup with me?"

For some reason the air between them seemed to shimmer as their eyes met. Dana had meant to say she'd had enough coffee, but suddenly she couldn't speak, couldn't tear her gaze from his.

Nico felt the thermos fall from his hand but he didn't

hear it hit the floor of the car, perhaps because the pounding of his blood was so loud in his ears.

As if controlled by invisible strings, they moved simultaneously, closing the distance between them in a blur of motion, their mouths joining hungrily.

They might have lost complete control, forgotten they were in a very visible car on a public street, but just then the glare of a spotlight washed over them, causing them to guiltily jump apart.

There were two officers in the squad car. One of them, in plain clothes, was Joe Lake.

Dana could see the embarrassment color his face as Joe recognized them.

"Sorry, we thought you were a couple of teenagers," he said, rubbing his mouth with the back of his hand.

"Come to that, what are you guys doing out here in the middle of the night?"

"I...we...you see—"

Nico interrupted Dana's stammering attempt to find a plausible story.

"We were supposed to meet a witness here, but the guy never showed. We were just getting ready to give up, call it a night."

Joe looked at the uniformed driver and turned back, shrugging. "Not smart to sit out here at this hour, this is a rough neighborhood."

"Aren't they all," Nico commented dryly. And then, as if an afterthought, asked, "What are you doing out so late, Lake, and in a squad car? Been demoted?"

Joe looked past Nico to give Dana a pained look. "I was keeping a promise to a friend."

Dana felt a wave of nausea stir in her stomach, sickened by having been discovered in a compromising situation by Joe. On the other hand, maybe it required something this drastic to convince Joe that there was ab-

solutely no future for them. Maybe now he really would
start looking for the right woman for him, one who de-
served him.

They were silent as they watched the squad car move
down the street. An uncomfortable silence. Nico pulled
away from the curb and kept his eyes on the road until
they were back on the freeway.

"I'm sorry, Dana, I don't know what got into me back
there."

"Don't be silly, Nico, that was as much my fault as
yours," Dana snapped.

He decided not to argue the point. Beside, she was
right, they were mutually culpable. Further proof that
they were an accident waiting to happen when they were
in close proximity to each other.

JOE LAKE CALLED the next morning, just as Dana poured
the first cup from the pot and settled behind her desk.

"Just thought I'd fill you in on the details of our little
impromptu inspection last night," he said, his voice as
cheerful as ever.

"I…well, I just want you to know I'm grateful for the
extra time and effort you're making, Joe," Dana said.

"Yeah, well, I'm not sure you owe me any thanks. We
really didn't accomplish much. We questioned the skeleton crew that work the graveyard shift and discovered
nothing new. But I'm not giving up, Dana. I'm going to
show up at odd intervals until they get so tired of me,
somebody talks. Or maybe I'll get lucky and walk in on
something going down when they least expect me. Any
little misdemeanor and maybe I can scare them into revealing something concrete."

Dana thanked him again. Profusely.

He interrupted her speech. "I just want to add one

thing, Dana. Leave the surveillance to the cops. It's our job, not yours, and not the job of that toy cop you hired."

"What does that mean?" Dana held her breath.

"It means I know you, girlfriend, and I know when you have a bee in your bonnet." He hung up before she could protest.

"Well, at least our friendship seems to be intact," she said aloud to the empty room as she hung up the phone.

"You talking to me?" Nico asked, coming through the door with a handful of computer printouts.

"Please don't feel you have to knock before entering," Dana snapped. "After all, since we're joined at the hip, I shouldn't expect to have any privacy."

"Bad night, boss?"

"In your dreams, Scalia."

"And so you were, love, which is why I'm in such a good mood this morning. Willing to overlook your grumpy disposition."

"I was perfectly happy until—"

The phone rang, causing Dana to flinch. She grabbed it up and swiveled away from Nico's smug gaze.

"This is whom?" she asked, sure she'd misunderstood.

"Alphonze Caprezio, Ms. Harper. I hope I'm not calling at a bad time."

And when would be a good time? Dana silently asked. Aloud, she said, "What is the reason for your call, Mr. Caprezio?"

Out of the corner of her eye she saw that Nico was making some kind of hand gesture. She swiveled another couple of inches, ignoring him.

"I was just thinking how much we have in common, Ms. Harper, each of us ending up a single parent, sharing the worries that brings. I know the expense of raising children, the joy when they do well, the heartache when they get in trouble. How is your lovely little girl, by the way? Krystal, isn't it? A beautiful name.''

"What do you really want, sir?" Her hair seemed to rise on the back of her neck as she listened to the old don gush in her ear. How did he know Krystal's name, what she looked like?

His tone rang falsely, with pain, or disappointment. "It must have been difficult for you after Zack's death, raising the little one on only one income, and without even the emotional support of a husband and father. Having a child of my own, I'm more sensitive to other parents' needs.

"I thought there might be some way I could help you, Mrs. Harper, help ease your load.''

Dana was silent a moment, trying to shift through the words to find the hidden messages of threat, collusion. *Zack! He'd referred to her late husband by his first name.* What did that mean?

Rage, outrage, indignation. Emotions warred with reason—and won.

"Attempting to bribe—or threaten—an officer of the court is a criminal offense, sir, and I warn you that if you call again, I'll be ready. Our next conversation will be taped.''

She slammed the phone onto the cradle and spun around to find Nico shaking his head, his arms crossed, his eyes glinting disapproval.

"What?" Dana asked through clenched teeth.

"Do you think that was a good idea? The Caprezios have escaped conviction over and over, but it's widely believed that they've been behind most of the major crimes committed in this state, not to mention a few in Wisconsin, Iowa, the Dakotas, and even Illinois. The don is reputed to have a long memory and a deep thirst for revenge.''

"Are you saying you think I should have played into Caprezio's hands, tipped the trial in Marcus's favor in exchange for what—a life of luxury? If I wanted that, we could be living on my parents' estate, with never a care in the world but what we want to order for dinner."

Nico chuckled. The sound didn't ring with humor.

"I was suggesting that you needn't have blown the don off so brutally. A little soft soap and tact could have accomplished the same thing, without offending the man."

"'The man,'" she emphasized, "is a scuzz, a lowlife murderer with or without the convictions, and I wouldn't humor him if he had me tied to a rack with a lit fuse of dynamite under my butt!"

It was obvious they were never going to see eye-to-eye on this subject, Nico realized. Using the kind of diplomacy he'd wished her to use on Caprezio, he held up the printouts.

"I could use your help deciphering some of your notes," he said, "but if this isn't a good time, I can come back later."

"No. Let's get this over with now, I have a ton of work ahead of me and I have to fit a couple of witness interviews and a deposition in, as well."

THOUGH THE SUBJECT hadn't come up again, it seethed, unsettled, between them whenever they saw each other through the day and on the silent drive home at the end of the day.

A note from Heather, propped on the kitchen table, didn't improve Dana's mood.

It read, "Hi, guys. I've taken Krystal to the early showing of *The Hunchback of Notre Dame,* and pizza afterward. We should be home around nine. Heather."

Dana crumpled the note, threw it in the wastebasket and stomped up the back stairs.

Nico retrieved the note, smoothed it out and read it. "What the hell?" he muttered. There was nothing in the note to set her off again, he mused. But maybe he was missing something here. Whatever. He knew exactly what Dana needed after a long and frustrating day. He set about to make arrangements.

Upstairs Dana turned the jets up high and swore under her breath.

"I wanted to take Krystal to see it, myself," she stormed, throwing a sopping loofah at the wall. It sprayed water, emphasizing her anger.

"What right does she have to take my child anywhere without consulting me first?" she demanded of the wall, sending a bar of soap after the loofah.

She snatched up a water-laden washcloth, aiming it at the abused wall.

Just then she caught her image, reflected in the huge mirror over the double sinks. Suddenly the rage seemed to explode and diminish like a huge bubble in her chest. She dropped the cloth back in the tub, turned off the jets and sank down, immersing her head in the hot water until she couldn't hold her breath any longer. She came up gasping, sputtering, and laughing all at the same time.

Sinking back against the plastic headrest that hooked over the back of the tub, she pondered the extremes of emotion she'd experienced through the day. All out of proportion to what was warranted, she recognized, and all inspired by one single emotion she'd been afraid to examine too closely.

Love. Wasn't it petty to be angry at Heather for doing something nice for Krystal?

Love. Nico was right, she tended to overreact without

considering consequences. There was a better way to deal with people like Caprezio.

Love. Maybe she could show Nico she was sorry for her temper tantrum. She'd go down and fix something really special for him for dinner, for a change. Since it was just the two of them they could eat in the living room, maybe light a fire.

He was already in the kitchen when she came downstairs in blue satin pajamas and matching robe, her hair wrapped in a towel. He'd set out a tray with cheese and crackers, and two wineglasses. He was opening a bottle of Cabernet Sauvignon, her favorite, and she could smell something exotic cooking on the stove.

"If I'd known this, I'd have dressed. Can you wait a minute while I run up and ch—"

"No need," Nico interrupted, "you look beautiful, your outfit brings out the blue of your eyes." They exchanged a look of awareness. Nico was first to look away.

He cleared his throat. "Anyway, I wanted you to be as comfortable as possible for this meal."

He handed her the bottle and led the way into the living room, carrying the tray. The fire was already lit and the logs were chirping as flames nipped at the bark. Dana sank into a wing chair flanking the fireplace and set the bottle down on the low serving table that separated her chair from its twin.

Under Nico's thoughtful nurturing, Dana's mood continued to improve and her energy renewed itself. When he removed the cheese tray and brought out plates of stir-fry spooned over lo mein noodles she gasped in wonder at his instinct for picking just the right meal for her every mood.

"How do you do this?" she asked.

"In a wok," Nico retorted.

Love. The word seemed to be attacking her from within at every turn.

"Not what I meant, Scalia, but forget it. I should know not to ask anything about your secret life in the kitchen."

He laughed and the sound thrilled her, reminding her she still wanted to do something nice for him. Nothing came to mind except apology.

She made it prettily, adding, "I know I have to work at controlling my temper.

"Don't worry about it, Dana, I understand."

"Yes," she said, searching his face, "I guess you do." *Love.* He just wasn't like most men, she decided. She wondered why no woman had snatched him up long ago. This was a guy who would take out the garbage without being asked, seemed to have none of the usual ego hang-ups, didn't ascribe to separate male and female roles, and could be totally understanding and sensitive. She wasn't even going to touch his incredible sexuality. If she belabored that one in her mind, she'd lose it.

"This is so sweet of you, Nico," she said, lifting her glass in a toast, "and more than I deserve."

"This isn't a reward for anything, Dana. This is just a little bit of buttering up the boss."

They grinned at each other over their glasses.

A sudden gust of wind blew down the chimney, scattering ashes and sending flames shooting up with a roar. Nico knelt on the hearth and adjusted the damper.

But Dana was focused on the sound of that roar. It reminded her of the roar of fury she'd heard in her mind as she listened to Caprezio Sr.

"Nico, I know I overreacted to Caprezio's call. You were right and I was way out of line."

He brushed ash off the knees of his chinos and took his seat. "It wasn't that bad. You could say I overreacted a little, too."

He replayed the incident in his mind. A flash of inspiration struck.

"Come to think of it, Dana, I don't think it's Caprezio Sr. who wants you out of the way, or wishes you harm."

"How did you arrive at that?"

"Well, the don would know you'd only be replaced by another prosecutor, so it's not as if your death would exonerate Marcus. On the contrary, if anything happens to you, the Caprezios would be the cops' number-one suspect and the rumors alone would prejudice the jury."

Dana considered that. She started to agree. "Maybe you're right...but..."

"But?" Nico prodded.

"What if the don thinks—even knows—that he can control my replacement. Maybe he already knows who that would be."

"Do you know?"

"Of course not. We don't have understudies as they do in theater."

"Then the only way Caprezio could know is if he's in cahoots with Yearling. Does that feel right to you?"

"No way!" Dana almost leaped to her feet in defense of her boss. "If there's one thing I'd stake my life on, it's that John is clean. Maybe he's a little too politically ambitious, but he's not without integrity."

"Okay. Scratch that for a minute. How likely is it that the Carter clan would go after you?"

"In a fit of rage? Plausible. But as part of a long-range, premeditated plan? Not likely. They aren't bright people. I don't think they could think ahead and come to the conclusion that taking me out would do them any good.

"We have so much physical evidence on the boys that even the most corrupt prosecutor couldn't let them get away, and they still don't believe that.

"But Pa Carter is like a keg of dynamite waiting to

blow, so if—no, when—the boys go down, he might well want to take his vengeance out on me. Do you see what I mean? They're the kind of people who react to stimuli, real or imagined, but that's after the fact. They'd be my last choice for threatening notes, leaving abstract messages, or setting up a plan.''

"Yeah, I see what you mean. Even the crimes they're accused of are based on impulse, spur-of-the-moment violence."

Dana nodded. "The worst kind of killer. You never know what will set that type off and where he'll attack next. And two of them on the loose is twice as frightening."

"Yeah, the intelligent killer works within a prescribed pattern you can ultimately figure out."

Dana sighed. "Does it feel like we're on a treadmill, working our buns off, not getting anywhere?"

"Hmm. Wait. I've just thought of something." He went to get his briefcase from the console in the foyer.

"Here it is," he said, pulling a page of notes from the case and going back to his chair.

He read from the page. "'You have more to lose than I do.'" He looked up. "His exact words?"

Dana nodded.

"An oblique threat," Nico mused.

"Not if you understand. Win or lose in court, Donegan for instance has already forfeited the trust of the financial world. But if I lose the case, it's a direct hit at my record."

"That doesn't add up to a threat on your person. A guy like our Charlie would count loss in terms of dollars, or real property."

"Treadmill. Back to square one." Dana moaned.

Nico shoved the notes back into his case and stood.

I'm going to get the coffee. Why don't you refill our wineglasses?''

Dana watched Nico leave the room, carrying their empty plates with him. Watched the way his cute, tight buns moved beneath his chinos, the long stride that moved him quickly but always with grace.

She stood and stretched and then poured the last of the wine. Looking around, she decided the room could do with less light. She turned off the lamp on the table beside her chair, pleased with the way the fire lit up the little area there and left the corners of the big room in shadow.

Getting down on the floor in front of the fireplace, she removed the terry turban and let her hair cascade to her shoulders. It was still damp. The heat of the fire would dry it in no time.

Nico returned with the coffee and stopped short in the doorway, taken aback at the sight of Dana's natural beauty, enhanced only by firelight.

As if in a trance he set the tray on the table and knelt in front of her. He touched her hair, a golden web with individual strands of red glinting in the firelight. His eyes filled with wonder and desire and his breathing turned shallow.

Dana saw the change come over him. *Love,* she thought. *I love this man.* The room felt charged with their chemistry.

They were both relieved when they heard the car pull in and the garage doors open. A moment later Krystal called out, ''We're home, Mommy. Where are you?''

Chapter Fifteen

"Close call," Nico muttered, passing Dana as she went up to tuck Krystal in. He was on his way to her study, a fresh cup of coffee in his hands.

Dana turned and whispered, "Not close enough." Her dimple flirted and her twinkling eyes dared him to take her to task.

He shook his head, his eyes smoldering. "We were lucky they came home when they did."

"You call that 'luck,' sweetie?"

Nico stared after her as she ran up the stairs, the blue satin pajamas flashing between the rails.

What happened to their agreement? It seemed they both forgot it every time they were alone together. What had happened to change him from a man who always held a part of himself back, who was always on top of any situation? And Dana had changed, too. It was as if she'd declared open war on their treaty, enticing him at every turn, flirting, teasing, daring him to give in to his deepest feelings.

Was love like this? he wondered. But love, he knew, was what his parents had. He had such confidence in their love for each other and for him, that he'd never felt compelled to go out and look for it elsewhere. That it might strike unexpectedly had never occurred to him; he'd always supposed it would happen when he was ready, when he made the choice, the situation well under his control.

He saw the pink flesh of her bare foot clear the last step. No situation that involved Dana would ever be under anyone's control but hers, he ruefully admitted.

He looked down at the mug in his hand and tried to recall where he'd been headed when he'd run into her.

DANA CAME AWAKE with a jolt, her nightgown uncomfortably bunched around her legs, her breathing raspy from an erotic dream. She realized she'd been dreaming of making love with Nico. And then she heard it again, the sound that had penetrated her sleep.

It was the neighbor's dog barking, intermittently howling.

She slipped from the bed and went to the window that faced the front of the house. The street was vacant.

But the dog continued barking and she couldn't get back to sleep.

She tiptoed out of her room to the window at the end of the hall, the one that overlooked the back of the house. Nothing stirred in the tree-shadowed yard, either. From this vantage point the roof of the gazebo was almost directly beneath her so that she couldn't see into its screened interior.

Suddenly she thought she saw something move beneath a tree beside the path leading down to the lake. A shadow or the figure of a man? Rubbing her eyes, Dana strained to adjust to the dark, to be able to make out which it was.

There! It had moved again.

Nico was sleeping just across the hall in the guest room. She considered waking him but decided to make sure there was cause to disturb him.

Carefully she eased down the stairs, praying they wouldn't creak and alarm the household. She reached the first floor without incident and began going from window to window, first to peer out into the night and then to make sure each was locked. All of them were, probably the result of Nico's nightly check to make the house secure. As she passed the front door she saw that the alarm panel was engaged and remembered, just in time, to avoid the intruder beam that was fixed to cover the length of the long hall from the front door to the kitchen.

She went around through the dining room into the kitchen and though she'd not seen signs of a prowler through any of the windows, she realized the dog's barking had reached a level of hysteria. When she went into the little powder room off the kitchen she saw the kitchen light come on in the house next door and in the dense, middle-of-the-night stillness she could clearly hear her neighbor, Max Shayle, yell at the dog to shut up.

The dog responded immediately but then started whining and barking again a couple of minutes later.

She heard Max swearing and she almost laughed aloud as she heard him pleading with the dog to be quiet.

The Shayles' kitchen light went out just as Dana was sure she saw a shadowy figure dart from the brick patio wall to the oak tree beside the glass-enclosed porch on the side nearest the kitchen.

"But there's a cop car out front," she softly mused aloud. She remembered they'd waved at it before turning into her drive when they got home from the Scalias'. As far as she knew, the police were keeping a watch there in case the shooter came back.

Maybe she should call 9-1-1, have them alert the cop out front. She didn't think the prowler could actually get into the house, but she wasn't prepared to take chances.

Sighing, she turned, planning to go up and wake Nico.

No sense having a bodyguard on the premises if she didn't use him in the threat of danger.

She felt her way back through the rooms, avoiding the intruder alarm in the hall, her hands out in front of her to keep her from bumping into anything. Suddenly her hands did touch something and it took her only a second to realize it was a human chest.

Her screams mingled with Nico's shouts and right behind that, the sound of footsteps pounding down the back stairs and Heather and Krystal calling out, their voices thick with fright. Lights sprang on all around her and Dana screamed again until she saw it was Nico beside her.

"Stay with your mom," Heather rasped, pushing Krystal toward Dana. Dana saw that Heather and Nico were both carrying guns and flashlights.

"You take the back, I'll do the front," Nico told his partner, already heading for the front door.

Mother and daughter huddled together in the kitchen, their chairs close together at the table, Krystal whimpering softly and Dana patting her hair.

Nico came in shaking his head. "Nothing," he said. "If there was someone out there, they're long gone." He went to the pair and lifted Krystal up in his arms. "Probably just a potential burglar, scared off by all the noise we made," he said, holding Krystal close. "He could never have gotten in," he assured her, "but it's just as well he didn't get a chance to try." He handed the child back to Dana.

"I'll make us all some cocoa so we can get back to sl—"

The front door slammed, footsteps running down the hall toward them. Heather burst into the kitchen gasping, her face white and panic-ridden. She looked wildly around and headed for the phone, yelling, "The cop across the street is dead!"

DAWN WAS A FUZZY PINK, blurred by an overcast sky, when the last cop left and the blinking light of a tow truck signaled that it was on its way, the dead officer's patrol car hooked up to be hauled back to the police garage.

Dana had gone out to the crime scene the minute Heather started dialing the phone, grabbing a mini tape recorder on the way.

Nico was only seconds behind her, a notebook in his hands.

Each working with their own system, they'd examined the body, noting the wound in the cop's forehead, and the car interior, looking for clues, all without touching anything with their hands.

They were done by the time blue-and-whites began showing up, their red lights flashing, giving advance warning of their arrival, through the trees that lined the street leading to their road. The ambulance had been alerted that this was a morgue pickup rather than an emergency run and came without sirens. No hurry in this case, Dana had thought as she stifled a sob that broke in her throat.

Now Dana, Nico and Heather were seated around the table in the kitchen, drinking coffee, mulling over the situation, each answer raising a new question. Their shoulders slumped with defeat and fatigue.

"That takes care of my theory about an aborted burglary attempt," Nico mourned. "Burglars don't kill cops. Statistically, they don't even carry weapons."

Dana wasn't interested in theory or statistics. "The worst part is that Krystal has been exposed to so much violence in her young life, most of it right here on her own home grounds, and none of us can guarantee her that it isn't going to keep touching her life.''

"The worst part is that if it weren't for that neurotic dog, we might all be dead in our beds," Heather stated, her face still pale, etched with the dregs of remembered horror.

"I want Krystal out of here today," Nico ordered. "Can you think of a safe place?"

Dana shook her head. "My parents' estate, but everyone knows who my father is and besides..."

The other two waited, looking at her expectantly.

"What?" Nico finally demanded.

"She doesn't like my mother," Dana admitted in a small voice, embarrassed to have to confess such a thing. Especially to someone with the kind of parents Nico had.

He stood up and went to the phone, dialed, and then apologized for the early hour.

"Listen, Mama, I know this is an imposition, but I need your help. I need to move Krystal and a woman from my agency today and—"

Rose Scalia must have interrupted him at that point because as his sentence trailed away, a smile came over his face and he gave the others a thumbs-up.

"Thanks, Mama, I knew you'd feel that way but I owe you a big one, and I won't forget."

He listened again and then silently held the phone out to Dana.

Dana started, but didn't get the chance, to express her gratitude.

"No more of that," Rose scolded, "Krystal's like family, where else would she go but to us? We have plenty of room now with most of the children gone and I'm sure the lady from Nico's office must be a very nice person."

Dana slipped in a weak word of thanks and was about

to hang up when Rose added, "Besides, now we'll get to see more of you, yes, Dana?"

Dana laughed. "Yes, Mama. Lots."

When they woke Krystal to tell her of the plan, she beamed with pleasure.

But then her face sobered and she stared up at Dana. "But I'll miss you so much, Mommy."

"I'll come and see you every evening after work, I promise," Dana assured the child. "And maybe, if it's not an imposition, I'll come back and tuck you in at bedtime."

"What about school?"

Nico answered. "Heather will drive you back over here for school and be there when you get out."

Dana flinched. Wasn't this a terrible job for Heather? She'd have to stay at the school, in her car, keeping surveillance on the doors from eight in the morning until two in the afternoon. Six hours of eye-fatiguing ennui.

She mentioned that to Nico while Krystal was in her bathroom getting dressed and Dana began making piles of clothes on the little girl's bed to be packed for the move.

"What will probably happen is that Stella will contact the principal, explain as little as possible, and get him to help with the situation by letting Heather come in undercover as the teaching assistant in Krystal's class or as an education student doing internship."

"Will Heather like doing that?"

Nico shrugged. "Beats sitting in a car doing nothing for six hours. You'd be surprised the jobs we've done as cover. This one actually sounds like fun."

Dana grinned. "That's because you're a nut about kids," she said.

"Well, Heather seems to have hit it off with Krys, so

I would assume she'll like a whole classroom of eight-year-olds.''

Dana plopped down on the bed and put her head in her hands. "God, I'm going to miss her. We've never been separated before."

Nico came over and held her head against his hip, stroked her hair, murmured words of comfort.

Dana raised her eyes to his, tears streaming down her face.

"I think my life is falling apart at my feet," she said on the edge of a sob.

"Nah-hh," Nico mused, "it hasn't fallen beneath knee level." He tilted her chin up. "Hey, don't think of it as being separated from Krys, think of it as getting a little vacation from the kid." He grinned lasciviously. "And we've got the house all to ourselves, Ma, so don't you fret none."

She had to laugh, in spite of her anguish.

And instantly sobered as she realized the truth in all that nonsensical drivel. They would be alone in this big house, night after night, for who knew how long.

Nico thumbed the tears from under each eye and then lifted his gaze to her eyes. Time seemed to stand still as he read the message in them.

"Dana...I—"

"I'm ready, Mommy," Krystal announced in a mournful voice from where she stood in the open doorway from the bathroom.

"Okay, honey," Dana gasped, surreptitiously dashing the residue of tears from her eyes. She stood up and avoided Nico's eyes. "I'll go get your suitcases from the attic."

"I'll do it," Nico said.

"Thanks." Still keeping her face averted. "It's the

blue set just to your right in the corner.'' Dana expelled a sigh of relief when Nico had left the room.

What was he about to say when Krystal interrupted? Half a dozen dialogues flashed through her mind. They made her blood alternately freeze and burn, sending chills down her spine.

She had a scenario of her own: they could really let go, make love; wild, passionate, totally uninhibited love…for about forty-eight hours. Get it out of their systems once and for all. The fantasy almost made her weak.

"Mommy, can I take my Barbie dolls with me?" Krystal was at the shelves between the two beds, looking for things to take that she simply couldn't live without.

"May I," Dana corrected automatically. She sat back down on the bed and shivered. "Oh, baby," she said with a sigh, "of course you can."

Dana cocked her head to the side, propping her chin on her palm, her elbow on her knee. "You really like these?" she asked, nodding at the Barbie dolls Krystal held in her hand.

Krystal giggled and said, "Yes."

"So? What do you see in Ms. Barbie's future?" Dana insisted.

"Well, she could be a model."

"True." There was just a tinge of irony in Dana's voice. "What else?"

"A dancer, or maybe an actress? How about a housewife?"

"Sure, she can be anything she wants."

Dana stood. "She could be a sumo wrestler!"

They were still on the bed, rolling around, holding their tummies and laughing hysterically when Nico returned with the luggage. He stood in the doorway, bemused. Hadn't he left Dana in tears, Krystal looking like she was being sent to the gallows? He shook his head, who would ever understand women, even when they were only eight years old.

Dana was first to recover herself. She got off the bed and took the nested cases from Nico.

"Come on, Krystal, fun time is over. How about packing your overnight bag with the things you need from your bathroom? Oh, and run down and ask Heather if she wants to put her bathroom articles in there, too. There's plenty of room."

An hour later they caravaned in two cars to St. Paul. Nico and Heather in Heather's car, Dana and Krystal behind them in the Lexus.

"Feels good to be driving again," Dana said as they came up on the freeway. "Nico's been driving so much lately that I haven't needed to."

"Mommy, how long do you think I'll have to stay with Nico's folks?"

Dana's expression saddened. "Don't know, honey. I certainly hope it won't be long. But, Krystal—" she glanced over at her daughter "—you do like the Scalias, right?"

"They're great, Mom, honest." She sounded so forlorn as she added, "But they're not you."

They clasped hands, Dana squeezing Krystal's to signal a shared sorrow.

Krystal seemed to sense that Dana's sadness was as deep as her own. "Don't worry, Mommy, I'll have fun there. When I get home from school, I'll have Myranda to play with and maybe Chianne and Maria, too."

She gave her mother a tremulous smile. Dana nodded.

"And Mama and Papa Scalia are the best grandparents in the world, even if you're not their own."

They nodded in agreement.

Both of them were feeling better when they followed Heather's car up onto the driveway of the Scalia family home.

Chapter Sixteen

On Saturday, with less than two weeks before the Carter brothers' trial was scheduled to begin, Dana sat down with Lincoln Adams, a department paralegal, arranging the man's research notes for her brief when the phone rang at her elbow.

She was still talking to Lincoln when she picked up the receiver.

"*Johnson versus Allen*... Oh, sorry," she said into the phone. "This is Dana Harper."

The voice was unfamiliar, the words horrifying.

"You'll be a lot sorrier if anything happens to your daughter. If you want to see Krystal alive again, you will meet me in thirty minutes. You will come alone and you will tell no one that you are leaving or where you are going. Is that understood?"

Dana's heart was pounding so loudly, she couldn't hear herself agree to his demands. "Yes, yes," she repeated, desperate to make sure he knew she was willing to cooperate.

"Please," she begged, and blinked, bringing Lincoln back into focus. She put her hand over the mouthpiece and said, "Linc, this is personal, could you give me a few minutes? I'll buzz you when I'm ready for you."

She caught only the tail end of the address, somewhere

near the Uptown area. "I'm sorry, I had to get rid of a colleague, could you repeat that?"

He repeated the address. She dashed it off on a memo pad. "Please, may I talk to Krystal, make sure—"

"You don't request anything," the voice rasped. "I tell you what I want you to know, what I expect you to do. I'm setting my watch. You have thirty minutes."

She was begging him to wait, to give her some proof Krystal was unharmed, when she heard the dial tone kick in. He'd hung up.

She sat a minute, trying to think, but panic overwhelmed her. She bent to put her head between her knees, afraid she was going to faint. The image of Krystal came into her mind and she felt her head clear as a surge of adrenaline flowed through her. Snatching up the phone, she dialed the Scalias' number.

"This is a mistake, a cruel joke," she said, her voice ringing with false confidence. She let the phone ring twenty times before she hung up. Thought a minute and dialed her house. Again, no answer. She glanced at her watch. She'd used up four minutes and accomplished nothing. She couldn't delay, she realized. She had no idea of the amount of traffic in the downtown area at this hour on a Saturday. Not to mention getting through Uptown, a place that was always teeming.

She snatched her bag out of her desk drawer and the jacket that hung on the clothes tree near the door.

At that moment she remembered that Nico was in his little cubicle, two doors down. She'd have to pass his open door to get to the elevators. Even the staircase was down at that end.

She ran back to her desk, punched in an interoffice number, got a busy tone, nervously banged on the disconnect bar and tried again.

"Scalia," Nico announced abruptly, picking up after the second ring.

Dana cleared her throat. Could she pull this off? She glanced at her watch. Almost six minutes down.

"Nico," she said, trying for a bright, breezy tone, "I'm down in the coffee shop. I was going to get carry-up, but then I decided it would be more fun to eat down here. Want to join me?"

"How did you get downstairs without passing by my—"

"Explain when you get here, sweetie. Hurry."

It seemed an interminable time until she heard his door open and close. She pressed her ear to the door, listening for the clang of the elevator bell as the car reached their floor. *Thank God it's Saturday,* she told herself, or the office would be teeming with activity, phones ringing, voices raised to din level. When she finally heard it, she tore out of her office and ran for the door marked Exit, barely breathing as she raced from landing to landing until she reached garage level.

It took her a moment to catch her breath, control the shaking in her hands so she could get the key into the ignition slot. Another couple of minutes getting her pass out to wave at the parking guard in his little booth, what seemed like an hour at the red light on the corner. She didn't dare draw the attention of the cops. She was walking into an unknown setup with no idea of the kidnapper's field of vision, should she have to relay to an officer why she was speeding and risk his following her.

Nevertheless, when she saw that she had only thirteen minutes, she stepped on the gas and pushed her speed up to fifteen mph over the limit. She ignored the honking horns that blared their outrage as she passed by, moving in and out of lanes, trying to shave off precious minutes.

NICO MADE his second search of the coffee shop and stopped up at the cash register, totally bewildered. Dana was not here. He'd spoken to her less than three minutes ago and now she wasn't even here. He went to the door and peered through the glass, thinking she might have stepped out to the ladies' room or something. But after a couple of minutes he began to get an uneasy feeling. He went back to the register. The cashier was counting the drawer.

"I beg your pardon," Nico began.

The cashier raised her hand to stop him and kept dealing bills into piles, her lips moving as she counted.

When she jotted a number down and reached for the coins in the nickle compartment, Nico raised his voice.

"Lady, this may be an emergency, do you mind?"

Exasperated at the interruption, the woman threw the coins back in the drawer. "What is it?" she snapped, "Can't you see I'm busy?"

Nico bit back a nasty retort, this was no time for amenities.

"I'm looking for Mrs. Harper. Dana Harper?"

"Why didn't you say so in the first place?" the woman snapped.

"Then she's been here?"

"Nope. Haven't seen her at all today. Didn't even know she was working today." Her face creased with the effort of thinking. "That's funny, usually if she comes in on a Saturday, she calls down for sweet rolls, but not today. Do you suppose she's on a diet?"

She looked up and did a double take. The good-looking guy was gone.

Nico only had to hear that Dana hadn't been in the coffee shop, hadn't even been seen today. He ran.

He arrived at the elevators just as a car landed, and

jumped inside, pushing the floor button and Door Close button over and over.

She was not in her office. He ran to her desk, pulled open all the drawers, glanced over at the clothes tree. Her bag and jacket were gone.

He fell onto her chair, rubbed his eyes and stared at her phone. Had she called from outside the building? She wouldn't have needed her jacket to go down to the coffee shop. Had she left the building, or planned to leave it? To run an errand nearby? Maybe that's where she'd called from, expecting to be back in the coffee shop before he made it downstairs.

But no, she'd clearly stated she was *in* the coffee shop, that she wanted him to *join* her there. She'd told him to hurry.

He returned to the lower level, praying he'd find her there, hoping they'd just missed each other some way. She could have used the ladies' room, stopped in the lobby to use the phones there.

The coffee shop had a Closed sign on the door window. He peered in and saw only waitresses, and that cashier, bussing and wiping down tables and counter.

He turned around, refusing to let panic obscure his reasoning, and his glance fell on the security guard near the revolving doors.

"Haven't seen Ms. Harper at all today. But that's not so unusual, when she parks in the garage she doesn't come in through the lobby."

Now he was faced with the big questions; where had she called from? What had made her leave her office without notifying him? What had made her leave the building?

The garage. She'd insisted on taking the Lexus that morning, saying she missed doing the driving lately.

He raced around the corner to the stairwell down to

the garage, praying this was all a crazy mix-up, that she'd just stepped into another office, that her car would still be parked where she'd left it. He ran to the space reserved in her name. The car was gone. He collapsed against the side of a Blazer and tried to catch his breath as he stared at the vacant space. He hadn't really paid attention that morning, could she have parked in someone else's spot, knowing they wouldn't be in on a Saturday morning?

His search proved another futility.

It dawned on him that he had no wheels. Worse, he had no idea where to begin looking for her.

It struck him then! Something must have happened to Krystal, in her panic to get to the child, Dana had run out without thinking of letting him know.

He tore back up the stairs to the lobby and ran to the phones. He rubbed sweat from his forehead with the sleeve of his sports coat and dialed his mother's number. Twice he dialed, muttering under his breath as the ringing continued unanswered.

He looked up and saw a yellow cab parked under the overhang that connected the two buildings that comprised the government center.

It wasn't until he was seated in the back, and the driver had asked his destination, that it occurred to him that he didn't know. "Give me a minute," he said, trying to get his thoughts straight.

Krystal may have been badly hurt and taken to a hospital. Which one? Had to be in St. Paul. About four hospitals to choose from. Which one?

But then how would that explain Dana's cheerful voice inviting him to lunch. Thoroughly confused and scared as hell, Nico did the only thing he could think of.

"Police station," he told the driver. If Joe Lake was on duty, so much the better, together they'd find Dana.

The driver took off his cap, scratched his head, replaced the cap. "That's a block away, practically across the street, mister."

Weary, with his energy seriously flagging, he told the driver to drive him there anyway.

Less than three minutes later the cabbie saw that his fare had given him a twenty and told him to keep the change. But the meter had registered at less than two dollars. He looked up, thinking he should call out to the guy, make sure he hadn't counted wrong.

The guy had already disappeared from the main entrance.

HEATHER RUBBED her cheek and took a last look around the mall entrance. Had she misunderstood Dana's secretary? But no, she'd written it down. Heather was to bring Krystal to the west entrance of the mall, next to Waldenbooks. Dana had decided to take a couple of hours off to do some last-minute shopping for school things for Krystal.

"It's been an hour, Krys," she said to the little girl whose high spirits were lowering by the minute. "What do you think we should do? I called both your mom's office and the house, and there was no answer either place."

"Then she's on her way," Krystal announced, clamping her lips together in a thin line. She seemed to be holding back tears, stoic in the face of disappointment. Heather loved the child's decisiveness, her squared shoulders, chin-high attitude.

Heather knelt in front of her. "I have a great idea, honey, why don't we go into that Pizza Hut, over there, and have lunch? We can ask to be seated in the window so we can keep an eye on this entrance and that way we won't miss Mommy when she comes in."

"Now that sounds like a plan, Heath, I'm starving and my feet hurt from standing so long."

Heather led the way over to the restaurant. Nico had her cell phone number; he'd have called if there'd been a change in plans. Dana must have been delayed but probably was on her way.

"Your mom will probably be here before our food is served," she told her little ward.

DANA PULLED UP in front of a nondescript stucco bungalow, set apart from its neighbors by a vacant lot on either side. The barren look of the place brought the Carters to mind for some reason. She could envision them living here.

"No cars," she murmured. She'd expect the Carters to have lots of junky cars sitting around, almost visibly rusting. As she got out of the car, her heart beating rapidly, she spotted a garage at the back. A car or two could certainly be hidden there. Or a pickup truck.

Walking up the path of weed-choked broken cement slabs, she noticed that all the windows on the main floor were barred.

The owners had to be pretty paranoid to have taken such precautions against burglars, and yes, paranoid is exactly how she'd describe the Carters.

But bars also kept people in, she reminded herself. Krystal. Were the bars put there to imprison her baby?

Her limbs shaking now, she stepped up to the bell and fumbled to push the small button.

She'd been so sure it was the senior Carter, for a second she was almost relieved when the front door opened to reveal Charles Donegan.

But this was a different Donegan. This man in bib overalls, holding a gun on her, his face set in grim lines, was no Prince Charlie. The darling of the press had disappeared and in his place stood a man who might well have been a member of the Carter clan.

"You're one minute late, Dana...oh, you don't mind if I call you Dana, do you?" He gestured her ahead of him, using the gun for a pointer.

"As I was saying, you're a minute late, but I've decided to be lenient with you, which," he emphasized by jamming the gun nose against her back, "is more than you were willing to be with me."

He snatched the bag off her shoulder, fumbled inside until he found her gun and threw the bag on the floor.

Dana, spun around by his action, glared at him. "I'm not taking another step until you tell me where Krystal is, prove to me that she's all right," she declared.

A terrible laugh erupted from Donegan's throat. He waved his gun as well as hers and in a voice edged with hysteria raged, "These aren't cattle prods, you know, but I'm willing to bet that after I plant a bullet in your leg, you'll be more than willing to obey my orders. Now turn around, keep moving toward that door ahead of you."

They were moving down a hallway with rooms on either side and a closed door at the end. He shoved her, making her move faster, but not before she got a glimpse of the rooms with their open doors. All bedrooms, vacant, except for the one on the right of the closed door. A bathroom.

She stumbled and almost fell down the rickety wooden stairs leading to the basement. But Donegan caught her arm and pulled her to safety.

"No accidents, please," he instructed. "Can't have you spoiling my plan."

He must be holding Krystal down here, Dana thought, and felt her spirits raise at the thought of seeing, holding, her little girl again.

But then, maybe he was just bringing her down here to kill her.

He pushed her over to a pair of washtubs and her stomach flipped as she considered his intention. Tubs to wash away her blood?

Thinking death was imminent, Dana almost felt relieved when Donegan ordered her sit on the floor and pulled out a set of handcuffs. Why bother cuffing her if he was just going to kill her?

As he cuffed her left wrist to the leg of the tub, she looked up at him, pleading, "Please, Donegan, at least tell me where Krystal is, what you've done with her."

Charlie leaned against the wall, still holding a gun on her. He shook his head. "This was all unnecessary, you know, Dana. If you'd heeded my warnings, I wouldn't be forced to go to such extremes."

"I don't understand. You're up on embezzlement charges—why are you adding kidnapping and murder to your agenda? If you kill me you're looking at life in prison."

"How did you get to be a lawyer?" he snarled. "You're so ignorant, you can't figure anything out. Don't you see that if I go down for embezzlement, my career, my life, is over anyway? With you out of the way I know I can beat the rap."

"How can you be so sure, because even if I die, the case will still go to trial, the evidence will still hold up. Nothing can change that."

"No, but evidence has been known to get lost, disappear as it were."

"Who would do that?" she asked, puzzled.

"Bill Henry. He put in a bid to Yearling asking to take over if you should become ill or incapacitated in any way. Seems Bill has handled many white-collar cases and prefers them. Yearling agreed. Seems you've had so many problems lately that there's a good chance you won't make it to trial." He gave another of those obscene giggles.

Dana gulped, resisting waves of nausea.

"Why would you expect Bill Henry to help you?"

"For money," Donegan gleefully crooned. "Money is the second best motivator in the world."

Despite herself, Dana asked, "What's the first?"

"This," Donegan said, sobering as he thrust the gun toward her. "Threat of death has surely got to be number one for inspiring someone to go along with your plans."

Dana shuddered, hoping she wouldn't anticipate *his* plans. The less she thought about them, the more likely she was to devise one of her own.

"Why are you holding me here, why not just shoot me and get it over with? And why won't you tell me what you've done with my child?" She pulled the shackled arm and held it up to the limit of mobility. "Obviously I can't use it against you."

"I'm sick of your whining about your kid," Donegan snapped. "She's not here and frankly, I don't really know where she is. For all I know, she's probably home by now. As for you, I can't believe you haven't worked it out. I'm waiting for dark and then I'm going to take you for a little ride in your very own car." He started walking toward the stairs and then turned to add, "Speaking of which, I think I'll just move your car into the garage where it won't be so noticeable."

She noticed now the sheen of perspiration covering his face. A wisp of hope drifted through her. Maybe Donegan didn't have the stamina for a scene like this. And if that were the case, she still had some slim chance of outsmarting him.

He was gone long enough for Dana to devise a scheme. Unless he was totally merciless, in which case, nothing would work.

When he returned, she claimed to be very thirsty. "Could you please get me a drink of water?" she begged.

"Ah, so remiss of me to forget my manners. As you're my guest, I should have offered you a drink as soon as you arrived."

She almost laughed aloud as he went back up the stairs. The pompous jerk loved to play the "prince" and because of it, he was going to play right into her hands. She glanced at her watch. Only two o'clock. She had about four hours until full dark. She should be able to pull this off by then.

"FRANKLY, SCALIA, I think you're overreacting. Dana Harper is a grown woman not a runaway adolescent."

"But why would she send me on a wild-goose chase," Nico argued, "unless she was in trouble and was forced to con me, to avoid having me go with her."

"Now, son, think a minute. She's going to turn up with a perfectly normal explanation and aren't you going to feel like a fool for running to the cops?"

Nico got to his feet, glaring down at the older man behind the desk. "I already feel like a fool, for expecting you to take this seriously, to help me find her. Thanks for nothing, Lieutenant."

He went out into the street, hailed a passing cab and gave the driver Dana's address. His car was there and once he had his own car, he'd figure out what to do next.

His heart was heavy as the cab joined the flow of traffic on 394. If anything happened to Dana, he didn't know what he would do.

DANA HAD HAD TWO full glasses of water. The minute hand on her watch seemed to be inching along by the second. She'd figured thirty minutes before she enacted part two of her plan, it had only been twenty minutes since she polished off the second drink. It felt more like a couple of hours.

Charlie had gone back upstairs for some reason and she was bored as well as nervous, frightened, depressed. She made an attempt to visualize the floor plan of the main floor. She knew the bathroom was to the right of the basement stairs, had glimpsed a kitchen through what must have been a tiny pantry to the left.

The front door had opened right into the living room and she'd seen a dining room beyond that. If her memory served well, that meant there was a traffic pattern that encircled, living room, dining room, kitchen, pantry and two of the bedrooms. Depending upon which side the bathroom door opened, she had a better than even chance of getting away.

She played a scenario using that floor plan over and over in her mind, rejecting some options and memorizing others.

By the time she heard Donegan's tread on the stairs, she was ready.

"Gosh, Charlie, am I ever glad to see you," she said sweetly, putting a little pant of desperation in her voice.

"That's a first," Donegan said. "Too bad you're too late, Miss Got-Rocks."

Panic welled. She swung her head to gaze up at the windows placed high on the walls. "It's still light out," she said.

"Too late meaning I'm not going to change my mind at this point."

"All I want is to use the bathroom, Charlie," she wheedled.

Donegan pushed away from the tub he was leaning against and then hesitated.

"Please, Charlie, I'd be so humiliated if I had an accident all over myself." She lowered her eyes demurely. "And I drank so much water, remember."

Charlie thought about it.

The thought of handling her after the accident she described was intolerable. And she couldn't get away with him right behind her after all.

He bent to unlock the cuff at her wrist. "Don't try anything stupid, Dana," he warned, retrieving the gun from his back pocket, "or we won't wait until dark."

The bathroom window was barred. She'd anticipated that but held out the tiniest glimmer of hope that she'd be wrong. She shut the door and turned the lock, waiting for Donegan to protest, to demand she leave it unlocked.

He was quiet on the other side of the door. She turned on both taps in the sink to cover the noise of opening the medicine cabinet.

It was empty! Her heart sank. Nothing, not even a dull disposable razor. Trembling, she turned off the taps and sat on the closed toilet seat. Now what?

"Hurry it up, Dana, I don't want to be standing here all day."

Donegan! She swallowed threatening tears. Her plan had come to nothing. At least if she'd had her purse, she could have tried her fingernail file or the little scissors in her emergency manicure kit. Even keys would have served if she could surprise him with a direct hit at his eyes.

But she had nothing. Not even a toilet plunger. She put her head in her hands and stared down at the floor, desperate to come up with another, instant plan. None came to mind.

She was about to give up, accept the inevitable, when her eyes glimpsed a familiar green bottle on the floor behind the toilet.

Of course! One of the most lethal of all household products. She had read the stats on the poison control pamphlet in the pediatrician's office when Krystal was about four years old. She recalled rushing home and gathering all the products listed as potential hazards. She'd thrown them into a leaf bag and tossed them in the garbage can set out for early morning pickup. This particular cleaner had been near the top of the list. More devastating than hot pepper, quicker acting than Mace, she was sure it would give her at least a couple of minutes to get away if she took proper aim.

Just then Donegan kicked at the door. "What's taking you so long in there?"

She stood, holding the green bottle slightly behind her in her right hand. She leaned forward and said, "I'm finished, I'm coming." His muttered response told her he was right outside the door.

She jerked open the door and threw her right hand up, aiming right into his face. She pulled the trigger back before he knew what had hit him. He yelled, staggered back, fell to his knees. His face was a mask of thick white foam.

Dropping the bottle, she pushed past him and raced down the hall, his screams echoing behind her.

At the end of the hall she veered to her right into the living room and made for the front door. Locked. No key.

She wondered about a back door, perhaps off the kitchen. But that would take her back in Donegan's direction and she had no idea how long the spray would affect his vision.

As if to prove her point she heard a gunshot from the end of the hall and a loud crash as Donegan screamed her name.

Mouth dry, heart pounding, Dana ran into the dining room, hoping that her fallen captor wouldn't spot her in the kitchen.

The kitchen door was not only locked, it had a wooden bar nailed across it and she didn't think she'd have time or strength enough to get it off without a crowbar.

A growl of rage, followed by guttural cries of pain from her right. Donegan lurching through the door, his face so red and puffy he was no longer recognizable.

She skirted the table and ran back toward the front of the house. More shots, though none hit her. She dived behind the couch and knelt, holding her arms around herself, biting her lip to keep from crying out.

It suddenly struck her that the shots had missed because he was firing blindly. He couldn't see well enough to aim true. She was about to stand when she realized that his aimless shooting could just as well hit its target by accident, that she'd be more at risk than if he could see her, direct his fire right at her. At least then she could try to stay out of his sight.

She got down on hands and knees and began crawling in the direction of the hall. His shots had seemed to hit high, perhaps she could stay beneath the line of fire.

She recalled that there had been a half floor above the first, with dormered windows. So there had to be either a second floor or an attic, and somewhere there had to be stairs leading up to it.

Her eyes were squeezed tight as she cringed at the thought of one of those bullets finding its target. Her left knee landed on an unexpected obstacle. Her eyes popped open. Her purse.

Shaking, she rummaged through it, seeking anything that she could use as a weapon.

Her fingers closed around a familiar, forgotten object. With a cry of triumph, she pulled out her pager.

Chapter Seventeen

Nico pounded the steering wheel, but even that didn't alleviate the anger and frustration. Maybe Lieutenant King was right, maybe he'd been getting himself all worked up over a simple misunderstanding.

Rational thinking didn't work. His gut told him something was seriously wrong. Especially after he'd called Heather to ask if Krystal was all right, if she'd heard from Dana.

"It's about time you called us," Heather said, sounding really miffed.

"Us?"

"Yeah, boob. Krystal and I. We've been waiting here over an hour and a half. I'd just decided to take her back to your mom's when you rang."

"Waiting for what? Where?"

Heather's sigh was heavy with impatience.

"Dana's secretary called me at Rose's and told me Dana wanted me to bring Krystal to the west entrance of the mall, next to Waldenbooks, so she could take Krystal shopping for more school clothes and stuff. We waited an hour, she didn't show up, we went into the Pizza Hut, had lunch, she still didn't show up. So where the hell are you guys?"

"Well, first of all," Nico snarled, "Dana doesn't have

a secretary of her own and she would never ask any of
the pool stenos or the receptionist to make a call for her,
let alone give you a message from her. And lastly, there
are no secretaries or receptionist here today. It's Saturday, people work on their own, if at all.''

There was a pause as Heather absorbed the facts Nico
had laid out for her. Guilt warred with worry. ''Dana
didn't send the message? Then who...why...''

''That's what I'm trying to find out,'' Nico yelled.
''And how did they get my mom's phone number? It
means they know where Krystal is. We're going to have
to move her again. But first, I've got to locate Dana. Get
Krystal back to Mom's. Make sure all the doors and windows are locked, keep your gun handy just in case, and
if I were you, I'd contact the S.P.P.D. and ask for cover.
No, call Stella to have her take care of that, she'll get
quicker results.''

He hung up the phone, got out of the car and began
pacing the driveway. It was as if Dana had disappeared
into thin air. He thought he'd go mad if he didn't come
up with an idea, soon. He slumped against the side of his
car and put his head in his hands. He was about to get
back in the car when his pager began beeping.

THERE WAS NO TIME to code in more than the address,
for just then a bullet whistled past her, barely missing
her. She scrambled to her feet and, changing direction,
headed into the dining room, away from the hall, from
Donegan's lurching progress toward her. If she could
only find a safe hiding place, until Nico got here. If she
was sure of one thing, it was that he would know the
message was from her, because by now, he had to be
tearing his hair out, wondering what had happened to her,
why she had sneaked off without him.

NICO BROKE every speed law, heading toward the Uptown area, to the address left on his pager. If the cops stopped him, so much the better, he'd have backup.

But no one stopped him and when he arrived at the house there was no car in sight. Furthermore the house looked deserted. It was already twilight and no lights were on and as far as he could tell, no curtains at any of the windows. A vacant house?

He moved stealthily around the house, looking for a way to see inside when suddenly he heard a sound like gunfire from within. No time to waste.

He ran around front and made a lunge at the door. Locked. Yelling Dana's name, telling her to get back if she was near the door, he shot at the lock. The door sprang open at the kick of his foot and Nico crashed into the hall in time to hear another shot and watch in horror as Dana appeared in the room to his left and fell to the floor.

Nico rushed toward her just as a man with a hideously bloated face stumbled in after her, waving his weapon. Nico aimed at him, ready to shoot, but the other man gave an unholy scream, clutched his face in his hands and fell to the floor before Nico could pull the trigger.

BOTH DANA AND DONEGAN were in the hospital, Donegan with a police guard stationed outside his door.

Dana no longer needed protection, now that the threats no longer hung over her head. In the ambulance, on the way over, she'd drifted in and out of consciousness, each time she came to begging to see Krystal.

"Shock," the doctor told Nico in the quiet of her room as they watched her drift off again. "More serious than that bullet in her shoulder. But she seems to be suffering from exhaustion, as well, and it will take a little while to get her vitals up to par."

"Can I bring her daughter to see her? I think that would help."

"Ah-hh, Krystal," the doctor said.

"Right."

"She kept muttering the name, even while she was under. I could only assume it was someone very special to her." He scratched his head. "Don't see why not. Probably will set her mind at rest. But let's wait until tomorrow, she's going to be in and out of it most of tonight. More out than in, is my guess, and she needs as much rest as she can get."

"If you don't mind, I'm going to sit with her for a while longer," Nico said.

"It's what I'd do if I were in your place," the doctor said with a grin, "that's a beautiful lady you've got there."

They shook hands and the doctor ambled down the hall. A man with tired feet but a wide-awake heart, Nico thought.

He went back into Dana's room and pulled a chair up to the side of the bed. He lifted her hand and stared at it. So fragile-looking, and like her face and neck, so pale.

He had a flashback image of those little hands holding that big police weapon and he softly chuckled.

Her hand twitched and he looked up and saw that her eyes were open.

"Thanks," she rasped. She seemed to have cotton mouth and he held her water up so she could sip through the straw.

He shook his head and took her hand in his again. "No thanks to me, love. You really saved yourself. I got there in time to see you go down and Donegan right behind you. I didn't save you from anything."

"You were there, you came and got me," she whispered.

"Oh, Dana, I pray I'll always be able to be there for you."

"Krystal?" she asked.

"Safe and sound with Heather. Your Prince Charlie had someone call and give Heather a phony message so they wouldn't be there when you called to check."

"Krystal was never..."

"Not for a minute. She's never laid eyes on Donegan up to and including today."

Tears slid beneath Dana's lashes and her grin was tremulous. She nodded, her mind at rest at last.

"I'll bring her to see you right after breakfast," Nico promised.

Dana tried to wet her lips with her tongue. Nico saw that and gave her another drink.

"Donegan?"

He cleared his throat. "We found the handcuffs on the tub in the basement, he didn't...hurt you, did he?"

"He was mostly a gentleman," Dana replied, squeezing his hand as firmly as she could manage. "He didn't mean me any harm but he did mean for me to die."

She flinched as she spoke the words and then her eyelids began drooping and she drifted off, still clinging to Nico's hand.

He carefully withdrew his hand and stood. Quietly pushing the chair back, he knelt on the floor beside the bed, took up her hand again and began to pray in a soft, beseeching tone.

Once started, he seemed unable to quit talking. It wasn't just about keeping Dana and Krystal safe, not only about asking God to give him a chance to bring happiness into their lives. Some of it was about helping him relinquish such things as pride, arrogance, the desire for control. To give him humility. To teach him to love with an open heart rather than an open hand.

And last, he asked, "Lord, let me always be worthy of her love."

A nurse had started into the room, seen him there, heard that he was praying, and quietly backed out, her eyes filling with tears. She was head nurse, Myra Jackson. All of her staff referred to her as Jack the Bear. She snuffled into a tissue before returning to the desk.

Nico was about to rise when he felt Dana's hand on his head, her fingers inching through his hair.

He lifted his face and saw that she was conscious again. He turned her hand over and kissed the palm. The floor felt like solid stone beneath his knees but he stayed there just the same.

"Go home...rest," Dana whispered.

Nico shook his head. "I want to be with you."

"We have...whole lives," she stammered.

He got the paper cup and held the straw to her lips.

"I want you to leave while I'm awake," Dana persisted. "Want to think about you...us."

He had to laugh at that. "You're adorable," he said, kissing her hand again.

She made a face and pointed to her lips. "Don't waste..." she murmured.

He laughed again and stood up to lean over her. His kiss, though infinitely gentle, lingered a long time, softly moving over her mouth, nipping with his lips at hers, his tongue laving the dryness. She opened her mouth to let him in and he drew back.

"None of that naughty French kissing tonight, my girl. Your doctor would kill me."

She gave him one of her adorable pouts, the one that showed her dimple and gave her lips that bee-stung look. Or was that from his kiss?

"Oh, you fight dirty, my love," he whispered with a growl.

"Go home," she ordered, grinning at him. "I have…reputation to protect."

"I'll see you first thing tomorrow," he reiterated.

"Yeah." She smiled and closed her eyes.

But she wasn't asleep. She felt him kiss her cheek, heard his footsteps moving to the door, heard the door close with a gentle snick.

She drifted off with a smile on her face, thinking about having Nico in her bed, in her life, forever.

SHE DIDN'T KNOW how much time had passed, but she came awake with a start, more alert than she'd been since Donegan's bullet brought her down.

The door was slightly ajar and a bit of light spilled into the room from the dim night-lights in the hall. Dana lay there, listening. Silence. Long after visiting hours were over, she guessed, a long time since Nico had left. Probably only a skeleton crew on night shift. She listened for the sound of rubber soles on the tiled floors, the swish of uniforms. Nothing.

She turned onto her left side, aware for the first time of the heavy bandages on her right shoulder. A throbbing there suggested she'd soon need pain medication. Would they come in at the scheduled time for her meds or was she expected to ring for them when the need arose?

Wait and see. She sighed happily. All the trauma and threats were over. She'd hold her little girl in her arms tomorrow. Well, one arm, anyway. And she'd see Nico again. Her heart seemed to want to burst from all the love there.

And then she heard a sound at the door. She started and then laughed softly as she turned onto her back. The door was closed, the room in full darkness. "Nico, you fool, what are you doing back here?"

No answer. She felt a tremor move down her spine.

She lifted her head, trying to see, making a ribald comment about alley cats and prowling at night.

The words were muffled as a pillow came down over her face, pushing her head against her own pillow.

She tried to fight, but handicapped by her shoulder, remnants of anesthesia and pain meds, her movements were slow, ponderous, ineffectual.

She was losing the battle, on the verge of suffocation.

Donegan. How had he found the strength to pull this off, and how had he got past the guard?

NICO WAS ALMOST at the Lexington exit in St. Paul. His parents had insisted he come no matter how late it was, and tell them everything that had occurred and how Dana really was.

He'd automatically put his hand in his pocket, reaching for cigarettes that he hadn't carried in years, when his hand closed around his pager. Funny, he thought, I never put it there.

He pulled it out. Dana's pager. He panicked for a moment and then realized she wouldn't really need it tonight. She was most likely down for the count until morning and besides, the villain was locked in a room on another floor with a cop stationed outside.

He put the pager back. He'd return it in the morning. He patted his jacket pocket and signaled his turn onto Grand.

He hadn't seen Grand Avenue in its late-night deserted state since he was in college and customarily come home well after closing hours. Come to think of it, it had been quite a while since he'd stayed out this late, even on a date.

He wondered why he'd been so averse to the idea of settling down. He *had* settled down. He just hadn't done so with a partner.

Well, he thought, grinning, all that was going to change the minute Dana was well enough to go with him to apply for a marriage license. He patted the pocket with the pager again, as if for good luck.

And then some impulse he was never able to explain made him take a right on Lincoln instead of a left, and he headed back to Minneapolis.

Only one thought kept playing over and over in his mind; he was never going to be more than a pager call away from Dana again.

A LAST DESPERATE SURGE of will gave Dana the energy to lurch her body upward. She heard a grunt, feet stumbling, felt the pressure leave the pillow as the assailant was caught off guard. She rolled onto her side trying to scramble out from under the covers, thinking only to break free, run from the danger. But the man had recovered himself and reached for her before she could clear the edge of the bed. His big hand closed around her injured arm and the blast of pain made her fall back to loosen the pressure of his hold.

Pain blinded her to everything else. She had tried to scream but her mouth and throat were so dry she couldn't do more than grunt. The pillow came down, shutting out even those meager attempts to cry for help. She put her hand up, tugging at the pillow, trying to let even a pinprick of air under it. It was no use. The man was too strong. Which once again begged the question, How had he got past the guard and where had he found the energy?

Dizziness prevailed and she felt her body go limp. She was going to die. Never going to see Krystal or Nico again…

NICO STOOD in the doorway, adjusting his eyes to the dim light, which was partly obscured by his own body.

For a moment he thought the figure bent over Dana's bed was her doctor, examining her.

He started to call out when it hit him that the doctor would have at least turned on the night-light. He took a step forward and saw Dana break away from the guy, heard her cry of pain, saw the man lift something that might have been a pillow and bring it down over her face.

The guy was big, as big as he. He fought with matching fervor, his fists landing on Nico's person over and over, though some fell short of their mark. In those instances it was because Nico had landed a few well-aimed parries of his own. Somewhere in the red haze of fury he was conscious of the sound of Dana crying and weakly calling for help, of the sound his gun made when it fell and slid away on the highly polished floor. But the guy wasn't going down and Nico wasn't quitting until he did.

The lights came on suddenly and a woman's voice cried out, "What's going— Oh, my God! Security. Somebody call security!"

In the moment that Dana had gulped that first unexpected gift of air, she'd not registered what had happened—was happening. She heard the sounds of men fighting, heard the grunts, the sound of air being sucked in when a blow landed, but her arm throbbed horrendously now and her mouth was so dry she felt she could suffocate from that alone.

Childishly she thought, This is not good for me, as her head fell back against the pillow. Did she pass out for a moment? The lights were on and there were shouts in the hall and the sound of a multitude of footsteps pounding up the hall toward her room.

She could see the two men thrashing on the floor and saw that Nico was pinned beneath the other man.

She tried to get out of bed, thought she could somehow

help him. But even if such a major feat had been possible she saw it was unnecessary when the room suddenly filled with people led by two security guards, their guns drawn.

"One of 'em's hurt," a guard cried. One of the nurses ran to the man on the floor and the other rushed to Dana's side, immediately starting up the machine that would take her pulse, blood pressure and heart rate.

Dana looked past the nurse at the scene in the corner. She blinked, shook her head, tried to focus. It must be delirium, she thought. She rubbed her eyes and looked again. Nico was leaning against the wall, holding his arm across his stomach, his eyes closed, breathing heavily.

The guard and a nurse were kneeling on either side of the man on the floor.

The man was Joe Lake.

Dana's head thudded against the pillow as she fell into a complete faint.

Chapter Eighteen

Nico Scalia waited for Mindy to signal that the boss was ready to see him. But when she did, he didn't seem to see her, his eyes transfixed on something beyond the window.

Mindy got up and went over to the chairs lined along the wall beside Stella Martinson's door.

"Nico," she said, touching his shoulder. He snapped to attention. "Stell is ready for you, hon."

Nico nodded, got up, looked around with a confused expression on his face and then seemed to connect with reality. He went into Stella's office.

Mindy stood there, staring at the closed door, shaking her head.

"Something wrong, Min?" Luke Avery asked as he passed by.

"Notice the way Nico's been acting lately?"

Luke stopped, stroked his chin, squinted his eyes in thought. "Now that you mention it. Scalia seems to drift in and out when anyone talks to him and I heard on the office grapevine that he's turned down two juicy cases. I happen to know firsthand that he quit our bowling league and refused our annual invitation to the S.P.P.D. Halloween Ball."

He frowned at Mindy. "Scalia used to be the most outgoing, fun-loving guy on staff."

"Well, let's hope Stell asked to see him so she could get to the bottom of it and find a way to get him back on track."

STELLA WAS ALREADY AWARE of what was bothering Nico. Heather Wilson had confided in her because she was worried about him. She couldn't just blurt it out, she had to finesse him. She pretended to be reading a file she already knew by heart.

"So, Nico," she began, "it looks like you've decided to take your vacation this month. Not the greatest time of year unless you're headed for the South Seas."

Nico stared at her, dumbfounded. "Vacation?"

"Or a honeymoon?" Stella slyly suggested.

His laugh was short, bitter. "From your lips to God's ear," he said, his eyes suddenly glittering with pain.

"Trouble in paradise?"

Nico expelled a ragged sigh and fastened his gaze on his shoes. "Let's just say, if you've got an assignment for me, I'd appreciate it."

"Nico, you turned down two assignments in the past two weeks."

Nico shrugged. "Something else," he said. But there was a definite lack of interest in his tone.

"I've got a case that's right up your alley. Industrial sabotage. Sort of a rerun. We did this one a few years back. Taylor Industries."

Nico's head sprang up and she saw that his face had paled.

"Is this some kind of joke?" he demanded. "If so, it's not very funny."

Stella gently shook her head. "No joke, Nico. This is a legitimate assignment. Nothing but surveillance and a little snooping around. Mostly waiting to catch someone in the act, actually.'' She hesitated and then added, ''Not much contact with the client or the employees. You'll be on your own for the most part and there's no time limit. The order read, 'As long as it takes.'''

In other words, a long, dull, brainless, routine assignment. Nico gave Stella a long searching look. Normally she'd never have suggested this kind of job to her best detective. But maybe he wasn't her best anymore.

''Okay—so it's legitimate. But is this a misguided plan to get me involved with Dana again?''

Stella shook her head, never breaking eye contact. ''I'm not running a mating agency here. You want the job or not?''

He thought about working for Taylor, Dana's father, a man he'd never met and didn't relish meeting now. Wouldn't everything on the job remind him of Dana? And wouldn't there be a chance he'd even run into her there? He knew she held her mother in low esteem, so if she had any kind of relationship with her father, she probably met with him at his office.

Dana had begged him to stay away from her, insisting she needed time to work through the past, and needed to be alone. If they ran into each other at Taylor Industries, would she think it was a setup?

He stood. ''May I have a little time to think it over?''

Her gaze never altered. ''Twenty-four hours,'' she firmly stated.

Nico left her office and the building immediately.

As if on automatic pilot, he found himself driving to the hospital. He parked on the street across from the side of the building where Dana's room was located. Her window was a blank screen reflecting the sky and the smoke-stack of a distant building.

Sitting there gave him some comfort though he'd never caught a glimpse of her at the window.

He'd been there maybe ten minutes when he heard a car pull up behind his. A moment later, heard a familiar voice.

"You and Papa go up to your mama, I'll be right along."

Before he could react he saw his father crossing the street, holding Krystal's hand. At the same moment the passenger door of his car was flung open and his mother climbed into the seat beside him.

"So, Young Dominick, this is what you've come to?"

"Mama, I didn't expect to see you."

"Of course you didn't. Maybe if you had you'd have shaved? You don't come to the house, you sneak around in your car and drive right by, you sit out here and moon for a woman who needs you but you don't go inside. My proud, arrogant son, a wimp now."

Anger flared and then dissipated. "You don't understand," he said.

"No, I don't," Rose admitted. "Krystal has been pining to return home and is confused by all the losses in her life. But you're too busy licking your wounds to give her back something she can depend on. Dana has lost her best friend, and worse, has to face that he murdered her husband and at least two other people, including a fellow policeman. That he tried to murder her. But you leave her alone with her pain, her guilt, her fear of ever trusting anyone again, instead of sitting by her side proving there is someone she can trust."

"She told me to stay away!" Nico yelled.

Rose leaned forward and slapped his face. "You don't yell at your mama," she said in a calm voice.

The slap had more stunned than hurt him. Nico put his

hand to his cheek and glared at his mother. "I'm not a kid anymore," he warned.

"No? Still you act like one."

They sat in a mutually stubborn silence for a few minutes while Nico mentally vowed he was going to buy a pack of cigarettes at the first convenience store he came to and Rose thought this would be a good day to make bread, to work her anger and frustration out on a massive hunk of dough.

As usual, Nico relented first. Mama's streak of mulishness could keep them sitting here without speaking for weeks on end.

"I'm sorry, Mama," he said.

Rose gave him a suspicious look with a tilt of her head. "Sorry enough to go up and see Dana?"

"She won't see me. I've tried. She refused."

"So, you'll try again. And if it doesn't work today, you'll try again tomorrow. Loving a woman doesn't mean giving up being a man, Nico. It should make you more a man." When she got out of the car she shook both her head and fist at him. He had to grin. Something about her reminded him of Dana.

NICO STOOD in the open doorway staring at Dana. She looked better than she had the last time he'd seen her, the day after Joe Lake tried to kill her. But there was still a fragile quality about her, as if a good wind could blow her apart.

A part of him that had shut down rose up and filled his chest, tautened his muscles, drove a burst of energy to stimulate his brain. He wanted to grab her up in his arms, hold her safe forever. Wanted to slay dragons for her. Wanted to fight her enemies, defend her causes, shower her with attention and gifts.

He stood and watched her as she stared out of her window, unaware of his presence.

And then she pulled her gaze from the window and turned her attention back to the TV set high on the wall beside the door.

That was when she saw Nico, her hand going to her chest, a gasp emitting from her throat, her blue eyes widening into circles of surprise.

"Nico!"

He took a step into the room and stopped. "Are you going to call Security?" he asked, wary of her reaction.

She blushed and the added color in her cheeks gave him a flash of the old Dana.

"I deserve that, I guess," she admitted.

"If you still don't want to see me, I'll go. But I warn you, I'll be back."

"In that case, you might as well come in." The sauciness of old but with a solemn expression on her face.

He went to the foot of the bed and pulled a chair over, sitting as far from her as possible. He wasn't going to stay away any longer, but he was going to let her set the pace.

Dana's head fell back against the headboard and her eyes closed for a minute.

"I want to thank you for respecting my wishes," she said when she opened them.

An alarm went off in Nico's head. His hands fisted in his pockets, his breath caught in his throat. He felt he'd choke if he tried to speak. He opted for silence.

Dana saw the tension in his posture and wondered what there'd been in her words to alarm him. She tried again.

"I know most men would have ignored those wishes, or read them as an end to the relationship and gone on to someone else."

"It's only been two weeks," Nico reminded, "not enough time to find someone else unless you're a cold-hearted person who has nothing but surface feelings for women."

He flushed as he realized he could have described himself in those terms before this year, before he'd met Dana Harper.

Her gaze was probing, made him feel exposed, but he didn't look away.

"You didn't even try to see me. I thought that was out of consideration for my feelings."

"It was. But it hurt like hell just the same. How did I know you'd ever let me back in?"

A look of true confusion dulled her eyes. "But you knew I was in love with you."

He pulled his chair closer, leaned forward. "Dana, when they brought you around and you looked up and saw me hanging over your bed, you screamed at me to go away, to get out. You got hysterical until the guard ushered me out.

"The next day was no better though your tone was altered. Very calmly, and with no hint of emotion on your face and in your voice, you told me you couldn't see me 'for a while.' That you needed to work things out alone. You literally begged me to stay away."

Dana twisted her fingers together, trying to wring some help from her hands. "It wasn't only you, Nico, I quit my job, as well."

"Wha-aat?"

She looked away. "I felt tainted, dirty by association, not worthy to be called an officer of the court."

It floored him. How had she fallen so completely apart in such a short time, and all because of a scuzz like Lake?

"I should have been here," Nico exploded. "I should have helped you make more rational decisions, helped you see none of this was an onus on you. Instead, I was off rubbing salt in my wounds and then whining when it burned.''

He pushed the chair back and strode to her side, taking her hands in his. "Dana, please, don't do this to yourself. If you don't want me, okay, I'll learn to live with it. But please don't throw everything else away. You're not responsible for Lake's twisted mind, his corrupt value system. And I've seen you in court, I know how much of yourself you put into your work. Don't let a fragmented ego keep you from the work you love and excel at. Don't let…''

His sentence trailed away, unfinished, as it struck him that he'd done exactly that with his own career.

"Nico?" Dana tugged at his hands, frightened by the look on his face, the way he'd suddenly paled.

He collapsed on the side of the bed and closed his eyes. "We are the most well-matched couple I've ever seen," he said in a hushed, almost reverent tone. He opened his eyes and looked into her face. "We make all the same mistakes, think alike, go off half-cocked in the same way. We'd make a great clown act together.''

Dana arched a haughty eyebrow, another look from the past he'd loved. "I'm not sure I like that image of us," she stated, sniffing.

For the first time in days, Nico grinned. "Calls 'em as I sees 'em, love.''

"So what do we do about it?"

"We could start by getting you out of here. Why are you still here, anyway?"

Dana lowered her eyes, plucked at the edge of the blanket. "I don't know. Apparently my vitals haven't been right.''

"Of course not," Nico snapped. "You've been in an intense depression all this time. I'd bet my medical career that sitting in this hospital has only increased your depression and kept your system from functioning normally.''

He stomped over to the locker and got her bag out. ''Come on,'' he ordered, ''get dressed. I'll wait outside.''

''I can't just walk...''

''Do you need help dressing?''

''I don't think so but...''

''Good. I'm going to tell the desk you're releasing yourself.''

''But Nico, I...''

Impatiently he turned back, his hand on the door handle. ''Do you trust me, Dana?''

She didn't hesitate. She nodded.

''Then just let me handle this. You're no more sick than I am.''

If he felt any qualms about his high-handedness, he squelched them when he reached the desk and told them Dana was checking out. The feeling that he knew her better than anyone, that he knew how to get her up and running again, was stronger than his fear that he might be way off track and might be endangering her.

The head nurse told him to wait, went into a glass-fronted inner office and picked up the phone. He watched her face as she spoke into it, watched her expression turn from indignation to surprise and then to meek agreement as she nodded her head.

Nico didn't wait but hurried back to Dana's room. He knocked and she called, ''Nico, I do need help.''

Now that was more like it, he thought, pushing open the door.

THEY WERE SEATED at the table, the three of them enjoying the first night back together at home. The TV was on, because Dana and Nico wanted to watch the news.

"Personally, I've never had any desire to go to Mexico," Dana said, eating the spinach on her plate because Nico said it was full of iron.

"I'd like to go to Disneyland," Krystal said, boldly shoving her spinach onto her bread and butter plate.

"Eat your spinach," they said in unison.

"I don't need iron," Krystal retorted.

"You will if you don't eat vegetables," Nico said, closing his eyes as he swallowed a forkful of it himself.

"See, Mom, he is closing his eyes. He hates it, too."

"Not at all," Nico said, avoiding eye contact with either of them. "I just got something in my eyes."

Krystal muttered something under her breath and ate her meat. If she took her time, they'd forget about the spinach and leave her alone.

"How about Colorado, for the skiing?" Nico asked.

"How about Disneyland."

They ignored Krystal.

"I don't ski," Dana said.

"You're kidding! Why?"

Dana shrugged and started poking at her chicken.

"Never had an interest in it. I watched most of my friends come back with casts and decided it wasn't worth the risk." She forced a bite of chicken. Nico had insisted it was a good source of protein. It was loaded with salt, which he figured should raise her blood pressure since people with high blood pressure had to limit their salt intake.

"I can't eat this," Krystal said, pouting. "It's too salty."

Nico had been covering the saltiness with his mashed potatoes and trying not to wince when that didn't work.

"We're trying to get your mom well with good nutrition," he reminded Krystal.

"I'm more in the mood for pizza," the child whined.

"Me, too," Dana blurted and then covered her mouth, aghast at herself for not thinking about Nico's feelings. He tried so hard, was so careful of her.

"I was just thinking of other foods that give you all the nutrients you need and pizza's definitely at the top of the list." He stood and gathered all their plates.

"Krystal, you call in the order while I scrape these and get clean plates."

He was just rinsing the last plate when the news came on. Dana had the remote and turned up the sound.

"In a late-breaking report from his attorney, Detective Joe Lake has pleaded guilty to three counts of murder, one count of attempted murder," the anchor reported. "Now here's Janice Mueller with an update on Detective Lake's apparent motivation."

A solemn, pretty woman's face appeared on screen.

"Though Detective Lake refused to be taped, he did agree to an interview with me earlier today in which he admitted he was on Alphonze Caprezio's payroll and has been for years. Apparently his attempt on Prosecutor Dana Harper's life came when he realized nothing would deter her from investigating the death of her late husband, police Detective Zack Harper. The murder of Mr. Harper is one of the three to which Lake has pleaded guilty. Sentencing will be passed by Judge Charles Yokum at nine o'clock Monday morning."

Dana silenced the TV and buried her head on her folded arms on the table. Nico went to her and took her into his arms.

"It's okay, love, it's better this way. You wouldn't be able to take days, maybe weeks, of a long, drawn-out trial and this way, you won't have to testify. It'll all be over on Monday and we can get on with our own lives."

She lifted her head from his chest and brushed tears

away. "I am grateful for that. It's probably the kindest thing Joe has ever done. But…"

Nico tilted her chin up with one finger. "But?"

"It doesn't bring the others back."

Nico's chin fell to the top of her head.

She pulled out of his embrace and went back to her chair. "It's so confusing, Nico. I love you as I've never loved anyone in my life before, and yet I hate that Zack is dead. Murdered by his partner and best friend because Joe knew he was going to turn in a report that proved the Caprezios were selling arms, drugs and stolen goods."

Nico went to the refrigerator and withdrew a couple of beers, popping the tabs before setting one down in front of Dana. He took a long swig of his own and sat across from her.

"Caprezio was paying big bucks for Joe's cooperation. Joe liked living high on the hog. The playboy bachelor."

"And his many proposals were part of a scheme to get me under his control, keep me from investigating."

"Something like that."

If Nico was going to say more, it would have to wait. Krystal's return put an end to the conversation.

Dana hurriedly dried her eyes and put on a cheerful smile.

"Say, I've just thought of the perfect place for a honeymoon," she said. "How about Italy? Have you ever been to your parents' homeland?"

"I've never been to Disneyland," Krystal said, a pleading look on her face.

"No, I haven't, and that sounds really great," Nico said. "But, Krys, honey, a honeymoon is a trip for just the bride and groom."

He turned back to Dana. "Isn't there someplace you've always wanted to go?"

"She always said she'd like to go to Disneyland," Krystal said, giving Dana a wistful look.

"Why should we go somewhere for me?" Dana asked. "That doesn't make sense if a honeymoon is for both of us. Besides, I'd love to see Italy again."

Nico gaped. "You've been there? When?"

"After law school, a graduation present from my dad. I did the whole schoolgirl tour—France, England, Germany and Italy. What little I saw of Italy was gorgeous. Yeah, I'd really like to go back, and especially with you."

"Why go somewhere you've already been when you've never been to Disneyland," Krystal asked, pouting.

The doorbell rang.

Nico pulled out a twenty and handed it to Krystal. "Tell him to keep the change," he said, laughing at the child's tenacity.

Dana started to get up, to go after Krystal.

Nico grabbed her hand and gestured her back to her seat.

"It's all over, Dana," he reminded her in a gentle tone. "She's got to get used to feeling safe and independent again."

Dana grimaced. "I know, it's just going to take some time to believe it."

"Well, they say kids are more resilient. She certainly seems to be in good spirits."

"You don't think it's too soon to go off and leave her again?"

"She thinks of the folks' house as her second home and they've made it clear they'll love having her back. Especially for such a good cause. They're so tickled about our upcoming marriage, they're like a couple of kids going to Dis—"

He stopped midsentence and shook his head. "How does she do that to me, every time?"

"Feminine wiles, they seem to be your weakness," Dana said, laughing.

"She's bullish when it comes to getting her own way."

"But cute."

"Yeah," Nico said, grinning. "Very cute, just like her mother."

"Nico, you can't be thinking of taking her on our honeymoon, that's so…"

"Still hot," Krystal said, plunking the Domino box in the center of the table. "And I've just been thinking—"

Their combined groans interrupted the speech she'd worked out. She wasn't about to waste it. She used a fork to put a slice of the pie on each of their plates and sat down, waiting for them to take the first bite. With their mouths full they'd never talk and interrupt her.

"See, the thing is, I hired Nico in the first place," Krystal noted pointedly, watching them chew. "And I'm the one who has to fire him. If I don't he's still my bodyguard, and he can't go off without me. So here's what I thought, as long as I have to go along, we really should go somewhere where I'll have something to do, too."

She sat back, giving each of them a grin of self-approval. Mommy always told her to use reason to win an argument. Personally she thought she'd done a swell job.

Nico and Dana exchanged an enigmatic look, and then both started applauding.

Nico raised his beer can. "A toast to the next Ms. Harper to knock the legal world on its a—er, buns."

Dana clinked her can against his and added, "The next Ms. Harper-Scalia."

Krystal stared at them. What had they said? "Does that mean yes or no?" she demanded.

"My parents will be disappointed," Nico said.

"You'll be missing school, you'll have a lot of work to make up," Dana added.

Krystal's mouth fell open and then she jumped up on her chair and threw her arm up in the air, her hand balled in a fist. "Yes!" She screamed. "Yes!"

Nico pulled her down and onto his lap. "Now listen, kid, you know what honeymoons are all about, right?"

Krystal nodded, afraid he was going to change his mind.

"Well, your mom and I are going to want to spend some time by ourselves, so here's my thought. We'll compromise. Yes, you're going with us. But we'll ask Heather to come along so you have an adult with you when Mommy and I want to go off by ourselves."

Krystal's exaggerated sigh of relief made the two of them laugh. She got off Nico's lap and started dancing around the room, singing some kind of foolishness at the top of her lungs.

"Italy next year," Dana said. She put her hand over Nico's. "I love you."

"And I, you, my darling." He stood and pulled her up out of her chair and swept her into his arms. Their bodies seemed to melt together as their lips met and clung, unmindful of the little girl looking on.

She stared at them, feeling a momentary guilt. Should she have explained that her whole reason for hiring Nico was to get a new husband for Mommy, a new daddy for herself?

Nah. No sense spoiling things when they were working out just the way she'd planned.

She left them, still kissing, wondering how they

breathed when they did that. But she had more important things on her mind.

First she was going to go up and put the daddy doll back in her dollhouse.

And then, just to make sure there was no change of plans, she'd start packing. For Disneyland.

EVER HAD ONE OF THOSE DAYS?

TO DO:

☑ at the supermarket buying two dozen muffins that your son just remembered to tell you he needed for the school treat, you realize you left your wallet at home

☑ at work just as you're going into the big meeting, you discover your son took your presentation to school, and you have his hand-drawn superhero comic book

☑ your mother-in-law calls to say she's coming for a month-long visit

☑ finally at the end of a long and exasperating day, you escape from it all with an entertaining, humorous and always romantic Love & Laughter book!

ENJOY
LOVE & LAUGHTER™
EVERY DAY!

For a preview, turn the page....

Here's a sneak peek at
Carrie Alexander's THE AMOROUS HEIRESS
Available September 1997...

"YOU'RE A VERY popular lady," Jed Kelley observed as Augustina closed the door on her suitors.

She waved a hand. "Just two of a dozen." Technically true since her grandmother had put her on the open market. "You're not afraid of a little competition, are you?"

"Competition?" He looked puzzled. "I thought the position was mine."

Augustina shook her head, smiling coyly. "You didn't think Grandmother was the final arbiter of the decision, did you? I say a trial period is in order." No matter that Jed Kelley had miraculously passed Grandmother's muster, Augustina felt the need for a little propriety. But, on the other hand, she could be married before the summer was out and be free as a bird, with the added bonus of a husband it wouldn't be all that difficult to learn to love.

She got up the courage to reach for his hand, and then just like that, she—Miss Gussy Gutless Fairchild—was holding Jed Kelley's hand. He looked down at their linked hands. "Of course, you don't really know what sort of work I can do, do you?"

A funny way to put it, she thought absently, cradling his callused hand between both of her own. "We can get to know each other, and then, if that works out..." she murmured. *Wow.* If she'd known what this arranged marriage thing was all about, she'd have been a supporter of Grandmother's campaign from the start!

"Are you a palm reader?" Jed asked gruffly. His voice was as raspy as sandpaper and it was rubbing her all the right ways, but the question flustered her. She dropped his hand.

"I'm sorry."

"No problem," he said, "as long as I'm hired."

"Hired!" she scoffed. "What a way of putting it!"

Jed folded his arms across his chest. "So we're back to the trial period."

"Yes." Augustina frowned and her gaze dropped to his work boots. Okay, so he wasn't as well off as the majority of her suitors, but really, did he think she was going to *pay* him to marry her?

"Fine, then." He flipped her a wave and, speechless, she watched him leave. She was trembling all over like a malaria victim in a snowstorm, shot with hot charges and cold shivers until her brain was numb. This couldn't be true. Fantasy men didn't happen to nice girls like her.

"Augustina?"

Her grandmother's voice intruded on Gussy's privacy. "Ahh. There you are. I see you met the new gardener?"

*A woman alone—
What can she do…?
Whom can she trust…?
Where can she run…?
Straight into the arms of*

HER PROTECTOR

By popular demand we bring you the exciting reprise of
the women-in-jeopardy theme you loved. Don't miss

#430 *THE SECOND MRS. MALONE*
by Amanda Stevens (August)

#433 *STORM WARNINGS*
by Judi Lind (September)

#438 *LITTLE GIRL LOST*
by Adrianne Lee (October)

When danger lurks around every corner, there's only
one place you're safe…in the strong, sheltering arms
of the man who loves you.

Look for all the books in the
HER PROTECTOR miniseries!

Look us up on-line at: http://www.romance.net

HPT

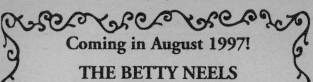

Coming in August 1997!

THE BETTY NEELS
RUBY COLLECTION

COLLECTOR'S EDITION

This August start assembling the
Betty Neels Ruby Collection. Six of the
most requested and best-loved titles have
been especially chosen for this collection.
From August 1997 until January 1998,
one title per month will be available to avid
fans. Spot the collection by the lush ruby red
cover with the gold Collector's Edition banner
and your favorite author's name—Betty Neels!

Available in August at your favorite retail outlet.

⬥HARLEQUIN®

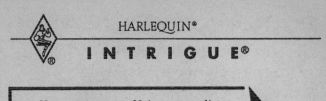

Let's Celebrate!

LOVE & LAUGHTER™

invites you to
the party of the season!

Grab your popcorn and be prepared to laugh
as we celebrate with **LOVE & LAUGHTER**.

Harlequin's newest series is going Hollywood!

Let us make you laugh with three months of terrific
books, authors and romance, plus a chance to win a
FREE 15-copy video collection of the best romantic
comedies ever made.

For more details look in the back pages of any
Love & Laughter title, from July to September,
at your favorite retail outlet.

Don't forget the popcorn!

Available wherever
Harlequin books are sold.

♦ HARLEQUIN®

Look us up on-line at: http://www.romance.net

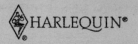

LLCELEB

FORTUNE COOKIE

Breathtaking romance is predicted in your future with Harlequin's newest collection: Fortune Cookie.

Three of your favorite Harlequin authors, Janice Kaiser, Margaret St. George and M.J. Rodgers will regale you with the romantic adventures of three heroines who are promised fame, fortune, danger and intrigue when they crack open their fortune cookies on a fateful night at a Chinese restaurant.

Join in the adventure with your own personalized fortune, inserted in every book!

Don't miss this exciting new collection!

Available in September wherever Harlequin books are sold.

HARLEQUIN®

HARLEQUIN WOMEN KNOW ROMANCE WHEN THEY SEE IT.

**HARLEQUIN AND SILHOUETTE
ARE PLEASED TO PRESENT**

Love, marriage—and the pursuit of family!

Check your retail shelves for these upcoming titles:

July 1997
Last Chance Cafe by Curtiss Ann Matlock
The most determined bachelor in Oklahoma is in trouble! A
lovely widow with three daughters has moved next door—and
the girls want a dad! But he wants to know if their mom needs
a husband....

August 1997
Thorne's Wife by Joan Hohl

Pennsylvania. It was only to be a marriage of convenience—
until they fell in love! Now, three years later, tragedy
threatens to separate them forever and Valerie wants only to
be in the strength of her husband's arms. For she has some
very special news for the expectant father...

September 1997
Desperate Measures by Paula Detmer Riggs
New Mexico judge Amanda Wainwright's daughter has been
kidnapped, and the price of her freedom is a verdict in
favor of a notorious crime boss. So enters ex-FBI agent
Devlin Buchanan—ruthless, unstoppable—and soon there is
no risk he will not take for her.

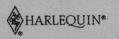